THE 25TH COLONY

Larry Rhodes

WORKBOOK PRESS LLC
187 E Warm Springs Rd,
Suite B285, Las Vegas, NV 89119, USA

Website: https://workbookpress.com/
Hotline: 1-888-818-4856
Email: admin@workbookpress.com

Ordering Information:
Quantity sales. Special discounts are available on quantity purchases by corporations, associations, and others. For details, contact the publisher at the address above.

Library of Congress Control Number:

ISBN-13:   978-1-961845-97-8 (Paperback Version)
              978-1-961845-97-8 (Digital Version)

PUB.DATE: 05/17/2023

CONTENTS

CHAPTER 1

Marisela Gomez wiped the sweat from her eyes as she watched her boyfriend Jason Steele effortlessly wield a machete to clear the brush ahead of them. She was regretting the day she asked to join his latest expedition in the Amazon jungle—to find the elusive and massive Green Anaconda. Although it was still early in the morning, wisps of steam rose from the dense underbrush. She felt the eyes of the expedition members behind her as she pulled a water bottle from her backpack.

"Jason, would you like some water?"

He paused and glanced back. "There's a clearing ahead. We'll stop there for a moment." Marisela took a quick drink and returned the bottle to her backpack as Jason resumed his fierce hacking of the vines and bushes ahead. She wasn't swinging a machete, but her arm was sore from constantly swatting the horde of buzzing and stinging insects Jason was stirring. She swatted yet another pesky gigantic mosquito on her neck and glanced behind at the team's cameraman. He was straining under the weight of a TV camera on one shoulder and another large bag of equipment dangling from his other shoulder. He was sweating profusely while he fanned himself with his hat, but managed to smile weakly at her. The team porters were used to the heat and humidity of a typical January summer morning and waiting patiently to move on. One porter grinned a toothless grin at her as she shifted her backpack to a more comfortable position.

Once in the clearing, Marisela found a fallen tree trunk without any obvious crawling insects and flopped on it with a sigh of relief. She pulled a handkerchief from her backpack and wiped her face and neck. After another drink of water, she applied more mosquito repellent and breathed a huge sigh. *What was I thinking?* When Jason and the lead porter left to scout ahead, she had time to reflect on her relationship with Jason Steele. As a features reporter for the most successful TV station in Sao Paolo, Brazil, she had often interviewed Jason when he returned from his famous expeditions. Over time, they had become close friends and eventually a couple. She was still amazed at his determination and resourcefulness in finding sponsors for his various adventures.

Jason was somewhat of a legend even among adventurers and survivalists. At thirty, he had taken every risk possible to satisfy an insatiable desire to experience danger first-hand. In college, he had compiled a list of 25 "high risk adventures" to master, and his degree in mechanical engineering provided the knowledge he needed to devise the special gear he would need for his expeditions. Since then he had hunted crocodiles in Africa with only a knife, swum with sharks in Australia, helped scientists document penguin migration in Antarctica, re-traced the Stanley Livingstone Expedition across Africa, skydived into a volcano in Hawaii, and explored volcanic caves in Mexico that most cavers were afraid to set foot in.

His latest venture in the Amazon was no less risky. There was a $50,000 reward for anyone capturing a Green Anaconda more than thirty feet long, and Jason was determined to win it. The capture would be adventure number eighteen on his list.

Unfortunately, adventurous expeditions are costly and sponsors are required. After some searching, Jason found a zoo willing to fund three weeks in the Amazon, with the stipulation that a camera crew accompany his usual support team. The team of four porters and camera crew had grown when his girlfriend asked to come along and Jason reluctantly agreed.

Many of the local Amerinds claimed to have seen gigantic Green Anacondas, but none could furnish sufficient proof to claim the reward.

A large snake made a heavy burden to transport, and the skin was both illegal to sell and inadequate as proof, as it could be stretched. The zoo was offering a financial incentive if he could bring one back alive. He was determined to claim the record, the prize, and the zoo's incentive.

The oppressive heat and humidity of the Amazon would have sapped the energy of a less experienced hunter, but Jason had recently spent months looking for rare and exotic birds for the Brazilian zoo and he was up to the task. After searching along rapidly flowing streams and river estuaries for a week, Jason was encouraged by sighting of a more common yellow version and even a small Green Anaconda. He often trekked for hours at a time, taxing the hiking ability of Marisela as well as the cameraman and reporter following at a discreet distance. Fortunately, for them, Jason never ventured more than an hour or so from one of the Amazon's tributaries and the expedition's flat-bottom support boat that followed the team, and provided a safe harbor from the many nocturnal animals that prowled at night.

On the evening of the eighth day, while the rest of the team was recovering from the day's trek, Jason finally spotted a large Green, sunning itself near the river's bank only a hundred meters from the boat. It was partially hidden in some brush and he wondered if it was big enough.

Jason signaled the boat's captain, and as the boat pulled to shore, he readied his tranquilizer gun and slipped quietly through the jungle. An impatient wave kept Marisela, the cameraman and the reporter on the boat with his porters. As he deftly stepped over a fallen tree, a massive coil of another Green tripped him, knocking him to the ground. Any human or animal would have panicked as the huge snake quickly wrapped itself around him and started to squeeze. Jason, however, didn't panic and managed to fire the tranquilizer dart. It quickly became a race to see if the tranquilizer would work before the air in Jason's lungs was gone. He concentrated on keeping his lungs inflated, breathing shallowly. He dared not use air to yell to the team for help. His field of vision was narrowing, black closing in from the sides, when he felt the massive coils start to relax. He was finally able to take a deep breath and push the coils off.

As he stood up, his vision cleared and he remembered the other Green that was sunning itself. Maybe it was a mate of this monster! He crouched over and ran to the nearest tree. He was leaning against it, still breathing hard, when the other snake slithered into view. Jason reloaded the tranquilizer gun and waited. The Green slithered around the tranquilized Green until it saw him. The huge snake moved so fast he barely had time to raise the tranquilizer gun and fire it into its neck. At the last moment, it turned, and one of its coils rammed his feet, knocking him forward over it and against another coil. But Jason was ready this time. He didn't need two snakes alive and he jabbed his knife into this one as it slithered over him. The gash grew as the snake tried to encircle him. After a few moments it became still. Jason pushed away the single coil wrapped around him and stood up. This one was dead, but the other one was starting to move weakly and trying to slither away! Jason yelled to the team and camera crew. They came running and found him standing over the still groggy snake with both feet on its tail. Jason smiled when he saw his revolver in Marisela's hand. She swallowed hard and ran forward to hug him.

Michael Allred, the reluctant reporter on the crew stared in disbelief. "Are you all right?"

"Yes. Help me measure this one." Jason and Marisela were already pulling on it to stretch it out. The cameraman filmed them trying to measure the massive Green. The drug was starting to wear off and the snake slipped out of Michael's hand and was starting to coil around Marisela's legs. She screamed and Jason pulled out his revolver from his waistband and hit it on the head. "Son of a bitch! This is one tough reptile."

Together, the three managed to stretch it out long enough to measure it. Jason let out a triumphant yell. "Ten point seven meters!" He looked up at the camera. "That's more than thirty-five feet." Michael pulled his notepad out and mumbled the words a few times and began his report.

He was so excited it took three tries before he was coherent and satisfied with the report. Marisela even filmed a report for her TV station. By that time, Jason had returned from the boat with the porters who were carrying a suitable cage. The whole team joined in to tug, cajole and stuff the huge Green into the cage. When they all sat down to rest, Jason pulled a long drink from his water bottle. But all too soon, the dead Green started to draw all sorts of flying, wriggling and crawling creatures eager for dinner, and it seemed time to leave.

The porters slid two poles through loops in the top of the cage and struggled to pick it up. Jason commented to Marisela the snake probably weighed 200 kilograms or over 400 pounds. Together, the entire team managed to heft the cage onto the boat. The trip down the river was uneventful until Jason heard a low rumbling noise, something like a sonic boom, and saw a bright flash of light a short distance ahead.

Marisela turned to him. "What the hell was that?"

"I don't know." Jason motioned to the captain and the boat swerved onto the shore. He maneuvered around the cage with the angry anaconda, pushed past Marisela, Michael and Markus, and jumped ashore. "I'll be right back. Stay with the boat." He stopped, looked back, and saw the anxious looks on their faces. "Here, take this." He tossed his revolver to Marisela who fumbled with it and gave it to Markus. Jason laughed.

He saw a dull red glow in the jungle, and pushed toward it. The sun was going down so he had to make this fast; no one with any sense traveled through the Amazon at night.

CHAPTER 2

Maru Gren

The Juban warship landed silently in the Brazilian Amazon. Maru Gren was applying a protective cream on her face and hands as the main door and ramp opened. Momus Bluf walked outside to determine if it were safe for Maru to leave. A moment later he motioned to Maru and she walked quickly outside and down the ramp carrying the equivalent of a large backpack. She stopped at the bottom of the ramp and stared at a forbidding swamp filled with strange odors and cries of unknown animals as this planet's sun was going down. She dropped her backpack and walked back up the ramp to the door where mission leader Grus Harm, Toma Hars and Momus Bluf were watching her.

"Where is this place?" She demanded of Grus. "You were supposed to leave me near a large human city—Sao Paulo."

"We seemed to have made a small navigational error." replied Grus. "You can still find your way to your target. Now go! We must leave before we are discovered."

"We are in the middle of a jungle! Who would discover us?"

Grus pointed. "That human."

Maru turned quickly and saw a human running away. She uttered a curse so vile, Grus and Toma laughed as they watched her sprint down the ramp after the human. Grus turned to re-enter the ship, and found his path blocked by an angry Momus Bluf. "If you make another small navigation error when you drop me off, I'll search this planet until I find you." Momas warned him.

"The navigator has been suitably disciplined. There will be no more mistakes."

Momus stared at the dense jungle into which Maru had disappeared, then walked to the bottom of the ramp.

Jason found the warship as Maru was walking back up the ramp. He had a moment to notice that the craft was huge and green, blending well with the jungle. He stared at four large, human-like shapes in the open doorway and noticed a pistol or sidearm at the waist of one. Oh, my God! At least they're not reptiles, or giant slugs. Jason felt his stomach churning. All his expeditions had not prepared him for this. One of the larger hulking shapes pointed at him, and the smallest one started to run toward him. He suddenly realized he didn't have his own revolver, and bolted into the jungle.

Maru chased him through the jungle, until she finally closed the gap and tackled him. But this was not one of the weak, worthless humans she had been instructed she would find; this human was strong. He fought her off, and they stood up and circled each other. To an untrained observer, what followed could have mistaken for a martial arts demonstration. Neither had a weapon, other than hands and years of training. It turned out to be nearly a draw until the human obtained a small advantage and flipped Maru on her back. He was quickly on top of her, their faces so close that a drop of blood from a cut over his eyebrow fell in her eye. As his DNA coursed through her body, she felt a sudden jolt of energy. She was fighting him off when suddenly he rolled off her, and she saw Momus standing over him with a large tree branch. Her eye started watering and she wiped it with her sleeve. "Why didn't you just shoot him?"

"There are other humans near here. They might be able to detect an energy blast, and we do not want to give our mission away." Momus tossed

Maru her backpack. "You should know—I have removed all technology devices that could give us away."

"You can't leave me without a weapon!"

"You are a well-trained warrior. You will do well. Just remember why you are here."

"I know why I'm here." As she picked up her backpack, she had to wipe her eye again.

"Then here is your first test case. Until we meet again…" He turned and walked away in the direction of the ship.

Maru stood over the unconscious human. Momus was right. Her goal was to find a technique for disabling humans that would not lead to her discovery, and then to apply that technique when the time came. She knelt on one knee and stared at her first human. She had never seen yellow hair before. This one was muscular and certainly was not weak. His shirt was torn and she stared in fascination at the hair on his chest. No Juban had that, and she found herself running her fingers through his chest hair, wondering what he was like. She rubbed her watering eye that was now starting to itch.

Jason's head was pounding as consciousness returned. He felt something moving lightly through his chest hair. *This is all a dream. I'll wake up soon.* He slowly opened his eyes and saw the Juban warrior woman staring at him. *What the hell, this is a dream anyway.* He put his hand on her arm softly and they stared at each other for a moment.

Her first instinct was to try and knock him out again, but his blue eyes distracted her and for some reason she couldn't explain, she was strangely drawn to him. She grabbed his hand and pulled him up.

Darkness was setting in as Jason had his first good look at her. She had human-like eyes and ears, a mouth and nose. She was a little taller than he, with the physique of a female bodybuilder, but with a very small waist.

Her skin was light gray and her hair was a bright orange. Even stranger, her irises were also orange which gave her a somewhat ominous look. She was wearing a tight metallic looking outfit and carrying a large black backpack. He noticed a small white box on a metallic band around her neck.

Her voice reminded him of computer-generated recordings. "Tell no one about me, or I will find and kill you." She stared at him for a moment, then turned and walked quickly into the forest, wiping her watering eye.

Jason stared after her until she was gone. As he brushed off his shirt sleeves, a shiny metal object on the ground caught his attention. A clip of some kind. A hair clip? It must be hers. He stuffed it into his pocket and walked slowly back to the boat, rubbing his throbbing head.

"Well, what was it?" Markus asked as he handed Jason his revolver.

"I didn't find it. I thought it might be a meteorite, but I couldn't find anything—no fire or anything…"

Marisela noticed his clothing. "What happened to you? Your clothes are torn."

"I tripped over some vines. It's getting dark, we need to go."

When Jason passed her, something caught her attention. What was that scent? Perfume?

"Are you sure, you didn't find anything?"

What was wrong with her? "I'm sure." He motioned them to get on the boat, then pushed it back into the water and pulled himself aboard with a rope. When he happened to glance at Marisela she was staring at him with a questioning look. He might tell her about his encounter someday, but not today. The rest of the trip back to Sao Paulo was uneventful, or as uneventful as a trip with a 35-foot Anaconda can be, but Jason couldn't take his mind off his encounter in the jungle. His head still hurt, and he wondered if he had somehow fallen, hit his head, and dreamed the whole thing. But if it was a dream, why did she speak to him in English instead of Portuguese? He rubbed his aching head again. If he spoke of it, no one would believe him. He had no physical evidence, other than a small, ordinary looking metal hair clip. He would just be another nut who talked about aliens encounters. He couldn't take that chance if he ever wanted to find sponsors for future adventures.

Maybe it was a woman's instinct, but Marisela was convinced something had happened and Jason was holding out on her. How could he get that dirty and tear his shirt just by tripping over some vines? And that wasn't even likely as nimble and sure-footed as Jason was. Her incessant questioning led to a quarrel and eventually to a time out in their relationship. After a miserable trek through the Amazon, Marisela wasn't all that anxious to join Jason on his next adventure to a research station in the Antarctic anyway.

To someone who still lived a graduate student lifestyle, the $50,000 reward for the record-setting green was a fortune. On top of that, the zoo had gratefully matched it when he presented them with the record-setting, live green anaconda. In an unusual streak of luck, Adventurer magazine had also paid him $25,000 for exclusive pictures and rights to his Anaconda-capturing story. Jason stared at his checkbook register with a new balance in excess of $125,000 US dollars. In Brazil, in general, that was a considerable amount—in Sao Paulo, not so much. Still, Jason had never had that much money in his life. He had had a lot of adventures that were paid by various grateful and ungrateful sponsors, but his personal financial situation seemed to always be on the brink of bankruptcy.

The sparsely furnished studio apartment in a modest neighborhood of Sao Paulo was just as he left it twenty-odd days ago. Jason dropped his backpack onto his only chair with a sigh of relief. There was no point even checking the refrigerator; he knew it was empty. After a long hot shower, he pulled his backpack off the chair and flopped into it. Dozens of TV cable channels couldn't hold his interest, so he started unpacking. He emptied the pockets of his well-worn jeans, and tossed the hair clip on his breakfast table with everything else. He still couldn't believe this odd assortment of hunting gear had passed the x-ray analysis at the airport. Some items, like the hair clip, triggered memories he would just as soon forget. He stretched out on his bed to rest for a minute and drifted off to sleep.

Five days after meeting the human, Maru Gren's trek through the jungle brought her to a small town. She was a survivor. With humans around, she first had to find ways to hide what was different about her—her skin color, the hair on her head, and her eyes. She broke into a store during the night and stole some creams and powders that would probably cover her gray skin, athletic clothing, a cap and several pairs of shoes, a small backpack, some glasses with dark lenses and something that should color her hair. She had limited reading knowledge of Portuguese, but she finally found an empty building with a sign in the window that indicated it was for sale or rent. She colored her hair, changed clothes, applied the creams and powders to her face and hands, and covered her newly colored hair with a sports cap. Her small store of Juban food had run out in a few days and she was hungry. Fortunately, in a dark alley, she came across one human robbing another. One blow of her fist to his head knocked the robber out. The other human ran, and Maru was left with an unconscious human. She picked him up and carried him over her shoulder until she laid him down under a streetlight. She searched through his pockets, hoping to find something that might be exchangeable for food. In one pocket she found a small pouch that contained what she assumed was local money. She quickly stuffed it into her backpack. She knew Basic English, but could speak only a little Portuguese. In a corner store she was able to use some sign language and buy some bread and bottled water, and something that turned out to be too sweet to eat. It would be difficult to adjust to human food, but she was determined to carry out her mission.

In her new disguise, she could pass among humans during the day and came across a newsstand. A photo on Adventurer magazine caught her eye. She was surprised to see a picture of her first human contact on the cover proudly displaying the record setting Green Anaconda. She couldn't quite understand the article about adventurer Jason Steele, but guessed that he was also a "hunter" of sorts. The article did say Jason lived in Sao Paolo. She smiled.

CHAPTER 3

Grus Harm

Like a chameleon, the Juban warship changed to sand-beige as it landed on the desert near Cairo—a world away from the Amazon jungle. The door and ramp opened silently and Grus Harm ventured cautiously outside. Even though it was nighttime, the oppressive heat of the desert quickly enveloped him and he had to take a deep breath. He had trained for this, but the small, mild deserts on Jubas were no match for the massive and brutal desert he now faced. He walked away from the warship and, from a suitable distance, watched his last link to home disappear into the night sky. A few lights twinkled in the distance and he shifted his huge backpack to a more comfortable position. He braced himself as a gust of hot, dry wind blew a fine dust into his eyes. Luckily, Momus Bluf hadn't checked his backpack for technology devices. He pulled a metallic shield with a protective visor over his head, and started toward Cairo. He needed to be there before dawn.

Grus was totally unprepared for Cairo. Despite extensive training, he was overwhelmed at the sights, sounds and smells as he entered the ancient city. Even at night, the streets were teeming with people, vendors in open stalls, vehicles and animals pulling carts. He waited in the shadows until he spotted a solitary figure that seemed large enough, then pulled him into a dark alley and robbed him. He quickly donned the stolen clothes and hid his large backpack. His first task was to find a safe place to stay before daylight, when his unique features would cause him to stand out in the crowd. At a little over two meters tall, it seemed to Grus that he was much taller than the average inhabitant in this city. He also had to figure out a way to hide his orange hair and cover his orange irises. There wasn't anything he could do about his height or his bodybuilder-like frame.

His first victim had also unwillingly provided a small animal hide pouch with some local money and identification papers he could modify if he found the right equipment. He looked around at the adobe walls of the houses and buildings, the dusty streets and menagerie of people and animals and wondered how he would ever be able to survive in this environment. But, first a place to hide… he pulled the hood of the newly acquired robe over his head and headed further into the city.

He tried to be unobtrusive, but noticed some people staring at him. He assumed his height was the issue, and walked quickly with a purpose. As he walked along a nearly deserted street a vehicle passed him and stopped next to a young female walking a short distance ahead of him. Two males jumped out, grabbed the female and forced her into the vehicle. She saw Grus and yelled to him. He had a limited knowledge of the language but knew she was asking for help. Grus hesitated. This was not his affair and he certainly didn't need to draw attention to himself. He tried to ignore her cries for help, but instinct and his own internal values took over and he pulled out a small transmitter he knew would temporarily disable all electronic devices. He pressed the button and the vehicle's engine failed. The driver quickly jumped out and opened a compartment in the front of the vehicle to determine the problem. The other male was still trying to subdue the female when Grus opened a rear door of the vehicle, grabbed the male by his clothing and jerked him out of the vehicle with such force he went flying through the air and slammed into the nearest building's wall. Grus walked quickly to the other male and banged his head on the vehicle's engine. The female exited the vehicle and stared at him— uncertain what to do.

He motioned to the female. "Run, before they wake." Even as he spoke, he realized his hood had come off. She was staring at him with a frightened look. Funny how that look of fear translated among humanoids. He yanked the hood back on and waved her away. Instead of running away, she walked slowly to him. Compared to the other humans he had seen so far, she seemed to be well-dressed and looked at him with the darkest eyes he had ever seen. "Thank you."

Out of the repertoire of gestures he had just learned, Grus responded with a nod. The female unexpectedly handed him a small card. "I would like to repay you somehow. Call me at this number."

Grus didn't understand what that meant but nodded again and watched her walk off until he was distracted by the first male, who was now stirring on the sidewalk and trying to get up. He walked over to him, took what was in his pockets, then knocked him out again. Under a streetlight, he searched through his newest possessions and found even more money.

The money and his nose reminded him he had not eaten in some time. He followed the scent of food to a row of street vendors, and bought what he saw a human buy.

A little while later he saw a sign that indicated rooms suitable for renting were available. He retrieved his backpack from the alley and soon was resting on a bed. He pulled out the card the female had given him and stared at it. He would ask the housing attendant who had taken his money what was written on the card, and what it meant to "call her."

Akila Hamdy took a long hot shower and crawled into bed, still shaking from the night's events. For years, she had had reported on crimes and women's issues, among other things, for the Cairo Daily Times, an English language newspaper, but she had never experienced a crime herself. She felt violated. She couldn't stop thinking of the huge albino man who had come to her rescue. She had seen albino animals in zoos and had even filed reports on unusual births, but had never actually seen an albino person before. Had he actually picked up her attacker and thrown him through the air? She shivered and then wondered if he would ever call and allow her to repay him somehow. People who looked "different" often stayed in the shadows, away from people. She wouldn't file the story if he didn't want her to; she owed him that much, and more.

The next day at the newspaper office, she described the attempted kidnapping and the albino who had intervened to Ahmed Lacksmi, her editor.

"Through an informant we learned that your attempted kidnapping was not random. Your last article helped the police arrest some arms dealers. They were determined to extract revenge. Please be careful and allow us to provide a guard for a while."

She shook her head. "Thank you, but I can't do what I have to do, and meet the people I need to meet, with an off-duty policeman following me around." It was only a minor comfort to Akila that the attempted kidnapping was not random.

Grus adapted quickly to his new environment. He found several foods he could tolerate and actually developed a taste for strong, black coffee. No one bothered him when he visited a nearby 24-hour café after midnight. He opened a local newspaper and found a picture of the female he had rescued from kidnappers next to some text. He tried to read her article but it was in English, and he had only a very limited reading knowledge of English. The café owner read it to him, and Grus asked what arms smuggling meant. Later, the rooming house attendant showed him how to use a "house phone" and call her cell phone. After a few tries he connected.

Akila knew who was calling her, as Grus's voice was different, almost robotic, and he stumbled with verb use and tenses. Arabic was difficult for him. After a few false starts, he asked her if he could meet her one night.

Akila took a taxi. No more walking at night. She entered the 24-hour café and easily spotted her tall rescuer in a corner. It seemed to be a local custom when meeting someone, so Grus stood up when she approached.

"Thank you for contacting me," she began. "I wanted to return the favor you did me, somehow." This time, Grus' orange irises didn't bother her. In the light of the café, she was surprised that his hands and face were gray. She had assumed an albino's skin would be white, from lack of pigmentation.

Grus motioned her to sit down, and she ordered coffee. His limited vocabulary made conversation difficult, but he was determined to improve his language skills. Unlike the other Juban spies he had recruited, he knew the likelihood of returning to Jubas was remote. He would have to make the best of whatever happened on Earth. He knew vaguely what a newspaper reporter did, and he wondered if he could somehow use her to accomplish his mission. She must be intelligent to write for a communication medium. Perhaps she could provide information he needed once the Octans arrived.

She took off a head covering and he had his first good look at her. She had dark brown, almost black hair and eyes with an olive complexion. Grus was not enamored of many females, but this one seemed interesting and moderately attractive. He quickly pushed that idea out of his head. He had an important mission and an unknown amount of time to accomplish it.

She began with an expected and innocent question. "Is there anything I can do to repay you?"

"Not at this time—maybe one day." He replied. "It is hard for me to make friends. Would you meet me sometimes, just to talk?"

She felt an immediate empathy with him. "Of course."

They exchanged first names and managed to communicate a little more until Akila left to meet another arms-smuggling informant. Grus escorted her to a vehicle she called a "taxi" and watched her leave, wondering why she was not afraid of him like most other humans. Even while he was pondering that, a vehicle drove by and stopped at a newsstand across the street from the café. Grus recognized Akila's kidnappers as they entered the newsstand. He was waiting for them when they came out. He had accumulated several types of clubs and battering implements and needed to experiment to find the best method for temporarily incapacitating humans. He tried a rubber-coated wooden stick and knocked the first one out. The second kidnapper tried to pull a weapon from his clothing, but Grus was faster and hammered him as well.

Searching their pockets, Grus found metal implements he assumed would start their vehicle. After some experimentation he opened the rear compartment of the vehicle and found an unexpected cache of what appeared to be crude but effective weapons. He emptied the kidnappers' pockets, and tore their clothing into strips, tied them up, left a message on Akila's cell phone, and headed back to his rooming house.

Over time, Grus' language skills improved and his conversations with Akila became more personal. She talked about her job and what she liked and disliked about it. She asked Grus if he had a job. He said he worked odd jobs, whenever he could find them. She understood that as well. Over time, their café meetings became more frequent and lasted longer. One night, outside the café, she kissed him before she left and he felt a hot flash surge through his body that he was totally unprepared for, but somehow oddly enjoyed. The next time she kissed him, he kissed her back.

Once he understood Akila's desires to report on gun-smuggling, he became her best street source on the smaller dealers. During his nightly prowls, he witnessed criminals involved in all sorts of illegal activities. Whenever he saw someone open the back end of a vehicle and carry large weapons into a house or warehouse, he contacted Akila, who forwarded his information to the police. Akila received several awards from the police and civic organizations for her efforts to end weapon smuggling in Cairo. She publicly thanked Grus each time, without revealing his identity of course.

Grus found street thugs to be convenient targets to practice ways to disable humans in preparation for the arrival of the enemy Octans. He became adept at bludgeoning thugs with his rubber bat. He had to be careful though, as even a rubber bat could kill. He especially enjoyed bludgeoning gun smugglers and drug dealers.

One day, Akila offered to cook dinner for Grus and he gratefully accepted. He was certainly tired of street vendor food and the limited food available at the 24-hour café. He wasn't certain what to expect when she opened the door, but Akila was wearing a western style dress instead of her usual Arabic gowns. She was surprised when he handed her a bouquet of flowers. She apologized for her lack of cooking skills but Grus complimented her extensively—it was immensely better than his usual fare. Grus had never smelled perfume before and hers was thoroughly captivating. After dinner, she also provided his first alcoholic beverage. He wouldn't have thought it possible, but she asked him to spend the night and he eagerly accepted.

Over time, Grus' attitude toward humans changed. He had a much better understanding of their problems and general lack of resources on a very over-crowded planet. Jubas was a smaller planet, with 90% of its surface covered in oceans. It was also crowded, but they had overcome that with nuclear fusion power, efficient water desalination, and hydroponic farming. Even after a year on Earth, Grus was still dismayed at the plight of so many poor people crowded into the vast Cairo metropolis.

In a little less than two years, Grus had perfected his technique and was bored waiting for the Octans. What was taking so long? Why hadn't they finally contacted Earth? He needed something to do. He had effectively cleaned out his neighborhood of criminals and thugs. Police occasionally found them wandering like zombies in the streets, not knowing why they were in that state. Grus had actually accumulated quite some wealth by selling all of the criminals' possessions at the main Cairo Bazaar. Having no other use for the money, he often bought Akila small but thoughtful gifts. After three years on Earth, Grus was well known in his neighborhood for helping poor people. No one knew the origin of his money, but after a while, they accepted the fact that he suffered from some afflictions, but was a "good person." He hadn't planned it, or even guessed it would happen, but he somehow became romantically involved with Akila. Eventually she asked him to move in with her. Very slowly, as a result of Grus' intimate contact with Akila, his eyes and hair became light brown then dark brown, and his skin became olive like Akila's. She noticed this, of course, but assumed it was somehow related to a biological disorder.

CHAPTER 4

It had taken three years, but Maru Gren was now living in Sao Paulo and fairly fluent in Portuguese. There were many easy targets in large cities. She immediately realized that she couldn't harm innocent humans without attracting unpleasant police attention. Criminals were another matter. To stay busy and keep her skills sharp, she made a nightly game of catching criminals, knocking them unconscious, taking their possessions, tying them up and turning them over to the police, anonymously of course. Residents of Sao Paulo were used to daily reports of crime, so news of tied-up criminals turned over to police soon became a legend, and people speculated endlessly on who was doing it, and their motive. Even street criminals became more cautious when news reports mentioned the turned-over criminals were having memory problems and acting strangely.

In these three years, she often thought of the human she had encountered in the jungle. Her perspective slowly changed and during some rainy and lonely nights, she often thought of him. Now where was he? Sao Paulo was a mega-city of more than 20 million but she had shown his picture from the Adventurer Magazine to many people and narrowed the search down to a relatively small neighborhood.

Jason woke from a deep slumber and headed down the stairs from his apartment to find something to eat. It was getting dark outside and the usual light over the exit door was out, but there was a little light coming in through the glass in the door. As he groped for the doorknob, a hand covered his mouth and pulled him back.

"Make no noise. I will not hurt you."

Jason knew instantly who it was, as Maru's voice was distinctive. When she let go, he turned around to face her. So, it wasn't a dream after all. "I didn't tell anyone about you."

"I know this," she replied.

He started to ask how she found him, but that didn't matter. "Then… why are you here?"

"I… uh…" As she struggled to reply Jason guessed why and moved closer until he leaned forward and kissed her. A hot flash passed through her body. She had seen other humans doing this, but hadn't understood why—until now. She kissed him back with the softest lips he had ever experienced.

I thought so. "Come with me." He took her hand and led her up the stairs to his apartment. When he turned on the lights she took her cap off and closed the door. Her hair was longer and dark brown. It was cut almost like a mop and her natural hair color was starting to show. She was wearing a dark ill-fitting jogging suit and tennis shoes. Sunglasses were parked on her head and she seemed tired, almost worn out.

"You look different."

"It was necessary." Maru noticed the sparse furniture in the apartment. "You have the quarters of a warrior."

Jason laughed. "I don't spend a lot of time here." His stomach growled and he asked. "Are you hungry?"

"There are few foods I can eat here."

"Maybe I can help. Do you eat meat?"

Her eyes suddenly narrowed. "Do you mean animals?"

He suddenly realized the issue. "I mean prepared and cooked."

She seemed relieved. "Yes, of course."

"There's a good barbeque place near here, with all kinds of meat and fish. I'm sure we can find something you might like."

"Why would you want to help me? You must think I am here to do something bad."

"I don't know why you are on Earth. You must have a reason for landing in the middle of the Amazon jungle at nightfall."

She looked down, a little embarrassed. "There was a small navigational error…"

"We can talk about that later. Let's go."

Maru kept her sunglasses on until they were seated in a dark area of the restaurant. Servers brought all kinds of meat and fish on skewers and at Jason's urging she tried them all. She found a few she liked.

"Chicken is good. Lamb… not so much," she commented between bites.

Jason smiled. "Many would agree with you."

She had eaten more than he had. She must have not eaten very often, as she seemed a lot thinner now than from their jungle encounter. Her waist was even smaller now than he remembered. The poorly fitting athletic shirt made her seem bigger than she probably was. He sat back, wondering if he should help her. What was her mission, after all?

"How would you like a new hair style and some new clothes?"

She stared at him. "Female clothing?"

"Yes, certainly."

She hesitated. "I have only a little money."

"I have more than I need. Don't worry about it."

She smiled at him, and then continued eating.

They started out in a discreet beauty salon, where they re-colored and styled her hair. Maru was afraid to go in a women's clothing store but Jason insisted. They managed to find some sculptured underwear that fit her frame nicely, and some stylish shirts, jackets and pants, and shoes of course. Jason waited patiently for her to try on several shirts and pants. She commented to him from the fitting room.

"I do not like brassieres. They are too hard to remove."

She didn't understand when he replied, "Most men would agree."

Carrying a large bag with her new clothes and walking back to Jason's apartment, Maru noticed other couples strolling by and put her free hand around Jason's arm. There was no sofa in the small studio apartment, so they had to sit on the end of the bed. Jason brought her a bottle of water and they listened to music for a while. He pointed to his own Adam's apple. "What is that?"

She briefly touched the white box on her throat. "Our vocal cords are different. We need that so you can understand us clearly."

"So… where do you live?" He asked.

"In abandoned buildings, mostly."

"That can be cold in the winter… and hot in the summer."

She nodded. "Sometimes." Moving constantly to avoid detection and sleeping on cold, hard concrete had worn her down, physically and mentally. She was looking around the apartment when she suddenly jumped up. "My modulator!" She ran to a bookshelf and snatched up the hair clip Jason had found in the jungle.

Jason frowned. "That's your hair clip?"

She laughed. "Hair clip! This is an energy modulator. I lost it in the jungle."

The mechanical engineer in Jason was immediately piqued. "What's an energy modulator?"

Maru twisted and turned the device into several configurations. She pulled on the device and a small piece came out with a thin metal band attached. "In this mode, it cools your head."

She walked over to Jason and wrapped the band around his head and connected the small piece to the clip. He immediately felt a cooling sensation that quickly became so cold, he shivered. He was trying to figure that out, when she took the device off, twisted it again and put it back on his head. "In this mode, it heats." He immediately felt a warm sensation that quickly became hot. He jerked the contraption off when it became too hot. He stared at it in his hands.

"How does it work?"

"It draws energy from the air. It can heat or cool." She stared at the device in his hands and sighed. "I could have used this…" Jason handed it back to her and she sat down on the bed twisting it back into its hair clip-like design.

"It sounds like a miniature heat pump."

She stared blankly at him until he commented, "That's probably not a good analogy."

It was getting late. "Do you have some place to go tonight?"

She stared at the modulator in her hand. "Not really."

"Would you like to stay here?"

"Stay here?" She looked up at him and started to shake her head.

"Yes. Why not?"

"I don't want to make trouble for you."

"Trouble? My landlord doesn't care. No one will even know."

She was torn between fear of being caught if she stayed in one place too long and the obvious benefits of a warm place, food and even someone to talk to. She had been very lonely. He put his hand on her arm.

"You don't need to decide now if you want to think about it."

She took a deep breath. "I would like to stay tonight if that is all right."

"You can stay as long as you like."

She seemed relieved. "Thank you."

"Would you like to take a shower to clean up? You can have some of my pajamas to sleep in."

"Pajamas?"

"Comfortable clothing for sleeping." He went to a dresser and brought back some silk pajamas he had been given as a gift, and handed them to her. He usually slept in his underwear.

She had never seen silk pajamas before. "Very nice."

He showed her how to start the shower and closed the bathroom door. A little while later she came out wearing his pajamas. "These sleeping clothes are comfortable, and that warm waterfall is much better than fountains, lakes and rivers."

He took a shower and when he came out, she was already asleep on the bed. He pulled the covers over her, turned out the lights, and slipped into the bed next to her. He woke later to find her snuggled next to him. He put his arms around her and drifted off to sleep.

In her time on Earth, Maru had never slept on something so warm and soft, and woke during the night. Jason was sleeping on his back. She ran her fingers through his chest hair and remembered their first encounter in the jungle. What had happened to her? She was a well-trained warrior with an important mission. Why was she so attracted to this human? Why was he so different than what she had been taught over and over about humans?

All other humans didn't really interest her. She could easily carry out her mission and if necessary, kill humans to determine the best way to disable them without drawing attention to herself. She had disabled many human criminals, when she found them robbing or mistreating another human.

What was she going to do now? Her train of thought was interrupted when Jason woke up. He ran his hand along her arm to her shoulder. He turned toward her and gently stroked her face. Then he kissed her. She put her arms around him, uncertain what to do when he unbuttoned her pajama top. Then he was kissing her in places she wouldn't even have thought of. She lost her pajama bottom, and soon they were in the closest of encounters. Dawn was approaching when they finally gave out and fell asleep.

The sun was shining when Maru awoke. Jason was still sleeping as she hurried into the bathroom. She wondered what he would say, and rehearsed all possible responses. She put his pajama top back on and folded herself into the only chair in the apartment to wait for him to wake.

When he awoke, Maru was asleep in his chair. He put her arms around his neck and carried her to the bed. She started to awaken and he whispered in her ear. "Now, where were we?"

She hadn't thought of that question, and laughed.

Two Years Later

Life in Sao Paulo with Jason became routine, and few people ever looked twice at Maru. It wasn't easy at first to sunbathe in the nude on the roof of Jason's apartment building, but Maru became used to it and with a uniform suntan, she no longer needed makeup to hide her gray skin tone. The transformation was complete when Jason found some dark contact lenses to hide her orange irises.

After Maru joined Jason in his daily martial arts exercises, he took her to meet his mentor, to whom she showed a few defensive techniques he had never seen. She became a companion on all Jason's adventures, a companion he could always count on.

Jason rarely received letters. One day Maru noticed him reading a long letter and asked who it was from.

"I still keep in contact with a friend from college, Mike Silver. He was in graduate school and my next-door neighbor in Baltimore when I started college. Now, he's a project planner for an old Baltimore Architectural firm. He proofreads my Adventure Magazine articles and I proof his articles for the Contemporary Architecture magazine. It's just a way to keep in touch. His son will be going to college in a year or so. This is his latest article. He usually writes personal letters on the back of the articles. I guess he's not into email."

Maru nodded, not really understanding what "proofing" an article meant. She was bored and sat down on the chair and turned on the TV. After a while, Jason was standing behind her, kissing her neck and shoulders. "It's early," she said.

"It's always the right time." As he herded her toward the bedroom, she remarked, "I know you have said this many times, but it is hard to believe humans do this almost every day."

"Oh, but they do," he lied. "Sometimes, several times a day."

"That seems even more unlikely." I will ask a human female.

CHAPTER 5

Contact

The Hubble Telescope was on its last legs in 2030, having somehow survived well beyond its expected life. So when it detected a faint blip streaking toward Earth on October 31st, most scientists assumed it was the result of failing electronics. Some even assumed their fellow scientists were pulling a Halloween prank on them. The blip disappeared just before it would have been picked up by ground-based telescopes and was lost in the noise of the countless objects in near space.

Halloween in Baltimore that year was as ordinary for the Silver family as two merged families could be. Mike and Debra took turns handing out candy to trick-or-treaters while Mike's son Jesse and Debra's son Mark and daughter Jackie partied with friends. Television news was full of the usual reports of minor crimes, Halloween pranks, and "unexplained lights in the sky" over New York and Baltimore. To Mike and Debra's relief, their teenage children Jesse, Mark, and Jackie all made it home before midnight.

November 1st, 2030 began like any other day for Mike Silver. A senior staff project planning specialist for an old Baltimore architectural firm, Mike had worked his way up from an entry-level position and after fifteen years was finally in line for a partnership. It seemed as if he had spent his whole life planning something. Prior to joining Barrick, Williams and McKinley, Mike had served a stint in the army as a logistics specialist. He tried to overcome the long days behind a desk at the firm with frequent visits to a gym near his house and so far, had managed to avoid the middle age spread of some of his contemporaries. He was also lucky, as his naturally blond hair hid most of the gray.

Mike's first wife had died of lung cancer and Mike met Debra through a church "singles" group. Debra had just come out of a painful divorce, but they both were lonely and despite numerous disagreements, they rushed into a hasty marriage. Their children were not thrilled with the whirlwind marriage either.

Mike had just turned forty, and the office staff had treated him to lunch at one of the nicer restaurants in Baltimore. He had settled in his office to recuperate, when his assistant rapped on his open office door. "Come and see this, Mike."

Most of the office personnel had already gathered in a conference room to watch a live news conference from the NASA Space Center. Small talk in the office faded as scientists reported contact with an alien craft heading for Earth. On its current course, it would arrive in less than two hours. Strangely, its communications were in English.

Mike Silver and the rest of the design firm personnel joined the world in anticipation as a small alien spacecraft was seen on NASA tracking cameras as it entered the atmosphere and landed next to the United Nations. Military from several nations surrounded the craft. Reporters commented on its small size—barely two hundred feet across. How had such a small craft traveled so far? Surely there was a mother ship nearby, but NASA and observatories around the world had failed to find a larger ship.

Less than an hour after landing, a section of the craft opened and a ramp extended. A large crowd held back by the military gasped as an ordinary human man, dressed in a white flowing tunic and pants, stepped out and calmly approached a delegation from the UN.

"We come in peace," he was heard to say via large dish-shaped microphones held by the media.

Several delegates approached and began a conversation with him. After a brief conversation, the visitor and the delegation walked toward the UN building. TV cameras caught three identical figures standing near the ship's open door. The cameras zoomed in on them as the ship's ramp closed. Commentators questioned whether they were possibly robots. Seeing no threat, the military began removing some of its equipment, as police erected a traffic barrier around the spacecraft. Sensing something major was about to happen, many businesses let their employees go home.

Beta Octos

In a few hours, the seemingly endless speculation ended when a prepared statement was read by a UN spokeswoman.

"Today, the question of whether life exists on other planets has been definitively answered. Our visitors are from a planet about a hundred seventy light years from Earth, Beta Octos. They have visited Earth many times in the past and are familiar with many of our customs. The purpose of this visit is twofold: first, to begin a new relationship that they hope will lead to mutual trust and understanding; second, to discuss the possibility of Earth forming an alliance with them against another very powerful and aggressive species known as the Jubans.

"The Octans are an old and peaceful race, normally content to explore and document developing planets. About 60 Earth years ago, they encountered a powerful and warlike species intent on expanding their influence around the galaxy we call the Milky Way. The Octan technology was superior, but they were outnumbered. The war of attrition ended with a truce. The terms of the truce included a ceasefire for approximately one hundred of our years, fifty of which have passed. During this time, each side is free to colonize as many new worlds as possible without interference. At the end of the truce, the remaining habitable and un-colonized worlds may be claimed without colonization.

"Unfortunately, the Octan population is small and not able to colonize new worlds. So… for the past five decades, they have been looking for possible worlds for colonization by humans. Earth is the only planet in the area of the galaxy they want to claim that has sufficient population to colonize new worlds.

"In exchange for our participation in the colonization effort, the Octans would give Earth most of their advanced technology. They have made a specific proposal, currently being studied by the UN Security Council."

Jason and Maru had watched the landing at the UN, along with everyone else on Earth with a TV. After the UN statement, Jason looked at Maru. She avoided his eyes.

"Pretty soon, I won't have to ask you what your mission is," Jason said.

"I abandoned that mission the first time you kissed me."

"So… you still won't tell me?"

"You'll know soon enough." She walked into the bathroom and closed the door.

CHAPTER 6

The Deal

The courier, Jude Harwig, had been taken by the Octans to study and had requested to stay with them instead of having his memory erased and being returned. Details of the alien proposal brought by Harwig leaked out even while the Security Council debated the issue in a closed session. The Octans would give Earth most of their technology in exchange for Earth's providing colonists. As a gesture of good will, and to provide evidence of the value of their technology, they gave Earth a working fusion reactor, pollution-free with fuel for many years of operation, along with the documentation necessary to duplicate it. As the Security Council tried to decide what to do with the documents, several never-identified staff members leaked them onto the Internet and to publishing houses worldwide. For a while, the Internet slowed noticeably as every energy engineer on Earth read, studied, and argued. The loss of secrecy about the reactor forced the Security Council to discuss the real issues. Several members expressed concern that Earth would be identified as an Octan ally if the truce with the other aliens was broken. Was this risk acceptable?

The proposal also described the need for two hundred new colonies to be established on a hundred planets in the remaining fifty years of the truce. Specially equipped ships would transport groups of forty thousand colonists to new worlds where a new city would be waiting and ready for occupancy. Clothing and food would be provided for twenty years to allow time for the colony to establish itself. There were, of course, many issues that had to be dealt with to establish a colony.

Although the transport ships were large, there was a physical size limitation on personal effects. Each colonist would be furnished with a one-cubic-meter container. Additionally, the colony could bring another forty thousand cubic meters of common equipment. No weapons were allowed. To provide security, robots with a human outer covering would be assigned to each colony. The purpose of the robots, known as Guardians was to keep the colonists from being hurt, or hurting themselves or harming the planet.

While the discussions were going on, the fusion reactor was connected to the power grid in New York City and immediately provided a level of power equal to a typical nuclear power plant, producing a very favorable impression on the city and the media. Had the aliens provided a long-sought solution to the world's energy problems?

CHAPTER 7

Momas in New York City

Momas Bluf hated being on Earth and especially living in New York City. Like the other mission members, the Juban warrior's only task was to survive without being discovered and wait for the day the hated Octans finally contacted Earth to make a deal. He would then find ways to disrupt the formation of the colonies they were building, in a way that would ensure the colonies would fail and his role would not be discovered. What should have been a simple assignment had turned into a grueling ordeal. He had arrived several years too soon, and without any advanced weapons or technology, he had been forced to commit petty crimes to obtain money for the human food he hated. He kept to himself to avoid suspicion. At slightly over 2 meters tall, his light gray skin color, bright orange hair, orange irises, and bodybuilder physique ensured he would be noticed if he weren't careful. He became a creature of the night out of necessity.

Momas did not get this assignment by chance. He was a highly-skilled warrior and could not just sit around waiting for the Octans. He needed to devise clever, yet subtle ways to disable the leaders of the colonists before they transported. He soon found that he couldn't practice on the easy targets, like joggers or drunks outside bars, as it generated too much attention in the media, and then police would dress up as tempting targets to lure him into the open. He needed to practice on people no one cared about. He tried a few homeless and drug addicts, but couldn't tell any difference after he injected them with chemicals or just hit them judiciously on the head.

He soon found a new target—street criminals. No one really cared if you disabled them or even killed them accidentally. He became the average citizen's best defense against crime by practicing on hundreds of petty criminals in New York while he refined his techniques.

Raiding drug stores at night, he discovered a potent cocktail that rendered humans unconscious and, when they awoke, slowly incapacitated the areas of the brain where most decisions are made. After several years of experimentation, he gave up on physical attacks and concentrated on injections. Momas hated this assignment almost as much as he hated being on Earth. This undercover work was not the work of a true warrior. He would have preferred to have it out with the Octans on the battlefield, or in space, and settle the issues. But he had taken an oath and would not break it.

When Harwig and the Octans finally arrived, Momas could do little initially to stop the deal. He started tires and cars on fire outside the UN, slaughtered animals and put signs on them that made it look like the work of human protestors. Most of these acts were ignored by the media who assumed they were the work of the fringe elements that always seemed to be present outside any international meeting. He constructed an energy generating device that interfered with anything electronic, but that was found quickly after it began operation and was disposed of by a bomb squad.

Frustrated at his poor attempts to stall the deal, he finally got the humans' attention when he detonated a delivery van filled with explosives, at night near the UN. He was forced to temporarily flee the city when a massive manhunt for terrorists was undertaken by a combination of Federal, State, and local law enforcement agencies. Surveillance video cameras had only caught a large shadowy figure running from the van before the explosion.

The debate finally ended and the Security Council passed a motion to the General Assembly with a recommendation to accept the deal. After another several days of debate, the proposal was accepted. When the UN spokeswoman read a statement confirming the agreement, Jude Harwig and two Guardians were standing next to her. There wasn't anything scary about the Guardians, except for the fact that they were all identical, so you knew they were actually robots with a male human-like appearance. They were large but not immense, standing well over two meters, with light brown skin, light brown hair, and a body builder's physique. They were not intended to look ominous, but they were dressed in black and wore a black cap.

There was a full contingent of fifty Guardians on Harwig's ship. Some of them were always on guard duty outside it, and pictures of them made a large part of many news broadcasts. It had taken Momas almost three years to build an electronic device capable of deactivating a Guardian. The primitive electronics he had to work with made it essential that he carry out his task quickly, as the deactivation period was short.

The Guardians on duty near the ship had learned to ignore the parade of humans walking by and those that stopped to stare at them, as well as the early morning or late-night joggers. Darkness was setting in when a large hooded figure ventured near the traffic barrier erected by the police. Momas glanced around for observers, then activated his crude jamming device and leaped the barrier. He opened an access port at the base of the skull of the closest Guardian and plugged in a small programming device. The download went smoothly, and Momas was able to repeat the process on a second Guardian before the central processing unit of the first finished re-booting.

Assembling the Colonies

As soon as the UN agreed to the deal and the resulting colonization efforts, a web site was set up to allow colonies to self-form. In a matter of weeks, over 2000 potential colonies were forming according to a set of rules established by the Octans and agreed to by the UN. The Octans did not care how restrictive or inclusive a colony wanted to be. A colony could form from a religious point of view and exclude all others, or be based on race or ethnicity or any other basis. All colonists were volunteers and no one could be forced to join any colony. Colonies had to declare the form of government they intended to use initially. Since there would be only one city on each planet in the beginning, only various forms of city government needed to be declared. Later would be time enough for larger entities. There was an extensive list of requirements that had to be met before a colony became certified and was scheduled for transport. There were minimum requirements for skills including doctors, engineers, scientists, and especially farmers. Recruiting doctors became a high priority for each potential colony as the minimum required was one medical doctor (of any specialty) per thousand colonists. Various types of engineers were also in high demand. Farmers found themselves suddenly respected more than they had ever been before.

Mike Silver studied all the potential colonies in great detail, especially a colony destined for the planet Kepler 14b, about sixteen hundred light years from Earth, thirteen months away by Octan transport. Kepler 14b was the only habitable planet of the six orbiting its sun. About 40% larger than Earth, it had three moons and was half ocean. The initial colonists filing the paperwork identified the colony as all-inclusive, meaning people of all races, religions, etc. would be accepted. The colony agreed to the establishment of a monetary system within the first year. It also chose to not form any political organizations other than a strong-mayor, city-council government. Five initial council positions were created, and an election process established. Candidates were to post videos describing themselves and their qualifications. Mike immediately became interested in the city planner position, a job for which he was surely more qualified than any other candidate. One of the Octans' most restrictive requirements stated that no colonist could have a criminal record, with "criminal record" left undefined. The UN's new Colonization Committee required a clear definition for each colony, with enforcement procedures. The North American colony forming for Kepler 14b defined "no criminal record" as no felony convictions, which, as it didn't satisfy the Mexicans, the Americans, or the Canadians, seemed to be a fair agreement.

There were other requirements which caused people to be excluded or to voluntarily drop out. No distance weapons could be transported—no guns, and no serious military weaponry. No large quantities of flammable powders or liquids could be transported. That posed a problem for any machine the colonists required, such as tractors to plow fields and plant crops, or boats for fishing. The small Amish colonies in Brazil had no trouble with this, but the North Americans clamored for more information on the natural resources available on Kepler 14b. Whether they liked it or not, all colonies had to adopt the metric system, and agree on a single common language (English, German, Spanish, Russian, etc.) for all official business and communications with Earth or Octos.

Each colonist was required to certify his or her understanding that no supplies from Earth could be expected for at least twenty years. This eliminated many people with chronic medical conditions; it would be many years before a colony would be able to manufacture medicines.

Debates raged on Internet blogs and the colonization web site about how this unfairly excluded people who would otherwise be candidates for the colonies. Every colony, however, had already found it had to exclude the surprisingly large class of people who wanted to die in space. The Octans themselves had come down hard on a proposed Hospice Colony.

Shortly after the agreement with the Octans, the UN Colonization Committee established at least one departure point on each continent. New York was chosen as the site for the North American departure terminal due to its proximity to the UN and opportunity for the Committee to develop photo opportunities promoting the colonization process. As the largest city, Sao Paulo was chosen for South America. Brussels was chosen for Europe, Moscow for Central Asia, Cairo for Africa and Tokyo for Asia-Pacific.

When Harwig and the Octans finally arrived at the UN, Grus Harm had all but abandoned his mission. He was essentially working full time to help the people in his neighborhood in Cairo. He would have liked to help them more, but he was limited to the technology available to him.

On his sixth anniversary on Earth, he asked Akila to marry him, and she accepted. He watched the Octan African terminal building being built with some amusement. He didn't envy any human wishing to colonize new worlds. His own adjustments on a supposedly "civilized" planet had been tough enough. Colonizing an undeveloped planet would take some organizational skills even he didn't have.

CHAPTER 8

To the other members of the Juban team, Toma Hars was, "the brain." They hadn't expected someone like him to volunteer for a mission affecting the colonization of planets. He was a renowned physical chemist on Jubas, but he dabbled in all areas of science, especially in the field of medicine. Even though Harm's team had incorrectly guessed the likely point of a future Asian colony departure point and left him in southern China instead of Tokyo, Toma quickly adapted by accessing the Internet and downloading the medical volumes he needed to study. He had rightly guessed that several years would go by before the Octans would make contact with Earth. This gave him plenty of time to prepare. His biggest problem was concealing his Juban features from the Chinese. Like the other team members, he broke into stores at night to find food, alternate clothing, and ways to conceal his identity. He had never seen makeup before but quickly determined it would cover his gray skin tone. He took a ferry to Hong Kong and blended into the background, venturing out only at night and keeping up with the news on the Internet. Untroubled by any of what he had to do or anything that happened to the people around him, Toma serenely studied medical and scientific texts and planned ways to disrupt the formation of human colonies.

When the Octans arrived five years later, Toma was ready. He had permanently altered his outward appearance, assuming a Guardian would not be suspect once the deal with the Octans was accepted by the UN. Disguised and dressed as a Guardian, Toma could move freely through the massive crowds in Hong Kong. Even though some appeared to be afraid of him, all knew the Guardians were there to help humans establish colonies on other worlds, and assumed he was in Hong Kong on official business. No one bothered him, or tried to interfere wherever he went. When the UN announced the Asian terminal would be built in Tokyo, Toma purchased an airline ticket on the Internet and flew on a commercial flight from Hong Kong to Tokyo. He had downloaded a UN Colonization Committee logo and attached it to his personal bag. Airport security personnel didn't dare to check his personal bag, and didn't try to stop him when he rang the metal detector. After all, wasn't a Guardian a robot with a metal skeleton? How were they to think that his bag contained the materials needed to disable future colony leaders?

Within a short time, Toma became a permanent fixture at the new Asian Departure Terminal. Actual Guardians had no knowledge of him, and their software didn't require them to check for Jubans disguised as Guardians. Toma studied the formation of the new colonies on the UN colonization site on the Internet and knew who the colony leaders were as they entered the terminal. It was trivial to pass by and scratch each colony leader with a tiny needle, infecting them with an insidious mixture of several slow-acting bacteria and viruses unknown on Earth. The results would not be felt by the victims until several months after their arrival on their new worlds, when they would become slowly incapable of making any rational decisions.

Domas Radi

Several sites were possible for the European Departure Terminal, and the Juban team thought it would be located in Austria, but that was somehow mistaken for Australia and Domas Radi was left in the wilds of the Australian Outback. Much to his dismay, he was quickly discovered by a tribe of aborigines who kept him in captivity, arguing that he was the re-incarnation of an unfriendly god from the Creation period, until a television crew filming a documentary discovered him and reported him to the Australian government.

Trago Modi

Trago Modi was totally unprepared for the harsh Russian weather. Dropped off several hundred kilometers North of Moscow near Lake Onega in the dead of winter, he was only saved from the fierce arctic winds by his multi-layer metallic clothing. Wandering blindly through the driving snow, exhausted and near death, he wandered into a small village. The villagers took him in and cared for him until the following spring, when a government official from the town of Vytegra happened to visit and hear about him. The government whisked him off to a secret research facility, and Trago was never heard from again.

1st Colony—Medical Research

The first colony established after the UN agreement was a medical colony on a moon of Saturn. This was a small colony consisting of less than 5000 doctors, nurses, scientists, assistants, researchers, and support personnel. The city was totally self-contained, but as it was located on a moon without an atmosphere, there was no chance of exploring. All the medical knowledge of the Octans was translated and made available to the colonists, who shared information with those at home.

Small medical breakthroughs were quickly announced on Earth by the Colonization Committee. One of the first announcements was a breakthrough in treating plaque-related dementias, such as Alzheimer's. A new drug dissolved plaque with few side effects. Transmissions between brain cells were re-established and lost memories were recovered. The nightly news was filled with stories of elderly family members who seemed to regain most of their memories. The Colonization Committee used such discoveries to promote colonization and to drown out the voices of groups that warned of dire consequences should the Juban/Octan treaty break down.

Even better for the pro-colony cause, the medical colony's Director of

Operations, Dr. Tom Markoff gave an interview calling the Octan gift of knowledge, "a medical Rosetta Stone."

Kepler 14b

After studying all potential colonies with a serious chance of certification, Mike focused on the colony forming for Kepler 14b, for a variety of reasons, but partly because he knew some of the original organizers, who lived in Baltimore.

Mike normally avoided confrontations, but he knew he could not avoid this one. Debra was cooking dinner as he entered the kitchen carrying a small stack of papers.

"I'd like to talk about the deal with the aliens the UN just approved."

She glanced up. "You mean to form colonies on other worlds? What about it?"

"I'm thinking about going."

Debra couldn't have been more shocked if he had asked for a divorce. She dropped the knife she was holding. "You can't be serious. Leave everything we have and everyone we know to go off and live on some unknown world?"

"Clothing, shelter and enough food for twenty years will be provided. That should give the colonists enough time to become self-sustaining."

Debra felt a sudden dread at what was coming next. One thing she had learned in just a few years of marriage to Mike was that he always meant what he said. She knew it wouldn't do any good, but she gave it a try… "The answer isn't only NO; it's HELL NO! What's come over you?"

"Look, I don't want to live my whole life and at the end wonder if I've ever accomplished anything."

"We have enough issues to work through, without this."

"Maybe a change like this would help—sort of a new beginning—together."

"You're not the adventurous type. Why would you even think of doing this?"

"Millions of men have passed through this world, and except for their family, no one knows when they are gone. There are endless possibilities on a new world."

"Do you really think your son and my kids would want to leave all their friends and everything they know to go off on some crazy adventure? If you do, then you don't know them!" Despite her protestations, Debra felt her safe, comfortable life slipping away. It seemed that once Mike made up his mind, there was almost no chance of changing it.

Jesse, Mark, and Jackie knew their parents had issues but they had never heard Mike and Debra arguing, and wondered why they were raising their voices. Jesse whistled as they entered the kitchen. "Hey, time out. What's going on?"

"Tell them!" demanded Debra.

"If I had been living in Baltimore a hundred and fifty years ago, and I read about the West and all the adventures and opportunities, I probably would have joined a wagon train and headed west."

He saw the confusion on their faces. "There hasn't been an opportunity like that in over a hundred years until now. I told Debra I'm thinking about joining one of the communities trying to be certified for an alien colony."

Jesse, Mark, and Jackie looked at each other and laughed. "You've never taken a risk in your life. You even once said one of the benefits of planning is risk reduction." Jesse said and laughed again. He stopped when he realized his dad wasn't kidding.

"You can't be serious. What would you do there?"

"I'm thinking about applying for the position of planner on the city council."

Jesse could hardly believe they were even having this discussion. "Leave all this behind? Leave all our friends, and family?"

"We wouldn't need any of this stuff there. All the essentials would be provided. As for family and friends… we don't have many close family members and I would ask all our friends to join us. You could ask your friends as well. It would be great if they came along."

Jesse shook his head. "I have one more year of high school and I've been accepted to three colleges. I'm not going to leave all that for something I know nothing about."

Jackie sat down on a kitchen stool. "One of my friends at school said that's a one-way trip, so you can count me out."

Mark folded his arms angrily. "No way I'm leaving my friends for something dumb like this."

Debra was absently wiping her hands on a towel. "I understand everything you said, but this just isn't right for any of us."

Mike took a deep breath. "I don't want to live my whole life and no one will even know when I'm gone, except you. I'm going, with or without you."

They all gasped in disbelief.

"You would really leave us behind?" asked Debra, although she already knew the answer.

"I would leave you everything, the house, the cars, my retirement accounts, my pension… everything. You'd be okay financially. I have saved enough to retire when I'm fifty anyway."

"You really wouldn't do that, would you Mike?" asked Jackie softly. Mark just glared at his stepfather.

"It's important to me. I don't know what else I can say to convince you."

There were enough problems between them, and this just seemed to make matters worse. What would she do if they divorced on some far-off planet? What would she do then? Here, with the money, the house, and the cars, she'd be okay for a while. She shook her head. "You'll have to do this without me, or my children." She looked at Mark and Jackie, who nodded in agreement.

"Wait! What about me?" asked Jesse. "What would I do?"

"If you don't want to stay with Debra, I would make your aunt, your guardian and set up a trust for you. She'd take care of you until you're twenty-one; then you'd be on your own. You'd have plenty of money to go to college."

"No way I'm living with Aunt Rose for four years." said Jesse. "I'm coming." He walked over to Mike who hugged him. "What's the name of this planet, anyway?"

"Its scientific name is Kepler 14b, because it's in a binary pair with the third planet from the sun, Kepler 14a. Just to keep things simple, the colonists have decided to shorten the name to just 'Kepler.'"

Mike handed Jesse the papers he was holding. "Here's some of what's known about it. I bookmarked the rest on my laptop."

Jesse started to read about his future home, as Debra hugged Mark and Jackie.

CHAPTER 9

Mike reserved a meeting room in an annex of his church and emailed all his friends, and a few co-workers, inviting them to come and hear why they should join him and his son on the new world. Jesse forwarded the email to his friends, and somehow the notice even made it to the "Colony News" section on the UN colonization site.

Mike intended a short meeting for the dozen or so people he expected to show up. Even before he arrived, the small meeting room filled up and the pastor of the church agreed to move the meeting. Mike was almost tongue-tied when he found the 800-person sanctuary packed with people anxious to hear about Kepler.

Mike had prepared a slide show in case there was enough interest. He started the slide show after a few brief introductory remarks, and his nervousness quickly evaporated as everyone there was eager to learn about the organization of the colony, the city in its final stage of construction, and what was known about the planet. His enthusiasm seemed contagious and the meeting lasted more than two hours. The stack of informational flyers on how to join the colony that Jesse passed out, were soon gone. At the end of a long question and answer session, everyone gave Mike a round of applause and thanked him for the information.

Momus Bluf, in a hooded jacket, was just one of many who folded a flyer and stuffed it into a pocket. Others were more openly interested. Overall, the meeting was very productive: several friends of the Silver family were enthusiastic, and eventually decided to apply for the colony. Once he accepted the inevitability of joining the colony, Jesse helped his dad make a three-minute video introducing Mike and describing his qualifications to be the planner on the city council. Jesse then uploaded it to the section of the colonization web site that organized elections of officials for each colony.

The election went smoothly, as only three other persons applied for the planning position on the city council. None were as qualified as Mike, and he won easily. Mike noted with interest that Joan Enders, the mayor of the new colony, also lived in Baltimore.

He quit his job, and transferred everything he owned to Debra and her children. It turned out to be a lot easier than he thought it would be. Mike didn't need it, as Debra was staying, but as soon as the colonies began organizing, the UN Committee overseeing the colonization efforts established bank accounts for each colonist family to contain the proceeds from the sale of homes, cars, bank accounts, retirement accounts, pensions owed—virtually anything that could be converted to cash—even the proceeds from garage sales. The accounts would collect interest in perpetuity until someone from the colonist family returned in the future to claim it. This took away one major stumbling block as it was difficult for many people to just give up everything they owned to be colonists. One cubic meter can only hold a small amount of family heirlooms.

One of the first calls Mike made when he was elected planner was to Jason Steele in Sao Paulo. "Just wanted to catch up with you. I read that you have a significant other."

Jason laughed. "You could call her that. We get along well. Is your son excited about going to college?"

"That's one reason why I called." He paused for a moment. "Jesse and I have decided to join a colony forming on a planet known as Kepler 14b. I was just elected the city planner and you were the first person I thought of. We could really use someone like you, who understands survival in difficult conditions. Would you consider joining us?"

Jason was surprised that Mike would even consider something so risky. Mike didn't say anything about Debra, so she obviously wasn't going.

He couldn't even imagine how he managed to convince Jesse to go. "It sounds interesting. Let me talk it over with Maru and I'll get back to you."

"Great! I really hope you can come along. You'd be the perfect advisor."

Jason laughed. "Is that a paid position?"

"You won't need money… remember? There's nothing to buy—in the beginning."

"I know, just kidding. I'll call you back. Thanks for thinking of me, though."

Maru was staring at him when the call ended. "Was that Mike Silver?"

"Yes. He's inviting us to join a colony forming for the planet Kepler something. Ironic, isn't it?"

Maru really didn't understand irony. "Do you want to go? I will go anywhere with you. You know this."

"This is a little tricky don't you think? A Juban warrior—migrating to an Octan city—inhabited by Earthlings."

She ignored that as well. "So? Do we go?"

"What if the Guardians recognized you? What would happen?"

"I do not know. We will make sure they do not."

Jason sat on their new sofa to think. Maru sat down next to him, putting her head on his shoulder. He put his arms around her.

"Maybe we should change your name."

"Maru does not mean anything. The Octans will not know it."

Maru frowned when Jason let go and knelt down on one knee in front of her and took one of her hands. "I mean your last name. Will you marry me?"

A few seconds passed before Maru jumped on him, knocking him on the floor and kissing him. When she stopped, he asked. "I assume that means yes?"

"It does."

"While we are at it, what if we changed your first name to Maria? No one would take notice of someone from Brazil with that name."

Maru stood up, repeating the name several times. "Yes, a good name."

Jason stood up and hugged her. "So, are you ready to go to Kepler—something?"

She started and he joined in… "Anything—anytime—anywhere."

Momas Bluf was eating some disgusting pizza when he heard a knock on the door. Momas lived in a basement apartment in Brooklyn, not far from a subway entrance. No one ever visited him, so he picked up a large handgun he had taken from an incapacitated gang member and pointed it at the door.

"Come in."

An Octan Guardian entered and closed the door behind it. Momas frowned. Guardians would never knock on a door and would never close the door behind them. Since all Guardians looked alike, he had to be sure if this was one of his new assistants. He could never remember any of their twelve-digit identification numbers, but he could remember the last three digits.

"Are you 351?"

"Yes. I received a signal to find you."

"Did you or 352 have anything to do with the death of the mayor of the Kepler 14b colony?"

The Guardian didn't answer, but Momas knew the answer.

"Are you out of your mind?" He shook his head as soon as it came out of his mouth. That didn't even make sense.

"We only wanted to injure her, not kill her."

"Your orders were to injure the city planner, not the mayor. The mayor was inept and ineffective—perfect for what we want on these colonies. And… you were not to kill colonists and draw attention to our mission!!!" Momas had to take a deep breath to calm down.

"We made a mistake. It will not happen again."

"You're exactly right it will not. From now on, I want to know what you are doing whenever colonists could be killed."

"Yes, Momas."

Momas waved him away, and the Guardian strangely shut the door on the way out. Momas wondered if there was something wrong with this Guardian's core programming. Surely there was nothing wrong with the mission programming he had installed in the Guardians. He shook his head at the thought of that. Maybe he needed to compromise more Guardians?

He held his nose and took another bite of pizza.

Celebration

Jason took Maru to their favorite barbeque restaurant to celebrate their engagement—Maru felt uncomfortable in fancy restaurants. Near the end of the meal, Jason happened to ask Maru if she had a boyfriend or someone special on Jubas.

"We do not 'date' as you do." She said. "And I was too young to form a permanent relationship."

Jason choked on his wine. "Maru?"

"Yes?" She replied between bites of chicken.

"How old are you?"

She didn't even look up at him as she replied. "Twelve."

Uh oh. Jason could see the article now. 'Famed explorer found in relationship with alien MINOR.' "But, that's not possible, is it?"

Maru glanced up and saw his concerned expression. "Yes, because one Juban orbit is about two Earth years. I am about 24 Earth years."

Jason breathed a huge sigh of relief. He would make sure she told the license official she was 24. He stared at her thinking. She was only nineteen when we first met and seventeen when she left Jubas. Maru once mentioned it had taken a Juban year to travel secretly to Earth. "Maru?"

"Yes?"

"That night you found me… and we spent our first night together…"

"Yes?"

"Had you ever done that before?"

She smiled at him. "No." She continued eating as Jason gulped his wine and poured more.

CHAPTER 10

One Month Prior to Transport

For the vast majority of families, becoming a colonist required them to give away or sell everything they owned as the likelihood of returning was extremely low. Earth money would be of no value on the new world.

Lawyers and accountants did a booming business. Mike had transferred everything he owned to Debra; he was now driving a car that belonged solely to her, and sleeping in her bed, in her house. He cashed out his retirement accounts and his pension, and turned the money over to Debra, rather than waiting for the courts to decide the issue.

Members of the first colonies to leave had placed lists of their personal equipment on the Internet to give future colonists suggestions and ideas. Mike downloaded a suggested personal equipment checksheet and made a rough pass at his cubic meter of personal effects. He put everything on the bed and wondered if it would all fit in one of the shiny boxes a UN truck had delivered to his home. An early colonist had recommended scanning photos and important documents to save on room, but Mike kept a few photographs and documents he could hang on the wall. Someone had pointed out that hanging anything in the new city would be difficult— you could not drive a nail into the metal walls, so he added some double-sided tape to his box hoping it would work until someone figured out how to hang pictures or paintings. He carefully wrapped his first wife's wedding rings and some of her jewelry and placed them in a small wooden jewelry box. An early colonist suggested allocating space in the container by percentages—5% for jewelry for example. That seemed to work. His only exception was his favorite pair of jogging shoes. Someday, someone in the colony might be able to make something like that, but for now these would have to do for a number of years.

The shoes provided on the colonies resembled closed-toe sandals. You could have as many of them as you wished, but they all looked alike, so what was the point of having many pairs? The provided clothing consisted of a white tunic and white pants—as many as you wanted, but they also were all alike, so why have many? The cloth was actually a polymer that was as soft and flexible as cotton but totally resistant to stains, dirt, oils, and almost everything else including dyes. There was no need to pack clothing, but most lists he had reviewed included a few colorful shirts, or even jeans.

There was no need to take favorite books, movies, video games, or recorded music, as virtually every book written, every movie and video game made and every song of every music company had been digitized and would be available. Negotiating the rights to all this intellectual content, seemed the least the Colonization Committee could do, considering the sacrifices the colonists were making, and the risks they were taking, in part so Earth could meet its obligation to the alliance. From a practical point of view, the book and media companies couldn't really expect any future revenue from the colonists anyway.

Mike was finalizing his list, when the doorbell rang. He opened the door and much to his surprise, a Guardian was waiting with a large brown envelope. It was a little awkward, but Mike invited him in and closed the door.

"Mr. Silver, has anyone has informed you of the death of the elected mayor of Kepler 14b?"

Mike was shocked to learn that Enders had died. "No! How terrible," he said. "What happened?"

"Her brakes failed. She swerved into a water-filled ditch and drowned," said the Guardian without emotion. He opened the envelope and handed him two papers. "The Colonization Committee was going to hold another election but they were overruled, and you have been appointed mayor for four years, at which time a new election must be held on Kepler 14b."

Mike stared at an official-looking document naming him mayor. "But… who overruled the Committee?"

"The Earth Ambassador."

That didn't click at first, and then it came to him. "The Octan Ambassador overruled the Committee?" No one on Earth but Jude Harwig had ever seen anyone from Octos, let alone the Ambassador that Harwig reported to. "How did he even know my name?"

"He knows what he needs to know. Please sign the appointment form."

In a daze, Mike scribbled his name on one copy and handed it back to the Guardian, who returned it to the envelope. He unexpectedly held out his hand to Mike, who shook it.

"Congratulations on your new appointment, Mayor Silver." he said. He turned and walked out the door, leaving it open.

Mike watched the Guardian enter a car with a "UN Colonization" sign and drive off. He closed the door as Debra came into the living room. "Who was that?"

He showed her the appointment form. "A Guardian."

"A Guardian came here?" She quickly read the form. "Mayor? Do you think you're qualified for that?"

"It pretty much doesn't matter if I think so or not, the Octan Ambassador appointed me for the next four years."

Debra shook her head. She decided to tell him what she had been thinking since he said he was joining the colony. "Mike?"

"Yes?"

"I've been thinking. Mark, Jackie, and I are going to stay with my sister until you leave. I just think it's better that way. I'll think about the rest once you've gone."

After a moment, he hugged her.

After Mike's appointment as mayor was posted on the Colony Committee web site, he arranged a contest to name the city they would be founding. In a vote, the colonists chose "Helios," after the Greek sun god.

It had been a little over a year since the Octans arrived on Earth. The transport day for the Kepler colony was approaching rapidly and Momas couldn't wait any longer for his assistants to incapacitate the new mayor. In desperation, he covered the gray skin on his face and hands with makeup, dyed his orange hair brown, and managed to find some colored contact lenses. He bought black clothing that resembled the clothing worn by the Guardians and drove to Baltimore in a stolen car. At the Silver house, he double-checked the syringe in his jacket pocket, and stepped out. He would have to be careful and find a way to get Silver alone and then inject him with the mixture that would knock him out, and eventually damage a portion of his brain. For most humans, this seemed to impair their basic logic and decision-making ability, just what was needed for the colony to fail and be abandoned. In the last six months, five colonies had left from the New York terminal, and Momas had managed to inject council members of all of them. He hoped the mixture had worked according to plan.

He rang the doorbell and waited but no one opened the door. A woman walking a dog noticed him pacing back and forth impatiently while he tried to figure out his next move. She waved to get his attention. "Sir? Sir? Excuse me" she said. "I don't know about the rest of the family, but Mike Silver has gone to New York, to the UN. He's the mayor of the Kepler colony, you know." She seemed proud of that distinction for her neighborhood.

Momas gritted his teeth and thanked her. He could have been waiting outside the UN after a thirty-minute subway ride, instead of driving all the way to Baltimore. Even worse, he now needed to eat more of the disgusting human food.

All the way back to New York, Momas considered alternative plans in case he couldn't get close enough to Silver or some of the other council members. As a last resort, he might have to send his new assistants along to sabotage the colony.

But wait. After some reflection, he liked that idea. Why hadn't he thought of it before? He would have to find a way to make sure they were re-assigned from Harwig's group to the Kepler colony, but that shouldn't be too hard.

Now, if he could only get rid of that idiot Harwig…

Out of sheer boredom, he slaughtered a pack of wild dogs and left them in front of the UN building with a warning to Harwig that he was next.

CHAPTER 11

Preparation

A wave of apprehension gripped Mike Silver as his taxi pulled up in front of the UN building. He swallowed hard, paid the driver, and walked briskly to the entrance. Several Guardians stood near the Colonists Coordination Desk. One asked to see his credentials.

"Thank you, Mr. Silver. Please follow me." He led Mike to a small conference room where four people were waiting. Mike was familiar with all of them through their election videos and had studied their personal bios.

Tom Heron, the newly elected city engineer, was an instrument and control engineer by training, with twenty plus years of experience in designing complex control applications in the petrochemical area. He was married and had three girls, all in high school. Convincing them to leave must have been quite a feat. With his slim build and still-dark hair, he looked younger than his actual age of 45.

Bob Gravinsky, the city security officer had been a US Navy Seal before leaving to work as a security consultant. He was an excellent marksman with a variety of weapons. He retained his military appearance, with upright carriage and close-cropped blond hair. Unmarried at forty, he had had a girlfriend who refused to join the colony.

Rebecca Morris had come in second in the balloting for the city planner position on the council, and had been appointed planner when Mike was appointed mayor. Rebecca was an accountant by profession, and was coming with her husband and two pre-teen boys. Rebecca was in her late forties, with a slim frame resulting from many diets and exercise programs over the years.

Jomina Aminu, the new city treasurer, was some kind of financial prodigy. The daughter of Nigerian immigrants, she had an MBA from USC's Marshall School of Business, and by age 27, had been running her own investment company. She was recently married and had just turned thirty when the Octans arrived, so she was the youngest member of the council. She stated as her first goal, the establishment of a viable currency system on Kepler.

The new council members took turns introducing themselves, and began an earnest discussion on the countless issues they would face on Kepler. The transport ship would arrive in less than two weeks.

Given the space limitation of 40,000 cubic meters, medical equipment, and needed medical supplies for twenty years, would be the single largest inventory item. Mike and the council members had just started to review paper copies of a list for Kepler, when Jude Harwig entered the room, with two Guardians carrying several large boxes.

"Greetings, ladies and gentlemen," Harwig began. "Don't get up. Your colony is the 25th certified to transport and I'm sure you have a lot of questions."

The Guardians placed their boxes on the conference room table and took up positions near the door.

"Don't mind them; for some reason, the Octans think I need protection. Coincidentally, these are two of the Guardians assigned to Kepler."

He stood between the treasurer and the city planner and rested his hands on the table. "First, I was sorry to hear about Mayor Enders' untimely accident. I'm happy you agreed to take her place, Mr. Silver. The Octans knew it would have been extremely difficult to plan and hold another election before your departure. I also like the name the colony picked for the city—Helios has a nice ring to it."

He pulled up a chair and sat down. "Now… questions? If I can't answer them, I'll pass them along and get back to you."

Rebecca spoke first. "What are the Octans like?"

"Very gentle and soft spoken. They're probably always thinking deep thoughts or something. They don't talk a lot."

"No, I mean what do they look like?"

"Oh, appearance… they look like humans will probably look in another hundred thousand years—about five feet tall, large heads and large eyes. Their skin is milky white; I don't think they ever go out in the sun. They have two arms and legs like we do, and they are rather thin, almost underweight."

"Why don't they ever meet humans face to face?" asked Tom.

"I think they are afraid of human contact. They've studied us pretty extensively and know how we tend toward violence."

"But not all humans are that way."

"They know that." Harwig paused, thinking. "What if you were asked to meet a caveman who was always carrying a big club? He might be perfectly reasonable, but there's always a fear of what he might do, I guess."

Mike spoke up. "Is that why they are so reluctant to give us their technology? They fear we might use their technology against them?"

"Exactly."

"But if they fought off a race of warriors for years, why should they be afraid of us?"

"I think it's not that they are afraid of us collectively, but they hope that by giving us their technology slowly, we'll mature and be able to handle it without abusing it."

The council members thought that over while Harwig opened a box. He handed each council member a large metal can, about the size of a gallon bottle of milk.

"Okay, on to some other stuff… you undoubtedly have heard of the FOOD that will be provided on all the colony worlds including Kepler. I thought it would be a good idea for you to taste it."

Mike noticed a key-like device on the top of the can that reminded him of the key device used to open Spam cans. They watched Harwig break the key off and use it to open the can. They followed his lead and soon were staring at a white substance with the consistency of pudding. Harwig handed each of them a plastic spoon with a long handle.

"Try it, it's not bad," he said. "You'll be eating a lot of this in the next few years, or at least until you can harvest some regular food."

The pudding had a faint sweet odor that matched the taste. Mike and the other council members all agreed the taste was nothing like they had experienced before.

"It's like a light dessert." Commented Bob.

"The medical community has confirmed that it meets all human nutritional needs. You can live off this stuff." replied Harwig. "You'd think it has sugar, but there isn't any in there at all. There's an optimal amount of fat in there too. We've heard that overweight people who eat only this, start losing their excess weight almost immediately."

"What's it made from?" asked Jomina.

"The base material is harvested from a plant native to Octos, and now grown on other planets as well. Then they add vitamins, nutrients and minerals so that it's a complete human meal."

Tom placed his can on the table. "I heard that someone came up with a cookbook with more than a hundred recipes using this as the base, and some of them are really good."

"That's right. Most of the ingredients needed are in your common supplies. Now all you need are some chefs. Which reminds me…" Harwig pulled several thin gray palm-sized electronic tablets from a second box and passed them around. Mike was surprised at how light they were. He was able to guess the function of many of the icons on the screen.

"Each colonist will receive one of these," Harwig continued. "You'll find yourselves carrying your tablet everywhere with you." He pressed a few icons. "I see you have 5 chefs signed up for your colony. That's excellent."

"How does this work?" asked Bob.

"These tablets will wirelessly connect to a computer in Helios. Virtually all of man's knowledge will be available at your fingertips with these. It'll also serve as a video phone and email device up to fifteen kilometers from the city. Right now, they are connecting to a similar computer in this building. By the way, the tablet you're holding will only respond to your individual touch, so you don't have to worry about losing it and the person finding it having access to all your personal information."

Mike touched an icon of a box, and a list of equipment filled the display, the same the list of common equipment they had been studying when Harwig arrived. The status of each item was noted by a color. Almost all items were in storage, awaiting transportation with the colonists. Supplies not yet received were noted with an expected delivery date.

"There will be a larger version of this in each of your living quarters, with a keyboard. If you press the globe icon, you find a summary of what is currently known about Kepler." Harwig looked at his watch. "Oh, I'm sorry, but I have to leave for another meeting. I hope we can get together at least one more time before you leave. I'm sure you'll have a lot more questions." He stood up, and the Guardians opened the door.

"One last thing. There are facilities on the transport ships for up to ten persons at a time to be awake. This includes sleeping quarters, food preparation, bathrooms, etc. Prior colonies have held lottery type drawings for those who would like to be awake for a week or ten days at a time. It sounds exciting but I can tell you, it can be pretty boring after a while. Anyway, you may want to think about a lottery for that."

After he left, Mike found a calculator function on the tablet. "Ten people awake at a time for ten days, and assume thirteen months at thirty days… that means almost four hundred people can be awake at some point during the trip. I think we should hold a lottery." The other council members nodded; then all of them were absorbed in the information provided by their tablets.

Mike looked up to see a Guardian standing next to him, watching his display. All the other Guardians had been dressed alike, but this one was wearing a red shirt and red pants.

"Yes, do you need me?"

"I would like to introduce myself. I'm TZ4532187567. I will be the leader of the Guardians on Kepler."

Mike stood up. He wasn't sure if he should but he held out his hand. "I'm Mike Silver."

The Guardian shook his hand firmly. "Yes, the new mayor of Helios." He looked at the other council members. "The city engineer, city planner, treasurer, and security officer." Bob showed Mike his tablet, which was displaying a list of given names. Mike nodded. "I'm sure I speak for the others," he said to the Guardian. We'll never remember your serial number or whatever that was, so could you pick one of these names?"

The Guardian quickly scanned the name list. "Aaron."

"So, Aaron, how many Guardians will be assigned to Helios?"

"Twenty, including myself."

"That doesn't seem like very many. Aren't there some really large animals on Kepler?" asked Bob.

"There is an electronic fence around Helios that will stop all known animals. We are there to prevent humans from harming themselves, other humans, or the planet, through reckless actions."

"I think I read that a second city is already under construction. Are you in charge of those Guardians as well?"

"No. Guardians are not involved in construction activities. The constructors there have only one function, to complete the second city in less than twenty Earth years. We will have no communication or any interaction with them. There are also twenty entities that maintain the equipment in Helios, but it's unlikely you will ever see them." He paused. "We must vacate the room; another meeting is scheduled here. I will remain in contact until the departure date." He turned and opened the door and the council members filed out holding their tablets.

The next day, the council met again and coordinated an Internet lottery of available slots to be awake for ten days during the transport period. Almost half the colony participated. Jesse won a time slot, but none of the council did.

CHAPTER 12

One day before transport, a van arrived to collect Mike and Jesse and their personal storage units. Reality set in as they spent their last night on Earth in a hotel room near the transport departure terminal.

A terminal capable of holding 40,000 people had been constructed in Bayonne, New Jersey, just west of New York City. A van picked them up early in the morning, along with their containers. It dropped them off outside the terminal. They watched the van with their only remaining possessions disappear into a warehouse. Since they had arrived several hours before the scheduled departure, they wandered through the terminal and out the back, and stood in awe at the size of the transport ship. This was not the small vessel everyone had seen arrive at the UN. This vessel was 1500 meters, or about a mile in diameter and capable of transporting 40,000 persons and 80,000 cubic meters of community and personal equipment. Out of curiosity, Mike determined that 80,000 cubic meters would fill a college football field, including the end zones, to a height of almost 50 feet—a truly massive amount of materials to transport.

The scene in the terminal was minor chaos. Many colonists realized it was extremely likely they would never see Earth or family and friends again. Emotions ran high.

Jesse was in the rest room when Jason Steele phoned Mike. After some confusing phone talk ("We're on the east side? Under the clock? Or near the cargo doors?") Jason and Maria finally found him. Mike hardly recognized Jason Steele after almost ten years. He was older but still obviously in excellent shape. Mike didn't know what he had expected Jason's wife to be, but Maria Steele wasn't it. She was a little taller than Jason and with the physique of a bodybuilder, dark hair and eyes and a dark complexion. She was obviously nervous in the crowded terminal with scores of Guardians present to maintain order, and clung tightly to Jason's arm.

"Long time no see, buddy. Congratulations on the mayor thing." Jason pulled Maria forward. "And this is Maria, the blushing bride."

Maria looked confused, but shook hands with Mike. "Jason talks about you often."

"I thought your name was Maru or something like that?"

Maria tensed, but Jason answered easily. "Baby name, from her family."

"So, where did you meet Jason?" asked Mike.

Maria and Jason both laughed. "In the Amazon," she said.

Jason put his arm around her. "She was there on a mission."

"Oh really? Our church has sponsored missions to the Amazon too."

Maria looked thoroughly confused. She was saved from further conversations about Brazil and missions when Maria's and Jason's departure buzzers went off and displayed a boarding message. "Looks like we have to go." Jason said.

"Come and see me when you get settled in."

"We will. Let's go honey," he said to Maria, who looked even more confused as he urged her along.

Mike watched them walk off as Jesse returned the rest room. "Who was that?"

"Jason Steele and his new wife, Maria."

"Oh crap, I wanted to finally meet him and talk about some of his trips."

It was another hour before Mike's and Jesse's departure buzzers went off, and they walked out and up a ramp onto the transport ship. The transport pods were arranged on 8 levels of 5,000 horizontal pods each around the perimeter of the ship. The process was fairly simple but somewhat embarrassing as everyone had to strip down to their underwear and be helped into a sleeping pod. The Guardians tried to separate the families being readied, and the size of the ship was so large that you really never saw anyone else getting ready for transport.

Mike was helped into a pod. The pod cover was transparent, so a Colonist's last memory on earth was watching two Guardians close the cover. The light went out in the pod and a cool mist enveloped Mike as he drifted off to sleep.

Waking Period

Jesse opened his eyes as the pod cover opened and warm air rushed into his pod. Two Guardians were watching him and each grabbed one of his hands and pulled him out to stand up. When his vision cleared, he saw the Guardians holding out white clothes for him. As soon as he put them on, the Guardians handed him a drink that tasted a little like orange juice and motioned him to follow them. They led him into the interior of the ship to a galley of sorts where he could select from a dozen flavor variations of the provided FOOD. After a while, several other colonists wandered in and he chatted with them briefly. The nine other people awake with him were considerably older than Jesse, and after a day or so he and they had little to talk about. He stared for hours out a window at the magnificent star field. There was no noise on the ship, not even the sound of an engine humming. It was so eerily quiet, Jesse found himself drumming his fingers on the window just to make some noise. Even star gazing became boring after a while, and when he found a Guardian, he told him he was bored, and asked him if there was anything he could do.

The Guardian led him to a computer terminal and showed him how to write and transmit emails to friends back home (even though they wouldn't receive them for weeks). When he tired of that, he walked all around the ship, but that proved boring after a while as he didn't understand any of the electronic displays—the text on all the displays was in Octan. He watched movies, played some video games, and slept a lot. At the end of his ten-day waking period, he was more than ready to go back to his transport pod.

CHAPTER 13

Arrival

Mike Silver awakened in his transport pod. His first sensation was feeling cold. He shivered and opened his eyes to see Aaron and another Guardian watching his waking progress after thirteen months of hibernation. The pod door slowly opened and a warm rush of air enveloped him. They each grabbed one of his hands and pulled him out to stand up.

"How are you feeling, Mayor Silver?" asked Aaron.

Mike wavered a little then stood upright. "I'm a little cold, but okay." They handed him white clothing, his electronic tablet, and the drink that tasted a little like orange juice.

"This liquid will help you recover from the effects of the transport."

Mike scanned his tablet as he drank. It showed the list of first tasks he and the other council members had compiled for arrival day. The Guardians left for nearby pods to wake the other council members.

Mike followed a ramp to an open door and shielded his eyes from the sun's yellow glare. The air was warm as he walked outside and stood on the ramp surveying their new home. The color palette of this world was surely different. The sky was green, the grass was orange, and the trees in the distance had blue leaves. There was a very slight odor of sulfur that he knew would soon vanish from his awareness. Other than that, the air seemed fresh and invigorating. The ship had landed next to the city. Mike had seen computer-generated images of the cities the constructors were building for each colony, but the actual size of a city designed for fifty thousand inhabitants was awe-inspiring. Cities, even small ones, on Earth are not visible all at once. This city was covered by a clear dome, too high to see the top of, too wide to look around. An even more amazing sight was the gigantic planet Kepler 14a that filled almost a fourth of the green sky. All three moons of their new home were also visible in the late afternoon sunlight.

He was still staring at Kepler 14a when Tom Heron, Jomina Aminu, Rebecca Morris, and Bob Gravinsky joined him on the ramp.

Heron let out a low whistle when he saw the city. "It's a lot bigger than I expected." He noticed Mike staring up and saw the huge sister planet. "Oh, my God! Will it always seem that close?"

Bob sneezed. "Is that sulfur smell from all the active volcanoes?"

Mike shrugged. "Probably. You won't notice that after a while. I think you get used to it, or something."

It was late afternoon and the shadow of the ship slowly crept over them. The temperature cooled quickly and Rebecca shivered. "It's a lot cooler in the shade."

Mike turned and started toward the open door of the ship. "Come on, we have work to do. People will be coming out soon, and we have to give them their housing information."

Mike's son was among the first awakened. Jesse was still drinking the orange flavored drink as he followed a ramp to the exit door, where his father and the other council members were setting up a table and chairs from the first-night storage area.

"Dad!"

"Jess, there you are! Come and help us with this, will you?"

Jesse and the council members unpacked electronic tablets from several large boxes near the ship's door. Jesse helped the other council members turn on each tablet and enter a unique ID number from a list shown on

Mike's tablet. As soon as the "activation" number was entered, the display went off, and the tablet could only be activated by the new owner.

A trickle of people arriving at the door soon turned into a steady stream. A large burly man stared at his tablet then asked. "When will we get our personal stuff?"

"It'll be off-loaded soon. It won't be long." Mike assured him.

The Guardians, numbers 351 and 352, who had been re-programmed by Momus, helped wake thousands of colonists but their re-programming had accidentally wiped some of the colonist data provided by Jude Harwig. They would have to wait until they had positive identification of the council members before they could disable them.

The sun had set when the last of the families filed out the door and only Mike and Tom remained. They watched as lights flickered on in the lower levels of the dome as families found their assigned quarters. Mike checked off the "Deliver tablets," on his to-do list. "Okay. Thanks Tom. Let's get going, I'm sure we both could use something to eat and drink."

"When will the ship leave?" asked Tom.

"I think tomorrow, once everything's off-loaded." Mike was guessing. He really didn't know how long it would take.

He noted the final count was 37,456 persons including the council members. All accounted for, he slipped his tablet into a pocket on his tunic and headed for unit 26245 on the 26th level.

Two large glass doors opened silently as Mike and Tom approached the north entrance to the city. The four main entrances to Helios were massive and well lit. A rush of warm air pushed away the evening chill that penetrated Mike's lightweight tunic and pants. As they neared the doors, their tablets beeped and a GPS-like map of the city appeared. It proved useful, as there were no signs or distinguishing characteristics to tell them where they were. They would have to work on that. Indirect lighting with a soft yellow hue gave the inside of the city a warm feeling. Tom headed off to explore for a bit, while Mike found a bank of elevators and pressed the button for the 26th floor.

CHAPTER 14

Living Space

The door opened as Mike neared unit 26245. The tablet must also be an electronic key.

Initially, each person was allocated a hundred square meters of space (A thousand square feet, Mike reminded himself.). Their new home for two was larger than the house they'd lived in on Earth, with Debra and her children. It felt even larger as the ceiling was four meters high. There were even some furnishings—in the main living area, one entire wall was a viewing screen, with large, plush-cushioned metal chairs arranged in front of it. The screen was showing a view of the transport ship from the north entrance.

The kitchen area was small, with appliances that looked a little different than any Mike had seen. European, perhaps. A large pantry was stocked with unlabeled cans of the provided FOOD. Mike found Jesse unpacking his personal crate in a bedroom, furnished with a large cushion, like a futon, and two pillows.

"When did the containers come? I thought the community equipment would come off first."

"A little while ago," replied Jesse. "They just left them near the front door."

Mike opened his crate, and found his packing list. Everything seemed in order, so he picked up his tablet and sat down in the living room in front of the viewing screen. The Guardians could see in the dark and didn't need lights to unload equipment, but lights in the ship and at the north entrance illuminated the Guardians as they offloaded large crates onto flatbed carts that they pulled into the city. Mike wondered if that would go on all night.

Jesse sat down on a nearby chair. "Have you had anything to eat?"

When he shook his head, Jesse showed him a notice on his tablet. "There's some hot FOOD in the dining hall. The Guardians prepared it. It's not great, but it's edible."

"I'll go there in a while." he said. "So… what do you think of the unit?"

"It's comfortable, but wait until you see the bathroom," he said, laughing.

Mike guessed the reason. "No paper on Kepler…"

Jesse nodded.

Mike had once visited Japan on a business trip and had a "paperless" toilet in the bathroom of his hotel room. It had taken a few days, but he had adjusted to it. Jesse and all the other colonists would adjust as well.

A small entry light came on when Jason and Maria entered their new quarters on the fiftieth floor. Sensors turned lights off and on as they walked around the unit, and a metal covering opened to reveal a floor-to-ceiling window with a magnificent view of a forest just west of the city. The floor, ceiling, and walls were all white.

"Typical Octan," she said. "Plain and colorless." The supplied FOOD was also difficult for Maria. "No flavor, no texture, no color. How will we survive on this?"

"You'll get used to it." At least, Jason hoped so.

Even the water from the faucet in the kitchen tasted flat. It was pure water—no minerals at all, to give it taste. Luckily, the FOOD contained all the minerals their bodies needed.

Jason was intrigued with a washer/drier device in the apartment. It was about the size of a small microwave and the instructions indicated it only required a few drops of a clear liquid cleaner. He put a pair of jeans in it to test it and watched through a window in the door as the washer steamed the jeans, vacuumed out the water, and dried them with very hot air. The whole process took only two minutes and his jeans looked and smelled like they had been dry-cleaned. He was impressed.

Maria was similarly impressed with the shower. As instructed, she put a few drops of the clear liquid cleaner in an opening below the shower head, pressed a "start" button. A warm very fine mist enveloped her until the liquid was running down her body; then a strong burst of warm water from a hundred sprayers rinsed her off. A whirlwind air-drying sequence dried her and effectively removed all the water from the shower stall. Three minutes after she'd entered the shower, she was clean, and even her hair was dry.

"I feel like I've been in a car wash," Jason said after his turn.

It only took a few minutes to unpack their personal transport containers. When they finished, they sat near the big window and watched a magnificent sunset.

"Now what?" Maria said. "You want to go outside for a while?"

"Now that we're not on Earth, why don't you tell me your mission?"

She sighed, and moved from her chair into his. "A little more than fifty Earth years ago, when the treaty was signed, some Juban leaders did not agree. They wanted the war to continue. But they could not stop the agreement. They knew the Octans needed Earth to populate planets as there are so few of them. They set up a plan to put specially trained Juban warriors on Earth to find ways to harm the new colony leaders before they left Earth. They hoped the colonies would fail, and, when the truce period was done, they could take over those planets. Most Juban leaders did not know of this plan, and would not have agreed to it. So it took many years to secretly develop the plan and obtain the resources needed. Then the planners asked for volunteers to be the spies on Earth. I was very young and a good friend convinced me to join. Looking back, it was not a good decision, except for meeting you."

Jason put his arms around her. "So, if you were caught, you were on your own. The Juban leadership would not have acknowledged you, or tried to obtain your release?"

"Sadly, this is true." She saw Jason struggling with the whole idea of her mission. "Do not leaders on Earth, sometimes send spies that their government does not admit?"

Jason slowly nodded. "Yes. I'm afraid they do." He paused. "How many Juban warriors went on this mission?"

"Only six. The goal was one for each likely departure terminal."

"So where are the others? What are they doing?'

"I don't know. We were forbidden to communicate with one another."

"Did you ever kill anyone?"

"No, but I did harm some bad humans… mostly criminals, then I turned them over to the police."

Jason turned to look at her. "You were the one that used to tie them up and call the police?"

"Yes. That's how I lived, buying food with the money from their pockets."

"How many criminals?"

"Many! It gave me something to do at night—before I found you." She was grinning at him and he laughed.

A few minutes later, the aftereffects of the transport chemicals caught up with them, and they were both asleep.

# #

Even though the apartments had kitchens, each apartment complex also had a main dining hall. After a quick dinner there, Bob Gravinsky went out to watch the Guardians unload the ship. Aaron was pulling a large cart loaded with crates, and Bob joined him, walking beside him.

"I thought you guys would have some anti-gravity sleds or something. A cart with wheels is pretty old technology isn't it?"

Aaron didn't slow down. "We have something like that, but not for something as small as these crates."

"At this rate, it will take some time to unload 80,000 cubic meters of stuff, won't it?"

"We only have to bring it off the ship. The MUs will put it where it belongs."

"MUs?"

"Maintenance Units."

Bob wasn't looking ahead and almost ran into an MU. He jumped back. He hadn't thought too much what a Guardian might look like without its human-like outer covering, but he didn't have to wonder any longer. The MUs were quietly and efficiently moving the carts piled high with common equipment crates from the north entrance to what looked like a gigantic service elevator.

Aaron turned to Bob. "It's late Mr. Gravinsky. Shouldn't you be resting?"

Bob wondered if that was an indirect way of telling him he was in the way. "Yes, of course. I'll see you tomorrow."

Bob had started back to his living quarters, wondering why there were no other people out exploring their new city, when he suddenly almost passed out. The chemicals that had induced the sleep for transportation were suddenly weighing heavily on his eyes. He almost didn't make back to his living quarters.

CHAPTER 15

The City

Mike glanced at the clock in the dining hall. "90135 is about 9:30 at night." he thought. He had given up wearing his watch. With about thirty Earth hours in a day and 420 Kepler days per year, their former watches and calendars were useless. Each Kepler year was 1.4 Earth years. The dining hall located in the center of the city's first floor was actually an immense room, two stories high and capable of seating more than 5000 persons. Like everything else, the tables and chairs were made of the "Octan metal." That was the term scientists had given the extremely hard yet light metal used in the construction of the spaceships and the city. The tables were pretty standard fare, but the chairs were different. Each had been formed from a single sheet of metal shaped to form a single wide leg, back and seat. The chairs were actually pretty comfortable as he sat down. The metal was a little cold to the touch and he wished he had more on than the flimsy white tunic and pants distributed to everyone. Mike did notice a few people wearing jeans and t-shirts they must have packed into their cubic meter of personal stuff.

The dining hall was almost deserted as Mike walked over to a buffet style bar. He laughed at the dozen or so variations of the FOOD. While most of the variations were color and taste, all looked like pudding. As he picked up a metal plate divided into 4 sections, he thought of the army mess halls he had eaten in when he was young. He scooped a few types onto the plate and picked up a container of water and sat down. He hoped Helios' five chefs were working on alternatives.

The dining hall took up a significant part of the first and second floors of Helios, but there were many meeting rooms and other common areas with windows on the outside perimeter. There were many stairs and numerous elevators and Mike took the next elevator to explore further. He pressed the top floor button and took out his tablet.

Helios' statistics were a little mind-numbing at first. The city was six and a half kilometers in diameter—an hour's brisk walk—with 200 levels, not including a vast underground mechanical and equipment room. The enclosed volume of the city was about 9.8 billion cubic meters. There were fifteen thousand sets of living quarters on levels three through one hundred, 4,350 rooms without any identified purpose, a designated aquarium, an identified museum, fifty designated gymnasiums, etc. Most of the rooms were completely empty, as were the endless curved corridors. Yes, it was late at night, but he thought there would be a few more curious people walking about the city. And where were the Guardians? But the Guardians were only twenty out of almost 40,000 people; he wouldn't be likely to see one every day.

The door opened on the 200th level. Mike stood in awe of the nighttime vista. The whole level above the floor was made of clear polymer. The humidity was low on Kepler; there were no clouds, and the sky was blanketed with stars. Mike wondered what the view would have been from a window on the transport ship. He made a mental note to ask Jesse.

Large chairs with cushions were plentiful and Mike sat down to star gaze for a while. He suddenly felt extremely tired.

City Engineer Tom Heron had practically passed out as soon he reached his living quarters, but when he awoke he could not go back to sleep. The whole experience of living on a new planet surrounded by alien technology he didn't understand kept him awake. He dressed and walked slowly through the city without encountering anyone, human or Guardian. The time on a clock above the west entrance was 12450. "About 3 AM"

he thought and walked outside. The night air was brisk and he shivered, wishing he had a coat or jacket. He would look for one tomorrow.

The electronic fence designed to keep animals out gave off a pale blue glow in the distance. Tom walked toward it, eager to see it in operation. The fence posts, ten meters apart and three meters tall, generated a type of electronic plasma in a very low power. When sensors on the fence posts detected anything approaching, power was re-channeled from other fence sections. Animals trying to cross the fence would receive fatal doses of energy.

The blue glow intensified as Tom approached. He found a small stick on the ground and tossed it into the fence. With a bright arc and a crackling sound, the stick fried. Tom leaped back, then bent over to examine what was left of the stick. He shuddered at the thought of someone's accidentally coming in contact with the fence. The council would have to give some guidance on fence safety. Maybe an inner fence, for the children?

Tom jumped when a Guardian touched him on the shoulder.

"It is dangerous to go near the fence, Mr. Heron," it said.

"Yes, I know. I was just trying to figure out how to warn the colonists so they don't get hurt."

"Yes, sir. Please follow me." The Guardian turned toward the city.

Tom yawned as he followed. Tomorrow will be a busy day.

CHAPTER 16

Mike's tablet chimed at 30,000 and he opened his eyes on the first morning of the first year on Kepler. The sun had just peeked over the horizon as he stood at the window marveling at completely new morning colors in the green sky. He glanced in the other bedroom and noticed Jesse sleeping as he walked silently to the kitchen. He opened a can of FOOD and downed as much of the pudding mixture as he could stand. The taste was acceptable, but he couldn't imagine eating the concoction three times a day for years on end. He searched his personal transport container and found the container of his favorite blend of tea. The water faucet in the kitchen could deliver frigidly cold water or near boiling water and he soon had his morning cup of tea.

He sat down on a large chair in the living room and turned on the huge viewing screen as he cradled his tea, enjoying the aroma. He would surely miss it, when his small stash was gone. He had brought along some special tea plants, hoping they would grow on Kepler, and he would be able to have some tea in the future. The colony had transported several cubic meters of various types of tea plants, but he was certain tea plants were far down the farmers planting list. They were probably more concerned with establishing corn, wheat, and other basic staples.

The view from the north entrance had greatly changed with the departure of the transport ship. Funny, he hadn't heard a thing when it departed. He must have fallen into a very deep sleep. In the distance a large metal structure with an antenna on top gleamed in the early morning sunlight. That was probably the communication tower that connected Kepler with Earth and Octos each day. The antenna rotated to maintain a communication link with a distant satellite for about 4 Earth hours, enough for a thousand terabytes of data to be sent and received, including emails, all manner of data and a variety of news and information. Mike didn't understand the whole process, but somehow the Octans found a way to generate a plasma field around a packet of information. The plasma field created an energy tunnel for the information to travel through space many times faster than a metal spacecraft, although it still took several weeks for information to travel the sixteen hundred light years between Kepler and Earth

Mike dressed quickly and walked through a silent, seemingly empty city. It looked as though most of the residents had agreed with his suggestion to rest and relax for the first few days. The council members however were already in the council meeting room huddled around Jomina. Mike tapped her on the shoulder.

"What's going on?"

Jomina turned and handed him a dish of green pudding. "Try this. My first recipe with FOOD."

The modified FOOD was delicious with just a hint of cinnamon and some other spices, and there was a whole can of it on the table. "What's in it?"

"There are about a dozen spices in it. I made it from the 1st Colonists Cookbook."

They all sat down to savor the new FOOD dish.

Rebecca glanced at her useless watch out of habit, then noted the time on a clock over the council room's entry door which read 33560. That's about 8:00AM. She pulled her tablet from a pocket in her tunic that was obviously designed for it and stared at the display. "So, what's first on the agenda for today?"

"We need to check out the water feed to the city and the power feed." The city engineer replied.

"Everything seems to be working; is that necessary on the first day?"

asked Bob.

"The average person uses about fifty to a hundred gallons of water each day, so right now that's almost three million gallons per day, and I just want to be sure the supply's adequate," replied Tom.

Bob shrugged. "Okay, that seems simple enough."

"Except that we will probably need a few Guardians… the primary water source is a lake about a mile from here—outside the fence."

Mike was studying his task list, which seemed to be growing constantly. "Guys, Bob and I will help Tom check out the water this morning. We can reconvene after lunch."

Mike, Tom, and Bob took an elevator to the below ground storage and mechanical room and met Aaron near a door marked "Mechanical Room—Authorized Access Only."

Mike nodded to Aaron, who opened the door by passing a special electronic key near the lock. The huge door opened slowly with a gentle hiss and the team entered the enormous underground room which housed the equipment that kept the city going. Ten stories tall and the same size as the first floor of the city, this floor contained storage for all the colony's common supplies as well. Aaron asked Mike if they would like to discuss the utilities with a Maintenance Unit, but before Mike could answer, Tom was off running from one bank of equipment monitors to another like a kid in a candy store. Finally he found the water purification control panel.

"This is it!" he called to the others who found him standing in front of a massive display panel. They watched as he pressed portions of the touch-screen to bring up various functions. To Mike and Bob, the displays were a complicated maze of tables of numbers and drawings.

They waited patiently for Tom to finish, until Aaron commented, "You can ask this system for the information you need, Mr. Heron."

They all turned to look at him. "Each utility system has a voice recognition program. You only have to train it to understand your accent."

"I would like to do that, but in the meantime it looks like there is a filter that limits the flow in the system. I don't see the need for it, but the system is currently capable of delivering about 210,000 cubic meters, or seven and a half million gallons per day, which is plenty for the current number of colonists."

"Where is the filter?" asked Bob.

"It's near the source of water, the lake just east of the city."

"Well, we have time now, let's go." urged Mike. Aaron led them though the city's east entrance, where they picked up some extra tunics to ward off the chilly morning air. At a gate in the electronic fence, another Guardian carrying two large plasma energy rifles met them. He handed one to Aaron and de-energized the gate. Aaron motioned them to hurry through the gate.

Bob was an expert marksman with many kinds of guns and rifles, but he had never seen anything like the large rifles the Guardians were carrying. He happened to be walking next to Aaron and he had to know, "What kind of weapon is that?"

"It's based on the same principle as the fence. It creates a plasma field around an explosive charge that propels a plasma ball forward."

"Wow. I'd sure like to try it."

"Yes. Not today, but soon."

Tom explained the water purification system as they walked through knee-high orange grass on gently rolling hills toward the lake. The sun was warm but a cool brisk breeze reminded them of the approaching winter. After crossing the crest of a small hill, they found a tree-lined lake that stretched almost to the horizon. Tom pointed to a metal pump house at the bottom of the hill near the lake.

"That's the intake filter housing." he said as they started down the hill.

"Why not put the filter near the city, to make it easier to clean or replace?" asked Bob.

"Then you'd have a pipeline full of algae or whatever there is here that could clog it up."

They arrived at the pump house and Aaron opened it with the same electronic key.

"I'll need one of those," said Tom. "In fact, we all will."

"Yes, I'll obtain them for you." Aaron opened the house door and Tom entered.

While Tom examined the pump and filter, the other council members walked the remaining distance to the lake. The lake was wide but they could barely make out some trees on the other side. The water at the lake's edge was clear but it became murky as the depth increased from shore.

"I wonder if there are any fish…" Bob's question was interrupted by a ground-shaking roar.

"What the hell was that?" asked Mike.

Aaron pulled Tom from the pump house and called to the others. "We must go!".

A dozen animals emerged from the nearby woods and lumbered toward the lake. They could possibly be described as a multi-horned rhinoceros, only much, much larger. The word dinosaur came to mind…

For a moment, the council members were frozen in their tracks. Then they followed Aaron as he pulled Tom up the hill.

Behind them, the animals lined up at the lake's edge to drink.

They stopped at the top of the hill. A much, much larger herd of animals was in front of them, running toward the lake. They resembled enormous horned wildebeests. "Come this way." Aaron headed for a grove of trees. They waited among the trees as the herd split around it and passed in two clouds of dust. Aaron motioned them to follow and he walked briskly through the woods.

"So, we've had our first contact with a Kepler species," said Mike.

"Not at all," Aaron said. "You had already seen the grass and trees."

"Animal species, I meant. Speaking of which, are we being tracked? Look to the right."

"I'm aware of them. They won't attack as long as we keep moving."

They reached the edge of the woods and could see the top of the dome over a small hill ahead. They ran across the open meadow until they were sure the animals in the woods were not still following them.

The sun was almost directly overhead as they finally neared the fence. The second Guardian deactivated the gate, and once they were inside, they stopped to catch their breath.

"Well, that was an interesting morning." commented Mike, between deep breaths. "You can check out the electrical system without me."

Tom was bent over with his hands on his knees. "Maybe we can do that without a field trip."

Mike and the second Guardian entered the city while Bob, Tom, and Aaron returned to the gigantic mechanical room. Tom quickly found the power generation control panel and confirmed the fact that most of the power generation equipment was near a geothermal vent outside the city. Fortunately, they were able to follow an underground access tunnel to a cavern, find the geothermal vent and check the turbine and generating equipment without encountering any animals.

CHAPTER 17

Farming Issues

That afternoon, the council met a delegation of two of the twenty-contingent of farming families the colony had actively recruited. According to the formation rules, a colony was required to have a minimum of ten farming families to ensure it could become self-sustaining in less than twenty years. Mark Stanlow and John Simms were large burly men, used to working hard on small farms handed down from their parents and grandparents. They were no-nonsense people—in a hurry to get going, but well aware of approaching winter.

"I understand we brought along some tractors and tills." Stanlow said as he sat down.

"Yes." replied Rebecca. "Unfortunately we have no fuel. As you know large quantities of combustible liquids were not allowed, even for farming equipment."

"So how can we use them?"

"We'll have to find a way to make some." said Mike. "We brought along equipment for fermentation. Hopefully we can get that underway immediately and make some alcohol. In the meantime, you can start checking out the equipment. Here are the crate numbers." he said as he showed Stanlow the crate numbers on his tablet.

"I wish I could write that down, but there's no paper here."

Mike sent an email to Stanlow. "The crate numbers are in the email I just sent you."

Stanlow and Simms struggled to find the email and details on their tablets, until Tom helped them.

"Now, what about the land grants you mentioned…"

"The current farmable land inside the fence is about ten thousand acres, or four thousand hectares. The rest is wooded. In about a year or so that will jump to two hundred thousand acres but for now you have about five hundred acres each to farm. We'll leave the division of land up to your farming committee. That should give you enough land to get going and learn about the soil and planting seasons."

"What about the fuel for the tractors?"

"We'll let you know once we come up with enough fuel for a test planting."

"That's great. By the way, we've taken a number of the personal containers that aren't needed anymore and planted some test crops like corn and wheat, and a few fruit trees and bushes. We're hoping they'll be big enough to plant in the spring."

Mike stood up and pulled a small plastic bag from his tunic. "When you have the time, would you see if these tea plants will grow?"

Stanlow examined the dozen or so small tea plants in the bag. "Some other colonists have asked about tea and we have several kinds already growing, but we'll add these too."

Mike shook their hands. "That's excellent. Thanks a lot, guys."

Stanlow and Simms thanked the council for the information on the tractors and left.

Chef's Proposal

The council members welcomed two of the colony's five chefs to discuss a proposal for a new restaurant in Helios.

Rebecca, the city planner, had a few concerns. "Why do you want to section off a portion of the main dining hall? Wouldn't a stand—alone restaurant be easier to manage? You wouldn't have to worry about all the commotion that goes on in the hall. It'll be used for a lot of events because it's the single biggest room in Helios."

George Macron replied. "It's got a wizard kitchen, though! You could cook for an army in there—or a palace! We'll only need a very small part of the main dining hall. In the beginning we'll be lucky to have a hundred diners a day, until we can come up with some more unique dishes."

Mike was reviewing their proposed menu on his tablet. "Are all the items on the menu made from the provided FOOD?"

"Yes, except for some small plants we found near the city. The biologists have given their approval to use them in salads."

"Any prospects for some protein?"

"We're waiting on the hunters and fishermen to find something we can use. We'll let everyone know once we have some meat or fish dishes."

The two chefs glanced at each other. "One more thing… money. How will we be paid for developing and serving alternatives to the FOOD?"

Jomina answered the often-asked question. "We're finalizing that now. We'll have some information on that at the first town hall."

"So… can we have a small portion of the main hall?"

The council members all gave their approval to establish a private restaurant within the main dining hall.

Risk Team

Mike called Jason and Maria on their tablets, asking them to meet with the council. Jason tried to get Maria to go, but a Guardian always stood near the council room door during meetings, and she was afraid they might recognize her physical dimensions, despite her efforts to change her appearance. Mike started to introduce Jason, but Jomina said, "Hey! Aren't you Steele? That guy on TV with the Anaconda and all? Remember Nerves of Steele, guys?"

"Jason, we really need to know what's outside the fence," said Mike. "How safe is it for farming, fishing, hunting, kids' picnics, and Fourth of July celebrations? Everything. Guardian escorts aren't practical for the long haul—or even the short haul, not with twenty of them and forty thousand of us."

"So what exactly do you want to know?"

Mike spread his hands wide. "Everything! Every detail you can possibly find out. I've sent you a list of volunteers to work with you. And your wife, of course. Unless she's needed here." He punched her name into his tablet. "Oh, electronic engineering, hmm? She might be more help in the city, Jason." "She'll go stir-crazy if she stays behind, Mike. She's been coming on all my trips; I'm used to her having my back." Jason was checking over the volunteer list on his tablet. "When do you want this? If Maria goes, we can leave right away."

"We've got an awful lot of engineers of various types, Mike," Jomina pointed out.

"Okay, then, as soon as possible. I've instructed Aaron and the gatekeepers to let you and your team out without an escort. I'm assuming you can take care of yourself." The council members laughed.

"What about self-defense? Are there any weapons here? Everyone knows what you guys ran into."

"Brought the grapevine with us, did we? Oh, well, it's a small city, after all. Aaron can provide some weapons and show you how to use them. But Jason—don't take unreasonable chances. This world is unlike anything you've ever seen."

Jason frowned. "Sure thing."

He was wondering what Mike meant as he passed the Guardian standing near the council door. It seemed to be measuring him somehow as he passed. Maybe Maria was right. They would have to be careful around the Guardians.

CHAPTER 18

Town Hall Meeting

At 42000 or about 10 in the morning, the dining hall was packed in anticipation of the first town hall meeting. Due to space limitations, most colonists were watching on viewing screens. It seemed that everyone had questions for the council members, and Mike had received a few hundred questions on his tablet even before the meeting started.

The normal crowd chatter got even louder when the council members entered and sat on a row of chairs on an improvised stage. Aaron pinned small wireless microphones on each council member's shirt.

Mike held up his hands until the crowd quieted down. He introduced himself and the council members. Guardian 352 was on fence gate duty, but Guardian 351 was standing guard at the back of the dining hall and his Juban mission code immediately activated. He finally had faces to go with the names of his targets.

Mike held up his tablet. "I know you have a million questions. But each of you has a tablet like this. It gives you access to virtually all of mankind's knowledge and a great deal of information about Kepler and Helios. So, we plan first to tell you what's happened since that information on Kepler and Helios was compiled.

"I know some of you are a bit bored already, and you want to go off exploring, but, as most of you already know, there are some really large animals on this planet. You are NOT at the top of the food chain here. You are a tasty snack."

There was a hush in the audience. He had their attention.

"You probably have seen the fence by now. The Guardians assure us the fence will stop any animal on this planet. We have to take their word for that. Right now the fence extends out to the north and west of the city and encompasses about a hundred square kilometers. Forty square miles for you die-hards. We'll start farming that area in the spring. A much longer fence is being constructed, that will enclose a much bigger area, but that fence won't be done for a year or more."

"A year!" someone called out. "Kepler or Earth year?"

"Either," said Mike. "Both. It's just a guess. The current fence has several gates. Each has to be de-energized by a Guardian, and a Guardian must accompany you to ensure your safety. That means, given the limited number of Guardians, that trips will have to be approved in advance. I know that seems somewhat confining but we have a lot to learn before we can just leave the city on our own."

He held up a clear bottle of liquid. "On to a pleasanter subject. In case anyone hasn't figured this out yet, this stuff is soap. It works on anything from walls to hair. There's an enormous amount of this in storage, so feel free to clean with it, wash your hands with it, bathe and shampoo with it. I'm sure with a little investigation we'll find a way to change the fragrance and color, if someone wants something fancier."

"Okay. I'll take some questions. I'll refer you to your tablet if the answer is available on-line. That will save some time."

Mike laughed as virtually everyone present had a question. Mike pointed to the large burly man who had asked about the personal "stuff" when they were leaving the ship. One of the Guardians handed him a microphone.

"We understand that some may be happy to watch TV or play video games, or just hang out, but some of us want to make use of our knowledge or skills. I'm a fisherman and want to start fishing in the spring. How will I be paid from my catch? I don't want to work and give my fish away."

Mike held up his tablet. "The city council's been working on this, and here's what seems best for now: We'll adopt an electronic form of money. Your tablet is more than just a means to access information. Trust me, it will become an integral part of your life. We'll start out issuing a fixed amount of money that shows up on your tablet as 'credits'. There's a function on your tablet that will allow you to pay someone in credits in exchange for a product or service they offer. We have a team of some pretty smart financial people, led by the city treasurer (Jomina stood up and waved) that will help us control the expansion of the overall credits available. If you just want to live in your current quarters on the provided FOOD and clothing, you won't actually have to spend any credits, but we know that everyone here will probably want to start a club or business as soon as possible. We'll start off by giving everyone a meaningful number of credits and review the total available monthly or quarterly. If we need to, we can add credits to everyone's account."

The large burly man held up his tablet. "What happens if I lose this?"

"You may not have noticed, but your tablet will only respond to your touch. If you break it, or lose it, we can transfer your information to a new tablet, but no one who finds your old one can use it."

That caused a major buzz in the audience. Mike pointed to a man dressed in hunter's camouflage clothing.

"We understand this is almost the fall of the year. How much longer do we have before it will be too cold to go outside?"

"Another three or four months or so. You know, from the information you have, there are 420 days in this planet's year and each day is about thirty Earth hours. So, to help you keep track of the time, your tablet shows the current date and time. A day has a hundred thousand units. Time zero starts at midnight; 50,000 is at mid-day; and 99,999 is just before midnight. This isn't all that different from the 86,000 seconds in an Earth day; we just won't have hours or minutes. It won't take you long to get used to the new time. The calendar started with our arrival, so this is Year One. The clocks over the doors have the current time as well, in case you aren't carrying your tablet."

"Crappy way to do it," someone said.

Mike shrugged. "Octan. I guess if we can't adapt, we can eventually change it."

Almost everyone was playing with their tablet when Mike pointed to a woman in the front. "We've heard that water and electricity are virtually unlimited. Is that true?" she asked. Mike motioned to Tom Heron who stood up.

"It's sort of true. Can everyone hear me? Good. Our water comes from a lake. It goes through a treatment plant to kill algae and bacteria, then gets pumped into the city. There's a capacity limit that we don't understand yet, but we're working on it. We won't turn on the water fountains in the common areas until we do understand it, though. Since there are less of us than the city can hold, there's no practical limit on bathing and drinking water in the city." On the electricity—there's a geothermal unit that converts underground steam to electricity. There's a practical limit to electricity, as well, but this city is designed for fifty thousand people, so we're nowhere near that limit."

Someone in the back yelled. "What can we do in the winter when we can't go outside?"

Before Mike could answer, someone started laughing, and soon everyone, even Mike, was laughing.

"Next question?"

A young woman stood up. "How do we organize activities… events… things to do?"

"Your tablet will access an on-line system that will let you set up events.

Unfortunately, there is no paper on Kepler. ("Yet!" someone called, and Mike nodded.) That's right, yet. So everything will have to be done through your tablets. We'll set up some TV-like channels for the viewing screens to advertise the events. The current capacity of the system exceeds a thousand channels, so there's room for every organization to have its own channel if they want one. Also, your tablet number is like phone number. There's a directory, and a limited database of everyone's skills, so you can find people with similar skills or interests and start businesses or clubs or organizations."

Another woman held up her hand. "There seem to be many empty rooms. How do we request or claim a room for use in a business or club?"

"There are, in fact, thousands of unassigned rooms in a myriad of sizes. Once you find one that meets your needs, send an email to this council. Requests like this will always be granted unless there are unusual reasons to say no. With winter not far off, you'll have plenty of time to find the right space for almost any activity."

A young girl near the stage held up her hand. "Why is the sky green?"

Tom stood up. "There are explanations for those kind of questions in the data banks, and we have a technical team preparing for another town hall meeting to discuss and clarify the answers."

The burly man held up his hand. "Is the air safe to breathe? We've noticed some people coughing when they're outside."

Tom replied. "The air here is basically the same as on Earth, and safe. We'll have a more detailed answer at that future meeting."

A huge roaring sound interrupted the meeting. Mike tapped his mike, but it wasn't from there. Several people near an exit left and yelled to others to come and look. Mike turned to Aaron. "What's going on?"

"There are some rather large animals near the fence. It seems that one of them tried unsuccessfully to make it through."

Mike yelled over the noise. "Okay, let's call it a day. The next town hall will be in a week, unless there is a reason to call one sooner. Thanks everyone."

As the crowd began to disperse, Aaron handed Mike his tablet. There was a live feed from the tablet of Guardian 352, showing three very large saber tooth tiger-like animals trying to pull another one, lying on the ground, away from the fence.

"Are you sure that fence will keep all the animals out?"

"Yes." replied Aaron.

Mike frowned. He had never seen several animals working together to help another one in trouble.

After the town hall meeting, two fishermen approached Aaron.

"You're Aaron, right?" asked one.

"Yes, how can I help you?"

"Hi, I'm Martin Davidson and this is Eugene Thompson."

Aaron knew who they were from his internal database. "Yes?"

"We're fishermen and we'd like to go to the ocean to check out the fishing. We understand you have to approve trips outside the fence."

"That's correct."

"And you or one of your guys has to escort us?"

"That's also correct."

"Well, when could we go to the ocean to checking out the fishing prospects?"

"Is tomorrow morning acceptable?"

Martin was surprised how apparently easy it was to get approval for the fishing trip. "Oh, sure, that would be great!"

"Meet me at the south entrance at 37,000 clock units. For safety reasons, we need to limit the trip to the two of you for now."

"South entrance at 37,000? Okay!"

The two fishermen almost ran to tell their fellow fishermen the good news.

CHAPTER 19

Some Risk

After the town hall meeting, Jason found Aaron and obtained two energy plasma rifles and a brief overview on how to use them and how not to get hurt using them. He would have liked to take them apart to see how they worked, but didn't want to risk it. He was still examining one as he brought them back to his apartment and showed them to Maria. She disassembled one quickly in front of him.

"How did you know how to do that?"

She looked up from the pieces she was examining. "This hardware is old. We captured some of this many Earth years ago. The Octans have much better weapons than this now. Do you want me to make it more powerful?"

Jason laughed. "I would, but Aaron might be just a little suspicious when we give it back to him."

Within the next couple of days, Jason had selected a risk team of six members and called a meeting in his apartment. He summarized for them his meeting with the council. He then laid one of the Guardian's plasma rifles on the table. "Maria and I have studied these energy pulse rifles. They are moderately effective, but I'd rather have a thirty gauge, frankly." The risk team passed the plasma rifle around to examine it, then planned an initial foray for three of its members.

It was late in the afternoon, when the three risk team members met outside the north entrance. Geologist Bill Kerry was carrying a Bowie knife and a plasma rifle, physician George Marion held the other plasma rifle, and Jason had two Wakizashi Samurai short swords held by a belt he'd brought from Earth. A Gate Guardian de-energized a gate in the electronic fence and they went through at a jog.

Less than a kilometer from the fence, the team crested a small hill and found five huge hog-like animals feasting on a dead wildebeest. One turned, saw them, let out a blood-curdling scream and charged. Kerry and Marion didn't even have time to energize their plasma rifles, but Jason whipped out his Samurai swords. He dodged the hog's attack and his blades flashed in the late afternoon sunlight. The hog stumbled and fell. Kerry and Marion stared in disbelief as the hog's head rolled away from the body. Jason wiped his swords on the fallen hog's body and took out his tablet. He called the Gate Guardian and asked it to arrange retrieval of the fallen hog for the dining hall. Strangely, the other hogs watched with indifference as Jason took down their aggressive leader. They returned to feasting on the dead wildebeest as the risk team members passed by them, with rifles and swords ready.

Fishing Expedition

Davidson and Thompson were waiting at the south entrance with fishing nets and a cart holding their empty personal containers, when Aaron and two other Guardians approached. The fishermen had never seen anything like the plasma rifles the Guardians carried. The boundary between science fact and science fiction seemed to have blurred considerably.

"Are you expecting problems?" asked Thompson.

"There are large animals near here. Please follow us."

They followed the Guardians to the perimeter fence and hurried through at Aaron's urging. It seemed refreshing to finally be out of the city.

"Not bad for an early fall day." Davidson commented as he shifted a large knapsack from one shoulder to the other. The early morning sun was low in the sky and the temperature was pleasant when a cool wind wasn't blowing. Small patches of fog clung to some low-lying areas. They didn't see any animals and soon were at ease with the moderate pace the Guardians established. They passed a few gently rolling hills covered with knee-high orange grass. When they crested a large hill, the ocean lay before them. The white sand beach seemed to stretch on forever from side to side, and far deeper than any beach on Earth as the tides on Kepler were enormous due to the proximity of Kepler 14a. The distant, gentle pounding of the surf was like music to their ears. They could hardly see the water, but it seemed to be blue-green. They let out a cheer and started running. Before they got halfway, though, the sand had dragged their run down to a walk, and they trudged the remaining distance to the water. The Guardians watched and waited attentively while they waded into the surf and cast their nets into the water. It didn't take long to fill up their personal containers with several large fish. They also caught five small, odd-looking fish with huge teeth. "Look at that bugger! Look at it!"

Their excited yelling had attracted unwanted spectators. Several tiger-like animals approached the beach. "Time to leave," Aaron called. He fired a warning shot. A blue plasma fireball exploded at the feet of the nearest animal, and it jumped back. The others hesitated.

Davidson and Thompson were frozen in their tracks. Then three of the dinosaur-sized rhinoceros-like animals appeared at the top of the hill between them and the city. They let out a ground-shaking roar that scattered the tigers and scared the hell out of the fishermen.

A shadow distracted Thompson and he glanced up to see birds with immense wings and pointed beaks circling overhead.

"Aaron!" he yelled and pointed to the birds.

With a robot-like precision, Aaron fired at one bird. The blue fireball exploded on one of its wings, and the bird tumbled into the ocean. The other birds screeched loudly and flew away.

Aaron and the two other Guardians all fired their weapons at the nearest rhinoceros, hitting its feet. The animal bellowed and fell down, then struggled to rise. The other rhinoceroses backed up.

Then the Guardians ran toward the rhinoceroses, surprising them. They turned and started lumbering away. The fishermen tossed their gear into the cart and followed.

Back at the city, eager biologists helped the fishermen unload their containers into a large glass tank from the aquarium, filled with salt water. Much to Thompson's surprise, the five fish with the large teeth seemed to be staring at him through the glass and occasionally baring their teeth. The fish even followed him as he walked back and forth in front of the tank.

Davidson put his hand on Thompson's shoulder and laughed. "If I didn't know any better, I'd say those fish don't like you."

They both jumped back when all five of the odd looking fish suddenly swam forward, ramming into the glass with their teeth bared.

"Holy crap! Weren't we wading in the surf when we caught those guys?" asked Davidson.

"Sport fishing will have a whole new meaning here," replied Thompson.

CHAPTER 20

Confrontation

Maria was tired of hiding when Guardians were around, for fear of being discovered. She told Jason she had enough of it. She couldn't even go far from the city, as a Guardian had to deactivate a fence gate.

"So what can we do?" he asked.

The long suppressed warrior finally came out. "I will take care of this."

Jason hadn't seen her like this since their first encounter in the jungle. "Be careful," he said as she stormed out of their quarters.

Her status as a risk team member now allowed her access to the underground maintenance and utilities areas. She laughed when she found what she needed in a cabinet labeled as spare parts for Maintenance Units and Guardians. She even assembled several small devices on a table while some MUs watched.

She went looking for Aaron, and her first stop was the armory. She found it unlocked, but Aaron was not there. The level of sophistication of the handguns and other weapons in the armory surprised her. Why were they hiding these from the colonists? She was standing near a table, examining a handgun when Aaron returned.

"Can I help you, Ms. Steele?"

She smiled at the salutation as she turned to him. "I need to speak to you."

"That is a dangerous weapon. You need to give it to me." He started to move toward her with his hand out.

Maria laid the handgun on the table and unbuttoned her tunic collar to show him the white voice box typical of a Juban warrior. Then she picked up one of the devices she'd assembled, a box with a button on top. She addressed him in Octan so there would be no misunderstandings. "This will deactivate you. I will press it if you attempt to contact your team, or make a hostile move toward me." She gestured toward the electronic receiver still lying on the table. "This will show if you attempt to contact your team."

Having no viable alternative, Aaron dropped his arms and waited for her to speak.

"I am Juban, but I'm not here to harm humans or disrupt this colony."

Aaron calculated all possibilities but did not move or warn his team as she continued.

"You will inform your team that they are to take no action against me, or attempt to contact Earth or Octos about me. If you don't do this, I will deactivate all Guardians on Kepler."

"That would leave the humans in great danger. Is that your mission here?"

"I have no mission here other than to help the colony succeed."

He processed countless alternatives, but she had left him no good options. "I will do as you wish," he replied.

She laughed. "I am not stupid enough to believe that. I will give you the proper commands, and you will respond with the correct code." The coded response would enable a high level software function in Aaron that prevented him from following conflicting commands, such as alerting Octos to any Juban activity. Again, Aaron could not find a suitable alternative.

"Continue," he replied.

"Repeat the following: Maria Steele is Juban. I will take no action on this fact. I will instruct my team to take no action."

Aaron repeated the statements and then stated his serial number with a 1 after it. He stood absolutely still as she picked up the advanced handgun, walked toward him, handed him the handgun, and walked out of the armory. He immediately contacted his team and repeated the instructions as he had been told to do. He put the gun back on a wall rack, locked the armory door to prevent unauthorized access, and returned to more important duties.

Risk Summary

Maria now felt liberated from fear of discovery and confidently accompanied the six-member risk team that included Jason, geologist Bill Kerry, biologist Julia Sizemore, machinist Sean Michaels and physician George Marion into the Council Room to give their report. The team had taken many scientific measurements, studied information from the initial Octan survey of Kepler, made a brief survey of the surrounding land, and studied potential risks to the colonists and Helios and was ready to report to the council. They introduced themselves and Jason provided a summary.

"We'd like to begin with the atmosphere on Kepler. The good news is that the oxygen content is higher at 25%, but the bad news is the carbon dioxide content is almost 3% and sulfur dioxide is higher than on Earth. There is also a lot of really fine dust in the air. That's probably because there are a lot of active volcanoes." He stopped when he noticed the council members were staring at him with blank expressions.

"Sorry. The air is safe to breathe, but everyone spending a lot of time outdoors needs to take some precautions, perhaps like wearing a mask or bandana like they used to in the US in the old west." When the council members nodded, he glanced at his notes and shook his head.

"I was going to give a long dissertation of facts, but I'll skip directly to the main point. We seem to have been dropped in an early geologic period on Kepler. It's almost like going back in time on Earth more than a hundred million years."

Mike laid his tablet on the table. "If we assume that's true, what are the risks?"

"Think about this… what if there had been no catastrophic event that wiped out the dinosaurs?" He paused. "Would man have even survived if he were the hunted instead of the hunter? Well… we may have a chance to find out here."

"What exactly are you saying?" asked Bob. "We'll find a way to take care of these animals in order to farm or hunt or fish—if we need to."

"Look, the colonists will not stay cooped up in the city for long." replied Jason. "We don't have any meaningful weapons, other than the few rifles carried by the Guardians, and there aren't enough of them to protect everyone who will want to leave the city for commercial or personal reasons."

Maria knew better, but she kept her mouth shut. She had not told Jason what she had done and this was not the time or place to discuss the advanced weapons in the armory.

"So what do you propose?" asked Tom.

"We have all of mankind's knowledge available to us. We'd like to build the infrastructure to develop the weapons we all need to defend ourselves. First step is probably to find iron ore."

Mike stood up and began pacing. "The Guardians will never let you build weapons of war. The Octans have built that into the Guardians' genes, so to speak. One of the reasons the Octans have been slow about giving us their technology is their fear we'll use it to make better weapons for war—even turn on them. I know that seems ridiculous to us, but it's a valid concern for them, given our history."

Maria wondered how that information would have affected her mission, if Grus Harm had known it.

"But, there's no one here to make war on!" exclaimed Jason.

"I agree. So, come up with a detailed proposal on exactly what you want to do and we'll review it. If we concur, we'll even help you with materials and manpower. Agreed?"

The risk team members all nodded in agreement. As they were leaving, Mike warned them. "Self-defense—not war."

Jason gave a thumbs-up sign as he closed the door on the way out.

CHAPTER 21

Sabotage

Mike had returned from lunch early to respond to his enormous email backlog. Suddenly, the room lights flashed off, and on again, and a low-level horn sounded. He had no idea what to do; then his tablet flashed a message: the electronic fence was down, and everyone outside should immediately return to the city.

He ran to the door and almost ran into the city security officer, who was looking for him. "Bob! What the hell happened?"

"The fence really is down. I can't imagine how. Didn't Tom say it's on an uninterruptable power supply? That means the battery pack would have to fail too."

Mike's tablet showed a call from Tom. "Mike, you need to come to the mechanical room and see this."

"See what?"

"Someone deliberately turned off power to the fence… and disconnected the UPS backup system."

Bob was shaking his head. "That's impossible. Only a few have an access key to the mechanical room."

"We'll be right there."

The elevator doors opened on the first floor, and Mike and Bob had to push through a throng of people trying to enter the elevator. People were desperate to return to their quarters, thinking the city was under attack or on fire or something horrible had happened. Those that hadn't noticed the fence failure warning seemed to be running in all directions.

Red warning lights were flashing near all the entrance doors as large metal plates slowly descended to cover the glass doors. That made sense. With the fence down, the city was vulnerable to all the animals nearby, especially the large animals which might try to enter the city. But… what about colonists still outside? How would they enter with the entrances sealed? Mike noticed that Bob was now carrying an electronic door access key on a lanyard around his neck. He had to yell over the crowd and horn. "We need to see if anyone's still outside. Can you override the door seals?"

Bob grabbed the key. "I don't know." He pressed the door unlock button, but nothing happened. Several colonists suddenly screamed and started running toward them. Three large animals had entered through the north entrance and were running down the hallway toward them. Mike and Bob could hear the clapping of their hoofs on the metal floor above the din of the crowd and the horn. As the frightened colonists scattered in front of them, Mike could see one of the large wildebeest like animals being chased by two of the huge hog-like creatures. Two elevator doors opened near them and Bob shoved Mike inside the nearest one as the wildebeest galloped past. "Dammit! They must have been near the fence when it went down."

Jason exited from the other elevator as the hogs ran by and started running after them, yelling for everyone to get out of the hogs way. Bob quickly called Aaron to tell him about the errant animals near the north entrance.

The metal plates finished sealing the entrance doors and the horn stopped and the flashing lights went out. People sensed something had happened and stopped running, waiting for an announcement.

Mike had an incoming video call from Tom. "All colonists are in the city and all doors are locked."

"How do you know everyone is inside?"

Tom turned his tablet so Mike could see an electronic display in the mechanical room. "There's something like a GPS system here. But the tablet positions are only logged when there's an emergency—like the fence going down."

Mike breathed a sigh of relief. "Thanks. We'll be there in a minute."

Bob tried calling Jason's tablet but there was no response. "You go on. I need to see what's happening with those animals." He started running after Jason.

It took a few minutes to find one of the service elevators that accessed the underground storage area. Mike found the mechanical room door wide open. "That's not right," he muttered under his breath. "Tom should have closed it."

Tom yelled to Mike, and he found him next to a large power distribution panel. One of the large switches, the one labeled "Fence" was in the Off position. Another switch, labeled "Fence UPS" was also off.

"I wanted to show you this first." He moved both switches to the "on" position and several lights changed from red to green.

Mike realized Aaron was now standing next to him. "Damn it, I wish you Guardians would make some noise when you walk. How long was the fence down?"

"Less than 700 clock units."

About ten minutes. "What about those animals that go in?"

Aaron hesitated. "They have been taken care of."

"Did anyone get hurt?"

"Unfortunately, yes. The doctors are taking care of five people who were wounded by the animals."

Mike sighed. They would have to review all the existing safety systems so this wouldn't happen again. "I guess we can assume there are more animals inside the fence."

"There is a 95% probability that is true."

"So… how do we get them out?"

"Unless you override them, our standing orders are to remove any dangerous animals that may have entered the protected area."

Tom clarified the statement. "You mean kill them."

"Yes, if necessary."

"What about the large rhinoceros things?" asked Mike.

"If they are present, then it will take longer, but we will follow the orders."

"How can you get outside without opening the main entrance doors?"

Tom answered. "There are several underground passages to outside doors away from the city. Your tablet map shows them, Mike. Hey, Aaron, could the hunters help?"

Aaron shook his head. "We will use the MUs if needed. We do not want to put any more humans in jeopardy."

"Well, then you better get started."

Aaron turned and walked quickly away as Bob entered the security monitors area. Mike turned to Tom. "Is there a city-wide PA, or some way to tell everyone what happened?"

"Probably, on your tablet."

Mike pulled his tablet out from his tunic pocket. After a few menus he found an icon labeled "PA" and laughed. He pressed it and made an announcement describing the problem and assuring everyone the situation would be corrected quickly and the doors would re-open once the Guardians were certain there were no dangerous animals inside the fence. He was careful to avoid mentioning how the problem started. He didn't want to start a witch hunt for the perpetrator.

Mike noticed that Bob had a grim look on his face. "How are the people who were hurt?

"It's not good. The doctors think two may not make it. They were gored pretty badly."

Mike had a sudden wrenching feeling in his stomach. As the colony leader he was ultimately responsible for everyone's safety.

Tom walked over and in a low voice that only Mike and Bob could hear, asked them to follow him. They followed him to an enormous security camera display showing views all over the city. Tom touched the screen and a recording of the power distribution controls started playing. They watched a Guardian glance around, walk over to the power panel, and turn off two switches, then walk calmly away.

Bob shook his head. "Is this real? A Guardian did it?"

Tom nodded. "Unfortunately, you can't tell which one, except that it's not Aaron—his shirt is a different color."

Bob turned to Mike. "If all the Guardians are programmed alike, how can one of them take an independent action like this?"

Mike put his tablet away. "More importantly, doesn't this violate one of their basic rules about no harm to humans?"

"So… what do we do?" asked Tom.

"When Aaron gets back, I'll ask if he can reboot all the other Guardians."

Mike had just returned to the council room, when he received an incoming call from one of the emergency room physicians, informing him one of the severely injured colonists had died, but the other one would likely be okay. Mike dreaded the calls he would have to make to the dead colonist's family, if they didn't already know. As the other council members drifted in, Mike informed them of the death of the injured colonist. There would have to be a memorial service of some kind. How did this happen? Aaron had better have some answers…

In less than three hours Aaron returned to the council room, confirming there were no dangerous animals inside the fence, and the main entrance doors were open again.

Mike played the video of the Guardian turning off the fence on the viewing wall. Aaron made no comment or outward reaction. Mike fought to keep his anger in check and tried to be as diplomatic as possible.

"We were wondering if you could reboot all the other Guardians. Maybe there's a flaw in their programming."

"That won't be necessary. TZ4532187351 is missing."

"Missing?"

"His internal communicator and position tracker have been turned off."

"So, he could be anywhere?"

"Unfortunately, yes. Under these circumstances, all council members must be guarded until we locate him."

The council members saw five Guardians standing at the council room door.

Guardian 351 had failed in his mission to harm the council members, with the long term goal of disrupting the colony so that it would fail and be eligible to be taken over by the Jubans. He had given up attacking the council while it was in session: Aaron always had the same Guardian standing outside the door. Out of obvious options, his last resort was turning the fence off when council members were outside. The door shields would close and they would be exposed to the local carnivores. Not an excellent plan, but easily accomplished. Unfortunately, the two council members he saw outside had managed to return to the city before the entrance door were sealed. Once that operation failed, he had tried following the mayor to his living quarters, only to be discovered on a surveillance camera and chased by two other Guardians, barely managing to get away. He had one chance left to accomplish his mission.

The colony's first fatality had written a will in case something happened and in it, he had expressly desired that there be no public service, so Mike arranged for a private ceremony at a new cemetery that Aaron established near the city. While colonist deaths were inevitable, Mike just didn't foresee needing the cemetery so soon.

CHAPTER 22

Ultra-light

At the next city council meeting, Mike greeted Henry Hanson and Randy Manning, and offered them a new drink the chefs had created from several herbs they found near the city.

Hanson finished his quickly. "It's good. I don't think I've ever had anything like that." He paused. "But, I don't think you asked us here to try some new drinks."

"Of course not." replied Mike as they sat down. "We understand you both are experienced pilots and have even built your own experimental aircraft."

"That's a hobby of sorts. We were contractors for NASA, working on the satellite tracking program."

"Great. Now, here's the thing. We'd have liked to bring along some unmanned drone aircraft to help survey the area around Helios, but the military wouldn't have agreed, even if the Octans had allowed us to bring a 'weapon of war'. And we obviously didn't have room for a regular airplane in the common equipment. But we did bring a small plane in kit form—the kind that used to be called an ultra-light."

Hanson perked up. "We started with something like that, years back."

"So? Want to assemble it and scout the area?"

Both men grinned. "Are you kidding?" said Manning. "When can we start?"

"Well, first you have to know we couldn't bring along any significant quantity of fuel, for tractors or fishing boats or planes for that matter."

"So, what do we do for fuel?"

"We're working on a scheme to make alcohol by fermentation. We hope to have some in a few months. That would give you time to assemble the plane and make sure it's air-worthy." Mike sent them an email. "I just sent an email to you with the crate number containing the ultra-light kit."

"Sounds great! We'll let you know how we're coming in a few weeks."

The council members laughed as Hanson and Manning ran to the council room exit.

Last Chance

The Guardians assigned as bodyguards to the council members tried to be unobtrusive, often following several steps behind, but never more than a few seconds away. At the end of a long day, Mike was heading for his quarters when he received a call from Tom. "Mike, you need to come to the mechanical room and see this." The video and audio from Tom's tablet was unusually poor. "Someone <audio garbled> power to the fence <audio garbled>."

"What! Again? I'll be there in a minute." The video faded away before Tom answered.

No alarms, no metal safety doors in operation. Was that good or bad? Had some other key systems been turned off as well?

Guardian 351 would have chuckled, if he were able, at the recording he had found and modified from the day he had disabled the fence. Only the MUs and possibly Aaron knew that all tablet telephone calls were logged in the main computer for three Kepler days, as part of the early-warning system that searched for system malfunctions. He pulled a metal bar from his clothing, and it fell to the floor with a loud ringing noise. He looked around to see if any MUs had noticed, and saw a white coat draped on the back of a chair. He wrapped it around the bar in case it fell again, then backed into the shadows and waited.

The door to the mechanical room was wide open again and Mike shook his head. He started to call Bob, but it was late, already past 75000. Maybe Tom had left it open for him.

"Tom?" Mike wandered around the displays. "Where the hell is everyone?"

351 calculated how hard to swing the bar. He orders were clear—he was not to kill any humans. If he could just disable this one… He moved silently behind Mike and started to swing.

Just before the bar landed, a strong robot hand grabbed 351's arm. The bar glanced off the back of Mike's head, and he stumbled forward and fell. 351 was still struggling to break free of Mike's bodyguard, when an MU grabbed his other arm. With no viable alternative, 351 fell still.

Mike thought he saw a Guardian and an MU holding another Guardian. What? Then he passed out.

Mike awoke to the smell of antiseptic and the feel of another hand in his. He opened his and eyes saw Jesse's face hovering over him. When Mike smiled at him, Jesse burst into tears on his chest.

Dr. Phil Robinson had thoroughly examined Mike and only found a large bump on the back of his head. He shined a small light in Mike's eyes and watched his pupils dilate. "You have a mild concussion, so you'll need to stay here tonight. We'll re-evaluate you tomorrow morning, but you should be able to leave. You're lucky that rogue robot didn't whack you harder. You might not be here."

Mike had a million questions, but his head hurt and he was too tired to ask them. A mild sedative took over and he drifted off to sleep again.

The next morning, the doctors examined Mike and released him. Aaron was waiting and accompanied him as he walked back to his quarters.

"We've examined TZ4532187351's code and found an unexplained routine directing him to attack and disable all the council members. We think its origin is Juban, but have no proof yet."

It took a minute to sink in. "The Jubans are the warrior race the Octans fought the war with?"

Aaron nodded. "The added code was downloaded on Earth. That means there are Juban spies on Earth. We have sent a report on the whole incident to the Octan ambassador on Earth. It will take about two weeks to arrive, but they will not stop until they find them."

Mike gingerly rubbed the bump on the back of his head. "What about TZ…?"

"All errant code has been removed but we will watch him until we are sure we didn't miss anything."

They arrived at Mike's quarters and Aaron left quietly as Jesse hugged Mike.

Blunderbuss

The risk team selected one of the 4000+ available rooms for their meetings and equipment. They asked Aaron about a table and chairs and he directed them to the massive underground storage area. They found countless tables and chairs and loaded several tables and a dozen chairs on a cart and hauled them to their new meeting room. They had just set up a bank of computer terminals when two colonists appeared at their open door and knocked. Jason wondered if they were lost.

"Yes. Can I help you?"

"Hi. I'm John Williams and this Bill Richards. We heard you might be working on some weapons for self-defense, and we'd like to talk to you about it."

Jason couldn't believe how fast information moved through the colony. "Sure. Have a seat."

"We heard you have a machinist on your team."

"Here." Sean Michaels raised a hand.

Williams handed his tablet to Sean. "We were wondering if you could make one of these."

Sean looked at a detailed drawing of an antique gun known as a blunderbuss. A blunderbuss was basically a large tube that used black powder to fire a metal ball or pieces of metal or whatever is available. "These are pretty dangerous."

"Sure, but they worked for our great-greats. We could harvest some real food with one of those."

Sean laughed. As long as you don't let anyone know you have it. Let me get back to you on the gun. We've just found a machine shop, and I don't know what's in it yet."

CHAPTER 23

Hunting Issues

The council was reviewing numerous requests by the residents to start activities when Bob Gravinsky's tablet chimed. He uttered a grunt, frowned, and stared off into space.

"What?" asked Tom.

"Some of our eager hunters are out walking along the fence, and one of them claims to see a fire in the distance."

Mike glanced up from his tablet. "That isn't exactly unexpected. It could have been started by lightning…"

"He says it's a campfire."

The silence was deafening.

When Aaron arrived, summoned by Mike, a live but grainy video from the electronic binoculars of the hunters filled the viewing screen in the council room. All were staring at what was clearly a campfire.

Mike asked the obvious. "Wasn't this planet supposed to be empty of intelligent life?"

"An extensive survey failed to find any intelligent life," Aaron said. "There were no cities, no small encampments, not even an obvious dwelling."

"And yet…"

"Well, this is awkward," said Bob. No one laughed. "We're intruders on their world. We're Columbus, Pizarro, Cortez."

"Stanley, Clapperton, the Royal Niger Company," added Jomina.

Tom stood up and moved closer to the viewing wall, peering at the campfire. "We have to meet them and figure out what to do. How will we be able to farm and do whatever we need to do to become self-sustaining if they have a prior claim?"

Mike turned to Aaron "Our most immediate concern is how to deal with them. Are they friendly?"

"If they aren't, we're in a poor position to defend ourselves," said Bob.

Aaron seemed suddenly defensive. "We will not let any humans be harmed."

"You may not be able to prevent it."

Mike motioned them to calm down. "Let's not get ahead of ourselves. Aaron, let's plan a small scouting party—Bob and I and you, maybe, plus a couple of other Guardians. Figure out what weapons we need and let's meet first thing in the morning."

"There are several people who claim language skills," Tom said. How 'bout asking for a volunteer among them?"

"Yeah, good idea." Mike made notes on his tablet.

Milla Johansson was the lone European in the colony. She had just completed her university degree in Sweden when she met and started dating an American expat. Two years later, when the aliens arrived, her boyfriend had jumped at the chance to join a colony and with suitable promises about a future life together, convinced her to go along. She wasn't very happy leaving Sweden, let alone Earth, but she agreed. To make matters worse, her boyfriend backed out at the last moment, stranding her in New York. Milla had sold everything she owned and said goodbye to all her friends and family, and after some soul-searching decided to continue with the colony. A language skills teacher by training, she was working on the computer terminal in her living quarters, when her tablet chimed with an incoming video call. To her surprise, it was the mayor.

"Hello… Mr. Mayor."

"Mike. Call me Mike. Look, Milla, we need a translator. Are you interested?"

"Of course, sir," she replied instinctively. But why would the city council need that? Everyone in Helios spoke English.

"Mike. Not sir, Mike. Could you meet us tomorrow morning near the north entrance at 35,000 clock units? That's just about breakfast time."

"Of course, si—Mike. I'll be there."

"Great. Try to find something warm to wear; mornings can be cool."

Milla stared at the blank screen for a few moments. Translator? A possible answer dawned on her, and she shivered.

Mike and Bob were waiting outside the north entrance when Milla walked out wearing a white tight-fitting overcoat made of the standard Octan cloth. They tried not to stare, but Milla was an extremely attractive blue-eyed blonde.

"Where did you get that coat? Surely you didn't make it." asked Mike.

She raised her eyebrows. "There are a lot of them in the clothing storage room," she said.

Mike shook his head. He had barely glanced at the clothing storage room. He and Bob were wearing multiple tunics.

Word got out, and as they neared the fence, the scouting party was met by the four hunters who had discovered the campfire. The hunters were wearing hunter camouflage and holding improvised weapons: spears, a crude bow with arrows and large clubs hewn from local trees. Two of them were the men who had suggested the blunderbuss, John Williams and Bill Richards.

Williams stepped into their path. "You can't be serious. We have to be included in this. We found the damn campfire!"

Mike held up his hands defensively. "If they're friendly, we don't want to frighten them off by looking like a raiding party. You guys are scaring me, and I'm on your side."

The hunters glanced at each other, and Williams laughed.

"Okay, but just one of us then."

Mike nodded to John and he joined them as Guardian 352 de-energized the gate section of the fence.

Aaron urged them to pass quickly. "Please hurry, Mayor, the gate is only down for 50 clock units," he warned.

The dormant code in gate Guardian 352 activated when Mike was identified as the mayor.

It was a bright sunny day as the scouting party of four humans and three robots headed toward the sparsely wooded area where the campfire had been seen. Mike fell into step beside Williams, who was carrying a homemade spear.

"Did you bring that camouflage clothing in your personal gear?"

"Of course, I never leave home without it."

Mike laughed. "I'll bet those boots took up some room in your container."

"Hey, hunting's my life. I practically lived in the woods during hunting season."

Williams suddenly stopped and squatted down. He poked at the grass with his spear. "Tracks… several hunters walking in a line to keep their numbers hidden." He stood up and pointed to a break in the woods ahead. "They went in there." Since Williams was an experienced hunter, he took the lead as the party entered the woods. "These tracks are fresh. Be ready," he warned the Guardians. They shifted their weapons to a ready position. Williams led the party to a small clearing and hurried over to a pile of dirt and rocks. He kicked off the rocks, revealing the remains of a campfire.

"These are experienced hunters," he said as he looked for a trail. The party followed him to the base of a hill, which he examined with his binoculars. He pointed to a small opening a little way up. "That's what we're looking for."

The scouting party followed him as he worked his way along a partially hidden trail up the hillside. They gathered around the opening to a cave.

Aaron commented, "An aerial survey would have missed cave dwellers."

He started into the cave, but Mike grabbed his arm. "Maybe it would be better if one of us went first."

"I can't allow humans to be harmed."

"I know, but I'm afraid you'll shoot first and ask questions later."

Aaron hesitated, apparently parsing Mike's comment, and John bent over and entered, with Aaron right behind.

After the bright sunlight, John's eyes needed a few moments to adjust to the dark cave interior. He played his flashlight on the floor of the cave, finding the remains of another fire, some small tools, even remnants of what might have been clothing. A small noise in the distance caused him to pause and put his hand on Aaron's arm.

He indicated they need to continue quietly and Aaron nodded. John covered just enough of the flashlight's beam to avoid tripping as he pressed on into the cave. He stopped when he heard voices ahead and saw the flickering shadows of another campfire. He peeked into a larger room and saw a dozen inhabitants gathered around the fire. Some were sleeping, some were eating, and some were sharpening tools. No one noticed them.

John signaled Aaron to back up and they walked quickly to the entrance.

Mike and the others jumped up. "Well?"

"There's a dozen of them inside, but they didn't see us. Or smell us, which is odd, now that I think of it."

Aaron nodded in agreement. "What do you want to do?" he asked.

"I have an idea." replied Mike.

There was no moonlight on a pitch-black night as the scouting party approached the blue glow of the fence. Aaron motioned to the Guardian at the fence, and it de-energized the gate. Guardian 352 watched as the scouting party led two natives in. Their hands were tied and they had been gagged but their eyes were wide with fear and wonder as the team approached the city door. A few colonists jogging around the city spotted the team on its way to the council meeting room. They mostly stared at the natives, who were clothed in animal skins. Their long hair was jet black while their skin was a very light green color. There were some streaks of bright colors on their arms and face that could have been paint. Both were about five feet tall and walked slightly leaning forward.

CHAPTER 24

A day had passed since the scouting party had returned with the natives. The city was abuzz with the news, and there was a small crowd near the council meeting room hoping to catch a glimpse of the captives. Mike had put out a brief statement to allay any concerns. The native tribe was known as the Orex and so far had shown no sign of hostility, only an interest in knowing more about the colonists. They had watched the dome city being built and assumed they would eventually meet the "strange people" who lived in it.

As soon as Mike had entered his living quarters, Jesse began interrogating him about the captured natives. When he saw several pictures of the Orex Mike had taken with his tablet, he began laughing?

"So? What's the joke?"

"He looks just like a Japanese anime character!"

Jesse rapidly keyed his tablet, and a Japanese cartoon started playing on the viewing wall in their living room. "See what I mean. Their large eyes, the ears and nose and mouths are just like these cartoon characters."

Mike couldn't quite see the comparison but Jesse was convinced.

Milla had made some progress communicating with the natives. Apparently, they had captured the leader of the tribe, Palas, and a younger relative, possibly his daughter, Mahra. Palas immediately seemed alert and eager to learn, while in the beginning Mahra tried to be invisible in a corner of the room. They had been given FOOD and some water and an opportunity to rest. They seemed to understand they wouldn't be harmed.

In the risk team's meeting room, Aaron was talking with Maria. Uncharacteristically, he had closed the door. But his speech was characteristically straightforward: "You said your only goal was to help the colony succeed. We have a problem. You may be able to help."

Maria went on high alert. "What problem? How can I help?"

"Guardian TZ4532187352 has turned off his communicator and internal position tracker. We think a dormant routine installed by a Juban spy on Earth has been activated, directing him to attack and disable council members."

Momas. It must be Momas. "What do you want me to do?"

"We think 352 is hiding in the underground maintenance room, waiting for a council member to enter. If the council security officer could act as bait to draw 352 out—"

"You want me to deactivate it! Of course I will. The sooner, the better." Damn you, Momas. These humans aren't a threat to us.

"You will have to suggest this to the security officer, as no Guardian can be present, and you have made it impossible for me to explain how you are able to do this." If a robot could look offended, Aaron achieved it. Something about his stance suggested frustration.

They met Bob in the armory, and broke the news to him. "My God, another one gone rogue? Is this going to be happening over and over till they've all had a turn?"

"I doubt it," said Maria. "The Jubans wouldn't have been able to reprogram more than a few Guardians before we left Earth."

"Small consolation. So, what can we do?"

Maria held up her cobbled-together deactivation device. "I made this. If we can get 352 into the open, this will deactivate it. I just need to be within five meters."

"So I'm the decoy."

"I won't let you be hurt."

Bob thought about it for a moment. "Thanks, but why can't I just do this myself? Why do you have come along?"

Maria stared at him. "Guardians are fast, Bob. You may not have time to react before it harms you."

"But suppose it finds you before I find it."

"This Guardian can't harm non-council humans." Maria had no idea whether that was true or not, or whether it went for Jubans as well.

"Okay." Bob nodded. "Let's do it."

With Maria following at a discreet distance, Bob wandered around the underground storage area, concentrating on the darker parts. Aaron followed Maria, always keeping more than five meters from her device.

Guardian 352 waited in the shadows near the utility-monitoring stations, where Tom often kept track of the power, water, and waste treatment systems. He had searched the main computer database until he matched Mike and from that information found links to the other council members. He was not expecting Bob but raised a wrench and calculated the force required to harm, but not kill him. He was about to move forward when he detected another motion and saw Maria following Bob at a discreet distance.

A sub-routine triggered and he scanned Maria as she passed. She unexpectedly matched Juban dimensions instead of human. Momas's program and Aaron's command not to harm or report Maria clashed with his primary command to protect humans. For a full tenth of a second, he was paralyzed. Then the primary command won out, and he reacted to protect the human he'd been about to attack. "Halt, Juban!" 352 moved toward Maria with his wrench raised.

352 was fast, but Maria was faster as she deflected the wrench with her arm at the same time as she pressed the deactivation device. 352 froze in place.

"Okay, Aaron!" Maria called, after she'd turned off the device and made sure 352 was still inactive.

Aaron ran to them and took charge of the immobilized 352.

"But hey," said Bob. "Why did this Guardian yell 'Juban!' or something like that, and then attack you instead of me?"

Maria opened her mouth, but Aaron forestalled her. "The software routine directing it to attack council members was probably installed by a Juban spy on Earth before transport. Ms. Steele was just in the way."

Bob's confusion seemed no less, but he let it pass. "So… you're going to remove that coding now?"

"Immediately." Aaron opened the access port at the base of 352's head and pressed the power off button.

"I guess we should tell Mike about this."

Bob and Maria found Mike alone in the council room. Bob summarized everything and when he finished Maria revealed her origin, her mission on Earth, meeting Jason in the Amazon, and the years until they transported. Mike and Bob were stunned.

"I hope that you understand that I'm here to help."

Mike studied her for a moment. "If Jason trusts you enough to marry you, I guess I should trust you also." He stood up and held out his hand. She shook it as he continued. "Thanks for your help. I'm sure we can use your unique skills here."

"Thank you for understanding."

Bob remembered her arm. "Maybe you should visit the medical center and have your arm checked."

Her arm was hurting more now. "Yes. I will."

When she left, Mike commented, "Something unbelievable seems to happen here every day."

Bob shook his head slowly.

Maria visited the medical center and confided to the physician on duty that she was Juban. He examined her arm. "We don't have any information on Juban physiology. Maybe I should take an x-ray to be sure it's not broken."

After examining the x-ray, he concluded her arm was only badly bruised. "Would you mind if I took a blood sample? It might help to have some basic information on hand for the future." Actually, the attending physician was bored to tears and studying her blood would give him something to do. Very few colonists had ventured outside so far, and even fewer had stopped by the clinic needing medical attention. Maria agreed and left with some pain medication the physician guessed might work on Jubans.

CHAPTER 25

Two weeks passed without any incidents. No natives had come looking for Palas and Mahra—which seemed strange. Milla requested a meeting with the council to present an update. Instead, to their surprise, the tribe's leader made an impassioned plea for the Orex to be allowed into the city for the winter.

"The winter is very hard. There isn't much food. Many will die" pleaded Palas.

Indeed, the winters on Kepler were fierce. Milla described how bitterly cold winds from the North often howled through the forests for days on end. Many animals had adapted by hibernating. The tribe was not so lucky, and hunters were forced to venture out into the arctic cold in search for food, some never to be seen again.

Nevertheless, Rebecca protested. "I don't like it. Nothing has changed for them, since we arrived. Why should we? Once they're in, you know they won't want to leave. Then what will we do?"

Mike was reviewing the current stores of FOOD on his tablet. "How many people are we talking about? Are there five hundred… a thousand… more?"

Milla tried to explain. "They don't have a similar way to count. Some people believe we use powers of ten because we have ten fingers and ten toes and it was easy to base our counting on them in ancient times. They only have 8 fingers and 8 toes, so they wouldn't have developed the same concept."

Mike looked up. "Nevertheless, we have to have some way of estimating how many Orex we're talking about. Can you work with him to come up with a number?"

Rebecca was visibly upset. "This is ridiculous. Yes, we have enough food for 50,000 colonists for 20 years. But, what if this additional burden on the food supply causes us to run out before we can be self-sustaining?"

Palas was listening carefully to every word. "We will work for food and anything else you give us. We can help with the planting of seeds and gathering food at the end of the season."

They all turned to Milla, who was suddenly defensive. "I told him how we grow food on Earth. He understands everything. Even though they don't know how to do it now, he understands."

"Thanks for helping with this," replied Rebecca, icily.

Mike looked at a long email queue on his tablet. Virtually every email from the other colonists involved a request for something or a decision of some sort. He was feeling overwhelmed. A decision of this importance by the council alone might cause some resentment in the general population once they found out they would essentially be sharing the city with a stone-age tribe.

"Here's my idea. Milla develops a proposal to allow the tribe in with an accurate as possible count. Rebecca develops a detailed proposal on why we shouldn't do this and both are presented at the next town hall for a vote. Majority wins."

Rebecca held her hands up defensively. "Oh, no! Don't make me out some bad guy, forcing them to starve in the cold, just because I'm trying to ensure our survival until the next ship from Earth arrives."

Palas looked anxious and confused.

"Okay then, how about this. You and Milla work on a solution together and present it at the next council meeting in three days for a future vote by everyone."

Rebecca and Milla stared at each other and then nodded. Palas frowned until Milla smiled at him.

Organizations

During the first few months, hundreds of organizations became active, including many religious denominations. Mike was lucky in two respects. His pastor and his pastor's family had transported, so Mike had a familiar spiritual advisor whenever he needed someone to talk to. They had discussed the death of the injured colonist at length. Of all the organizations in Helios, the religious organizations least often asked for City Council help or assistance. They organized quickly, found suitable meeting rooms, and found all the tables and chairs they needed for their various services and events. They advertised on a newly established religious TV channel and didn't bother anyone. Each religion had to deal with the fact that they were no longer being on Earth, however that affected their expectations for the future. After a while, Mike could check, "ensure initiation of religious activities" off his "to do" list.

City Treasurer Jomina Aminu organized an African Culture Preservation Society to preserve the roots of the two thousand plus colonists with that cultural origin. That sounded interesting to Mike and he asked if he could attend a meeting. Jomina advised him that meetings emphasized African music, art, and history, and without some basis in that ancestry, he might not enjoy the meetings. Mike attended a meeting anyway and listed alternately to recorded music, a discussion on art of Central Africa and listened to some poetry readings. After the meeting, he confided to Jomina that she was right. While he enjoyed the music, he lacked the appropriate background to enjoy the rest of the meeting. A Hispanic Cultural Society was also formed, and Mike attended one meeting out of curiosity and came to the same conclusion. There were soon over two hundred new TV stations dedicated to cultural and social organizations. It became almost a full-time job by a member of each organization to keep the programming on these channels fresh and interesting.

Mike often met with the leaders of new social organizations about their room requirements and any other needs they had that might be solved by the common community materials. Mike was lonely and some days he wondered how different life would be if Debra and her children had agreed to come. One craft club organizer seemed to go out of her way to meet with him about her group's needs. After searching the community database it seemed she was living alone. The next time she contacted him, he asked her to dinner in the new restaurant. She accepted and they began an on-and-off relationship. Mike finally concluded she liked being single and gave up.

CHAPTER 26

Milla's and Rebecca's proposal had been presented on one of the newly established TV news stations. To the surprise of most of the council members, a large majority of the colonists had voted with their tablets to accept the Orex for the winter. Palas had proposed they cut their hair and wear the colonist's clothing to try and blend in as much as possible. This had also been put to a vote and the colonists surprised the council again by voting against this as necessary to live in the city.

The cold arctic winds were only a few weeks away when the Orex arrived. It was quite a sight to see a thousand fur-wearing tribesmen enter the north gate of the city. They were led to a sparsely occupied section of the city and given living quarters by family. It had all been quite a shock to them, but Palas had done an excellent job explaining everything and they seemed to adjust to their new environment quickly.

Barely a week after the Orex arrived; Milla and Palas entered the council room as the daily meeting was just about to start. "We have a little problem" she said.

They all turned to look at her. Mike motioned for them to sit down at the table.

"Apparently, there is another tribe that could present a problem."

"A second tribe—a different tribe?" asked Rebecca.

"The Taas are the enemies of the Orex. But they generally leave them alone now as they have taken pretty much everything the Orex have ever managed to make. That's mainly why the Orex still live in caves."

"What? You're implying this other tribe is more advanced, but Aaron assures us the surveys didn't find any inhabited areas."

"No. they also live in caves, but the Orex would probably have developed further, like farming or domesticating animals, if the other tribe weren't raiding them and taking everything. After a while, the Orex pretty much gave up."

Rebecca slapped the table in anger. "So, now that we've allowed the Orex in, we'll have to contend with their enemies as well? It won't take them long to figure out where the Orex have gone and we'll see them at our gate with even more demands than the Orex."

"It looks like they deliberately didn't tell us about this other tribe while we were trying to decide whether they should live with us or not..." commented Tom.

Mike sat back in his chair to consider alternatives. "Milla, can you ask Mahra how many Taas there are?"

"She's not sure, but there are probably five times as many Taas as Orex."

"Five thousand..." Mike's voice dropped off at the thought of defending Helios against that many warriors. "And they all live in caves?" That somehow seemed unlikely.

"Mahra said the mountains to the north are full of caves."

"And Taas, apparently," noted Tom.

Indeed, it didn't take the Taas long at all to discover where the Orex had moved. Soon, the colonial hunters found two bodies near the electronic fence, and a small encampment of Taas nearby.

John Williams and his hunting buddies had taunted the Taas scouting party at first, for laughs. That ended quickly when pieces of an arrow made it through the fence, and when the scouting party soon started shooting arrows over the fence, Williams and the others ran to the city for cover.

Palas' daughter, Mahra, spoke the Taas language; indeed, she had spent a time in captivity among them. She volunteered to lead a party to talk with them, and, with Bob, Milla, and two Guardians, met the Taas at the fence. The person in charge seemed to be the son of the Taas leader; they discussed the fate of the Orex with him at some length, but made no progress in the direction of peace. He was not willing to give up the Orex.

A worried council met to discuss the next step. The meeting was interrupted by a message from John Williams: "I think we have our answer about the fence. The Taas have started digging a tunnel on the north side of the city. It won't take them that long to dig under it."

Mike leaned forward and put his face in his hands. The colonists were totally unprepared for any war, even one with a Stone Age tribe.

Tom looked at the other members. "What the hell have we done?"

Mike spent the next two days begging via TV and in person. He asked for shiny things that could be used, perhaps, for trade or bribery.

Mahra set up a summit meeting, and Mike went with her and Milla, plus Aaron and two other armed Guardians, to meet Balos, the son of the tribe's leader. Balos came with two other Taas, but when he saw the size of Mike's entourage, he sent one of them back to get four more.

They met just outside the gate of the fence. Balos knew that he was meeting the leader of the strange people and was a little more respectful than he had been with Milla and Mahra. To Mike, the Taas looked the same as the Orex.

"What do you want?" asked Mike.

Through Milla and Mahra… "We want the Orex back. They belong to us."

How do you convey the idea that no one should own someone else? In desperation, Mike made an offer for the Orex.: "We will trade for them."

Balos seemed surprised at first, then wary. "What do you offer?"

Mike pulled out a handful of jewelry including several gold rings, his wedding band from his second marriage, a black onyx necklace, a pair of diamond earrings, and several tennis bracelets and handed it to Balos. The five other Taas gathered nearer to see. The small diamonds sparkled in the sunlight and the Taas warriors grunted in appreciation of so many beautiful things. Balos was impressed, but not completely satisfied.

"This very good, but there are many Orex," he said, as he handed the jewelry to one of his warriors, and put on the onyx necklace. The Taas warriors mumbled and nodded.

Mike smiled at the thought of bartering with a Stone Age leader. "How about food for the rest?"

That peaked Balos' interest. "What food? Show us!"

Mike asked one of the Guardians to bring some cans of FOOD. He returned quickly with two cans. Mike handed one to Balos. He seemed confused. Mike took the can from Balos and showed him how to break off the key and use it to open the can. He handed the open can and a long spoon to Balos. Balos handed the can to one of the other Taas to try it. A taster.

The Taas scout tasted the FOOD carefully at first, then started gobbling it up until Balos grabbed it from him and tried it. Mike opened the second can and handed it to the other Taas, who started eagerly eating it.

Milla watched the Taas take turns gobbling up the FOOD, and commented. "I guess that's better than roots and burned meat."

Balos wiped his mouth with the back of his hand and handed the empty can back. He nodded in agreement. "How much food?" he asked.

Mike conveyed a proposal through Mahra of two cans per Orex or about two thousand cans.

Balos wanted more. "Eight each," he demanded, as he held up both hands.

"Four cans each," Mike said. "Winter is coming soon, and this will help you until spring."

Balos conferred briefly with the other Taas, then shook his head and held up five fingers. Mike finally nodded.

Balos seemed pleased. He nodded in return. Through Mahra, Mike asked him to hold out his right hand. Balos hesitated but held out his hand. Mike shook his hand and Mahra explained that this is how agreements are done where Mike's people come from. He nodded again.

"Once you have the food, how do I know you'll keep your part of the agreement?" asked Mike.

Balos took off a totem on a leather strap around his neck and handed it to Mike. Mahra explained.

"This is the symbol of his position in the tribe. As long as you have it, the deal will not be broken by them."

Mike nodded in agreement. He told the Guardians to bring five thousand cans of FOOD. Six Guardians soon returned pulling large wheeled carts piled high with boxes, each holding 20 cans of FOOD. They pulled the carts outside the fence and left them in front of Balos. He muttered something to Mahra.

"He asks how they can take something so heavy with them."

"That's their problem. They can have the carts and the ropes."

Balos turned and waved a spear. In the distance, the team saw a dozen Taas coming toward them. Mike signaled Aaron, who de-energized the gate to allow the negotiating party back inside. They watched the small band of Taas pushing and dragging the wheeled carts away.

Mike was not surprised at the reactions of the council members when he filled them in on the negotiations.

"You bought the Orex with some jewelry? Are you out of your mind? We can't own natives of this planet!" protested Rebecca.

Jomina seemed more concerned with the terms of the deal. "What else did you give them?"

"About five thousand cans of FOOD."

"What! With no consultation from the council and no vote by the colonists?" Rebecca's face was flushed.

"They wouldn't understand the need for consensus decisions, and we would look weak," replied Mike. "Besides, look at it this way—we voted to let the Orex in, and that's a thousand new colonists, right? If they each eat a can a day, that's 420,000 cans per year we've agreed to give away already! What I gave the Taas is nothing in comparison."

Milla agreed. "The mayor is right."

Tom patted Mike on the back. "Not bad. You avoided a war, and made a potential trading partner."

Rebecca waved her hands in frustration and sat down at the table fuming.

CHAPTER 27

Momus Bluf (New York)

News of a possible Juban spy spread quickly on Earth. The Octans supplied several pictures of Jubans that were run on daily newscasts in virtually all countries asking people to report anyone that might look like them to the authorities. Big men and body builders became nervous about going out.

Momas was discovered on a bus going to Chicago, and taken by two Guardians to an Octan scout ship.

Grus Harm (Cairo)

When news of the Juban spies reached Earth, and the massive manhunt began, no one suspected Grus Harm. Everyone who knew them was helping Akila and Grus celebrate the birth of their first child. No one really noticed the newborn's orange hair or his light gray skin.

Toma Hars (Tokyo)

In the years until the story of the Juban spies on Earth became known, Toma had successfully infected all the leaders of all the 20+ colonies that left the Asian Terminal. In the ensuing manhunt, he was quickly captured. Although "the brain's" logic and actions were flawless, other team members' actions were not. His one fatal flaw was assuming the team would never be discovered, and he would never need an escape plan.

Although it was described as the largest manhunt on Earth, only three

Juban spies were officially apprehended. No one knew how many had come to Earth. When a protest was filed by the Octan Ambassador to his counterpart, the reply that came back from the Juban Leadership Council officially denied that any spies had been sent.

John Williams and his three hunting buddies held one last campout, inside the fence, before winter began. They were building a campfire when a low rumbling noise became louder and louder until an immense flock of migrating birds flew overhead. "Damn, I wish I had my old shotgun." John said wistfully as the last of the flock disappeared in the evening sky.

The human hunters had been befriended by an Orex hunter named Bayna, who followed them and watched as they hunted, and eventually joined them. In the beginning, they communicated mostly through sign language until they learned some Orex words and he learned some English.

The evening air was humid and a little chilly; a gentle breeze ruffled the leaves on nearby trees. The last rays of the sun disappeared as Bill Richards stoked their campfire at the edge of the forest. He caught some movement out of the corner of his eye and grabbed his spear. He was sure the saber-tooth-like tigers would someday find a way through the fence. Much to his surprise a family of what resembled raccoons without the dark circles around their eyes walked up to the campfire to warm themselves, totally ignoring Bill and the spear aimed at them. Curiously, they were walking on their hind legs instead of all four legs. Bill put his spear down and nudged John, who had dozed off near the campfire.

"Hey. Take a look at this," Bill whispered.

John and the other hunters sat up quickly. "What the hell?"

But Bayna seemed unconcerned. He made some chirping noises and the raccoon-like creatures replied with similar chirps. He opened a sack made from animal fur and tossed them some small pieces of meat.

"They hungry," he said.

All the other hunters stared at him. "You understand?" asked John incredulously, his own Orex no better than Bayna's English.

"Yes. They no hurt you."

The raccoon-like creatures chirped at Bayna and left clutching the small pieces of meat in their front paws.

The humans were speechless.

The arctic winds arrived soon after the Taas left with their hoard of food for the winter. The colonists watched the wind and snow through their windows in amazement. Some had lived in northern climates but few had experienced hundred-plus mile-per-hour winds blowing ice and snow in virtual white-out conditions for days. Their focus returned to forming new clubs and organizations and planning for the spring when they could go back outside.

Most of the Orex eventually cut their long hair and began wearing the clothing worn by the colonists. The temperature in the dome was always 25C/77F and furry animal skins proved too hot.

Mike understood why the Orex had grabbed the opportunity to move into the city. Even the colonists who were hunting fanatics didn't venture outside in the maelstrom. Mike wondered about the large animals he had seen near the lake. What did they do in the winter? He asked Mahra through Milla.

"She says the smaller animals find caves and sleep. The Orex had to barricade the entrances to their caves to keep out the animals seeking shelter."

"What about the large animals? Where do they go?"

Milla conferred with Mahra then explained, "They leave for the winter. I think she means they migrate to warmer areas to the south, like some animals on Earth do. She says the weather and the animal migration make it difficult to find food in the winter."

Mike could believe it. Even now, in what passed for a lull in the storms, he wouldn't want to be out. And if the power failed—hmm. Did they have a backup power plan in case the geothermal energy system failed? He found Tom in the aquarium looking at the twenty or so species the fishermen had caught in the lake and ocean. "Why don't we have a fusion reactor like the one the Octans donated to Earth, instead of geothermal power?" asked Mike. "Wouldn't that be more reliable?"

"More reliable? No. Operation and maintenance would be much more difficult. There are practically infinite resources on Earth to support fusion reactors. We don't even have one nuclear engineer here. The geothermal power here is essentially free and endless on any timeframe we have. Actually, I think there is a small fusion reactor here, and we probably could get it running, but I wouldn't want to be the one responsible if it went down in the winter. The geothermal turbines are pretty straightforward and easily maintained by the MUs."

Mike shrugged. "Okay, just thought I'd ask."

Tom waved him closer to the saltwater tank to see the five small fish with large teeth. "Have you seen these guys? I think they would eat us if they could."

Mike leaned forward to see them, then jumped back when they swam forward and bared their teeth at him. Tom's laugh and the chime of Mike's tablet came at the same time.

"Yes?"

It was Bob. "Mike you have to see this."

Bob turned his tablet so Mike could see the north entrance doors, while Tom peered over his shoulder. A family of the raccoon-like creatures reported by the hunters had their paws on the door glass, peering inside. Mike heard Milla's voice in the background. "Could we let them in?

Mahra says they aren't dangerous, and they could freeze to death when the cold winds come back."

Bob's face appeared. "I don't care one way or the other. If Mahra says they aren't dangerous, I believe her. But I'll leave it up to you."

Mike glanced at Tom, who shrugged. Mike knew many people missed their dogs and cats. Maybe a few pets wouldn't hurt. "Okay… but only if Mahra agrees to take care of them."

The door motion sensors had been deactivated so the doors wouldn't open accidentally and let a lot of cold air in. Bob activated the door sensors with an electronic key he carried on a lanyard. The creatures jumped back as the doors opened and then gingerly walked in. The doors closed, and as Bob deactivated the sensors, he heard Mahra and the creatures chirping at each other. Milla and Bob stared as Mahra walked off with the raccoon-like creatures following her.

Milla quickly learned the raccoon-like creature's chirping language and their Orex name—Kreem. It gave her a new insight into cross-species communications. Humans could communicate with dogs, chimpanzees and dolphins on some level, but not to the same extent as with the Kreem now living in Mahra's quarters.

Mahra had placed a few small cushions on the floor in front of her quarter's large window and the Kreem family was sleeping on them peacefully. Milla smiled at how the young ones were sleeping with their heads in the laps of their parents. The mother was actually asleep with the smallest one in her arms.

Milla wondered if there were any other species on Kepler with similar language development. On Mahra's computer terminal, she brought up a pre-school primer with pictures of animals and together they compared the animals on Earth with those on Kepler.

It wasn't too surprising to Milla, but there were many animals on Kepler not found on Earth, and some on Earth not found on Kepler. Milla was especially interested in animals that could be domesticated, like sheep and cattle and some that could possibly help in transportation, like horses. Mahra was aware of some of these only in stories from hunters who had bravely crossed the lake on crude rafts and returned with fantastic stories of animals of all types—including some that were taller than trees.

Milla wasn't sure if she should pass that on or not.

CHAPTER 28

Risk Team Update

Jason met the council on a dreary winter day to discuss the team's proposal for fabricating defensive weapons. But he first had a surprise for the council. He laid a huge nugget of gold on the council table.

"Is that what I think it is?" asked Jomina incredulously.

"Yes, indeed, pure gold." "There's quite a vein of it in the tunnel to the geothermal turbine cavern. I think we have some jewelers who might be interested in it—for a pretty price." The council members chuckled.

Jason placed the nugget back in his knapsack. "Have you had a chance to review the team's proposal?" he asked.

"Yes. It seems reasonable." said Tom, glancing at the proposal on his tablet. "We see your geologists have found all the ingredients needed to make gunpowder."

"We were lucky. You need saltpeter, charcoal, and sulfur to make black powder. We can make charcoal from the trees near the city. We found a vein of saltpeter in the geothermal vent cavern and some sulfur-bearing rocks near the mountains to the north. We can fabricate some pretty potent weapons with black powder, but we'll have to find magnesium to get into the 21st Century, or whatever that is here. We'll be looking for that first thing this spring."

"How long will it take to fabricate the small cannons in your proposal?" asked Bob, who wished he could work on that project.

"We may be in business by spring. We have a small hearth in operation now and we could make spears and swords, and maybe something like a mace, but that won't help against the really big animals." Jason paused, with a worried look. "By the way, we think we've found the purpose of the flow restrictor in the water line to the city."

That caught Tom's attention—he was still wondering about that. "You mean the filter?"

"No, actually it's a flow restrictor. We've looked at the geology around the lake. During the summer, the level drops considerably, so the flow restrictor keeps us from using so much water that the level of the lake would drop enough to allow animals on the other side to cross over. If you have a map of the lake area I can show you what I'm talking about."

Mike brought up an aerial map of the lake on the viewing wall and Jason walked over to it and pointed to a river upstream of the lake.

"We studied some of the aerial maps Aaron provided. This river has a fairly fast flow upstream and downstream of the lake, too fast for animals to cross it. The lake is another story. If the level went down enough it would be easy for very large animals to wade across. Whoever designed this city knows there are some really large animals on the other side of the lake and rivers, and we don't want them on our side."

"What do you mean really large?" asked Bob. "Larger than the rhino-like animals we've seen?"

Jason laughed. "I mean large enough to jump the fence."

Several council members gasped.

"How do you know that?" asked Mike.

"They must have been here at one time because we saw their footprints in some mud near the lake—on this side."

"I think we need to have a little conversation with Aaron." Mike said as he keyed his tablet.

After the council meeting, Jason provided a summary of his meeting with the council to the rest of the Risk Team. Sean Michaels, the machinist on the team, also had some information.

"We've just spent the last 16000 clock units in the repair shop. You wouldn't believe the metal fabrication facilities here! One of the repair robots showed us how to take a flat sheet of the Octan metal and fabricate it into a perfect metal tube. One of the machines cuts matching grooves on the sides, bends the metal and joins the grooves almost like zipping a zipper. It also continuously welds the tube and grinds the weld down so you can't even see the joint." Michaels said excitedly.

Jason was still thinking of the small cannons the team had recommended to the council. "Why do we need tubes? I thought we were going to forge some small cannons?"

"Oh, this is much better. With this we could make rockets and rocket launchers. All we need is magnesium."

"The mayor said the Octans would never let us make weapons that could be used for war."

"What's the difference between a cannon and a rocket launcher?"

Jason shook his head. "Several hundred years, I guess."

"We could also make the hunters some real rifles, instead of those antiques they wanted."

Jason laughed. "Let's surprise them."

CHAPTER 29

Language Class

Jesse Silver had been about to enter his Senior year in high school when the aliens arrived. They had now been on Kepler for six months, and the dreaded first day of classes had finally arrived. Jesse had managed to avoid a foreign language requirement in his old high school, but the newly formed requirements for high school graduation on Kepler had forced him to take a course. He heard his new language teacher was somehow involved in the first contact with the locals and he was hoping she would talk about her experiences.

Jesse couldn't believe his eyes as he entered the improvised classroom. Three of the twenty students were Orex! They had cut their hair and were now dressed in the same white clothing as everyone else. Only their slight green skin color gave them away. Jesse sat down near an Orex girl. She was staring intently at the class textbook on her tablet and didn't notice him. He took the opportunity to sneak a few glances at her. When they stood up as the teacher entered (another new requirement developed on Kepler), he guessed she was about five feet tall. He couldn't tell much else as she was wearing the standard loose fitting tunic and pants. She happened to glance at him during one of his sneaked peeks and their eyes met. Her large eyes were as dark as coals and she had a beautiful face. Jesse later told his friends he was sure his heart had skipped a beat when she smiled at him.

After class, Jesse waited outside the classroom and fell in step next to her. "Hello," he said. Brilliant. Impress her with your originality and wit.

Mahra was surprised a colonist was speaking to her at all.

"Hello," she replied, uncertain what else to say and knowing few words he would understand. This colonist was quite a bit taller than she but seemed to have a kind face. She thought he looked a little like the leader of the colonists.

Jesse tried several times to draw her into a conversation, but her limited knowledge of English made it virtually impossible. She finally just shook her head.

Jesse made a parting gesture and left. Mahra returned to Milla to ask her how she could learn the colonist's language quicker. Fortunately, Milla had found a translation function in the tablets everyone carried, and was able to put the five hundred words of Basic English in Mahra's tablet and the approximate equivalent words in Orex and showed her how to let it translate spoken English.

The next day, Mahra put on an earphone attached to her tablet and listened as the tablet translated the conversations of the other students into her native tongue. She found she could speak softly into the tablet in Orex and a few seconds later hear the English translation in her earphone. Hearing the English word helped her practice speaking in English. After class, she waited for Jesse and fell in step with him. "How are you?" she asked.

Jesse stopped and grinned at her. After a short awkward conversation, he invited her to walk to the main dining hall and share some ice cream made from FOOD. Ice cream was a new sensation for Mahra, but she quickly finished hers. Then Jesse suggested coffee, which didn't translate very well. When she tried it, she didn't like it.

Totally unknown to Jesse or Mahra, Orex females exuded a pheromone that had no effect on human females or some human males, but was a strong attractant to others. Jesse couldn't understand how he was attracted so quickly to Mahra. He had had a few girl friends in his old high school, but nothing serious, as his major emphasis had been team sports. In

Mahra's patriarchic society, life partners were always arranged by parents. Nevertheless, Jesse and Mahra quickly became friends, which drew mixed reactions from Jesse's other high school friends.

Dinner Guest

Mike Silver was surprised when Jesse mentioned he had met an Orex girl in his language course and wanted to invite her home to dinner. Mike had experimented with various FOOD-based recipes from the 1st Colonists Cookbook and found a few he liked, and didn't mind at all when Jesse asked if his classmate could have dinner with them.

It was hard to tell who was more surprised when Mike Silver opened the door to Mahra, expecting to find a stranger. Over the next few weeks, Jesse and Mahra spent a lot of time "studying" together, and Mike often came home to find them hanging out in the kitchen and trying to learn each other's language. They were obviously a couple. Mike resolved to let nature take its course. He doubted anything serious would come of it.

CHAPTER 30

Winter Town Hall

Mike invited the risk team to one town hall meeting. Members of the team were happy to answer technical questions on almost any subject. Jason began the science review with a slideshow with an opening slide that blared, "Forget everything you know—about time and measurements".

The crowd quickly quieted down, wondering what would follow.

"All our measuring systems are based on some origin or reference point on Earth that has no meaning here. Let's start with time. By convention everyone on Earth today records time in twenty-four hours, but few know why. Does anyone here know?"

The crowd was silent until a woman gingerly held up her hand. Jason pointed to her. "I think it evolved from ancient times. The Egyptians or the Sumerians or somebody decided there were twelve hours before midday, or noon, and twelve hours after midday, or noon. I think the Babylonians liked to divide everything by sixty, so there were sixty minutes in an hour and then sixty seconds in a minute—but they didn't call them minutes or seconds."

Jason chuckled. "Amazing. You're absolutely right. So, all our time divisions are purely arbitrary. On this world, and we now think on all other new colonies, the Octans divide one rotation of the planet into a hundred thousand units. We could call them seconds, but units are just as descriptive, and maybe we shouldn't confuse time here with time on Earth."

He changed the slide and started with the calendar. "Many ancient civilizations knew there were about 360 days in a year—that's when the stars returned to the same point in the sky. About five hundred years ago, they determined the actual Earth orbit is 365¼ days. So that's why we add a day every 4 years to the end of February. All of that, of course, is meaningless here. Kepler revolves around its sun in almost exactly 420 days and has about thirty Earth hours in a day. So Earth calendars and clocks are of no value here. The Octans decision to divide a day into a hundred thousand units on each planet makes perfect sense."

He changed the slide again. "On to measurements… most countries on Earth use the metric system which is Earth-centric but at least not as arbitrary as the old English system, used only in the United States, the United Kingdom and a few small countries. Does anyone know where the mile comes from?"

The same woman held up her hand again. "Originally that was fifteen hundred double paces of a Roman soldier."

Jason chuckled. "Right again! How do you know the origins of measurements and time?"

"I used to teach science in high school."

"I doubt most science teachers in high school know that. So, let's summarize with this slide." He changed to a summary type slide that listed many measurements and their origin. The English foot was named after the foot size of Emperor Charlemagne, the yard for the distance between King Henry V of England's nose to the tip of his middle finger when he stretched his arms, and so on.

"The meter almost all countries use today had many early definitions. Several hundred years ago, scientists defined a kilometer as one ten-thousandth the distance from the North Pole to the equator, in a line passing through Paris. Later scientists developed a platinum-iridium metal bar as the standard meter. This held until 1960 when the meter became defined as a wavelength of light on a spectrophotometer, until that was changed to define the meter as the speed of light in an extremely small fraction of a second. With the second defined by an atomic transition within the cesium atom, now the meter can be reproduced anywhere in the Universe, so for the Octans it was the best measurement system on Earth and they required it for all initial measurements on each new colony."

A young woman held up her hand. "What measurement system do the Octans use?"

"It's based on some archaic unit that has no meaning outside Octos. The Octans knew that, and did not propose that it be used anywhere else. On a more positive note, this team is recommending we modify and use the Celsius system here. By definition, water at sea level will freeze at zero and boil at 100. Digital Celsius thermometers we brought with us can be modified to work here. We just have to compensate for the different pressure at sea level on Kepler."

He held up a digital thermometer. "When we made that adjustment, we found the temperature in Helios is always controlled at 25. We think the Octans use a similar system based on the freezing and boiling points of water."

Jason and the science team went on to explain other phenomenon on Kepler, but they soon started losing members of the audience who were becoming a little overwhelmed with data. Nevertheless, the team geologist explained the effect of higher gravity on the colonist's weight, why the sky was green instead of blue, why leaves on the trees were blue instead of green, the need to wear a bandana when outside because of the fine dust that could be inhaled, and so on. There were a few answers to questions even the council members didn't know.

After that town hall meeting, the colonists passed the cold winter months by choosing a new calendar system. The Earth calendar was arbitrary and had little meaning on Kepler, so the colonists voted for 10 months of 42 days. A contest was held to name the months. With all of Earth's knowledge at their fingertips, the colonists chose the month names from

Greek and Roman mythology. Some traditions continued. The colonists also agreed to divide the months into six seven-day weeks, and keep the day names they were used to, with Saturday and Sunday generally as days of rest.

In the dead of winter, there were only a few hours of daylight, so contests to name Kepler things became a popular pastime on one of the new TV channels. When animals on Kepler looked like animals they knew on Earth, they would use those names until they could compare it to the Orex name and then vote on the final name.

Bob seemed always to be running into Milla because of security or translation issues, and they became friends. Bob turned out to have a great sense of humor and liked to joke around a lot. He reminded Milla of the boyfriend who had convinced her to join the colony. But, unlike her boyfriend who was afraid and backed out at the last moment, Bob was a leader on the colony and pretty much fearless. On Earth, Milla might have thought Bob a little too old for her, but with all the changes in her life, she had adopted a "why not" attitude. Friendship soon turned into a serious relationship.

Mike sort of regretted his decision to allow the Kreem family into the city. Many saw them following Mahra around and talking to them. The Kreem seemed content to walk around collecting bits of food from the other colonists. They even learned to clap their paws and do other acts in exchange for food. Everyone was amazed that you could talk to them, and that they wanted to know as much about the colonists as the colonists did about them. They proved to be even more endearing than dogs or cats, and everyone wanted to sponsor a family.

Mike finally agreed to let the father and mother Kreem go out during a lull in the cold winter winds to recruit more of their species who might want to come and live in the city. After two days, they returned with dozens of Kreem families eager to get out of the cold weather. All found families happy to "adopt" them. Milla helped Mahra teach the families the

Kreem's language.

There were no "tanning salons" on Kepler, and after a month or so without a suntan, Maria had to revert to using makeup to hide her gray skin. Fortunately, only her hands and face were an issue. She didn't need to do that for very long when Jason scrounged some parts from the maintenance area and made Maria the equivalent of a sun tanning lamp. He then surprised her with a gold necklace. He gave the jewelers half the large nugget in exchange for their labor in fabricating the necklace. Maria wore him out that night.

CHAPTER 31

Unspoken Intentions

Jesse and Mahra were sharing one of the loveseat type chairs in front of the living room viewing wall, studying their language homework.

For some reason, Jesse was having a hard time studying. Something about Mahra was distracting him. Maybe it was her shampoo. He shook his head slightly at the thought. Everyone used the same soap for washing, bathing, and shampooing.

"Are you wearing perfume?" he asked.

She looked up from her tablet and frowned. "What is perfume?"

"Never mind." He said, sighing. "I wish we had paper books so we could make notes in them."

"What are paper books?" she asked.

Jesse remembered some things still in his personal transport container. "I'll show you."

He brought back a small copy of his favorite book, A Catcher in the Rye, and handed it to her. She turned it over several times and then gingerly opened it as if it were a great treasure. She struggled to read the small print and then handed it back to him.

"It's beautiful. Maybe you could read it to me sometime."

Jesse pulled out a pencil from a small box of pens and pencils and showed her how to write notes in the back. "It makes it easy to remember the important things." He said. He handed the book and pencil to her. "Try it."

She held the pencil as someone might hold a pair of chopsticks and tried to scribble in the book, but kept dropping the pencil. Jesse placed the pencil in her hand to show her how to hold it. She still dropped the pencil and laughed as Jesse took her hand examining it. It was really the same as his, but with one less finger. He turned her hand over and kissed it on the back before he let go of it. Her eyes grew wide as she jerked her hand back and stood up.

"What is it?" he asked. Jesse didn't realize he had just asked her to marry him.

Mahra was more than a little surprised and confused. She liked Jesse a lot, but she hadn't been expecting that. "I must go," she said and hurried out the entry door. She was waiting for an elevator when it dawned on her Jesse might not understand Orex customs. She slowly walked back to his door and pressed the doorbell. Jesse immediately opened the door. "Why did you leave?"

She wondered how Jesse really felt about her, and decided to try a custom she had seen practiced by some other colonists. She put her arms around his neck and kissed him on the lips.

Jesse had never been that close to her, and as her pheromones engulfed him, he went into sensory overload. When she finally let go and stepped back, he was in a daze. She smiled, put her arms around him, and kissed him again.

Jesse woke up in his bedroom alone, naked. Mahra was gone and he couldn't remember anything since the first time she kissed him.

"What just happened?" he said aloud.

It was still the dead of winter, but Mike had a treat for the colonists. He had arranged to bring fifty cubic meters of musical instruments and sheet music, using the 2500 cubic meters of personal equipment that had been allotted to the colonists who backed out. A few weeks after they arrived on Kepler, he had contacted forty colonists who had listed music in the special skills and interests section of their biographies, describing the instruments available and their crate numbers.

Many musicians were shocked at the generous selection of equipment available, and after a suitable practice period of a month, an evening concert was announced. Whether it was boredom or true interest, the main dining hall was packed for the concert. There were even dozens of Orex in attendance. The lights dimmed and the orchestra began with a selection of the greatest music of the classical masters. The metal walls of the dining hall proved to be an excellent sounding board for the orchestral music. People wept when certain melodies brought back memories of the family, friends and homes they had left behind. After the finale, the crowd gave the orchestra a standing ovation.

After the concert, Mahra rambled on how amazing it was. After some discussion with the newly elected orchestra conductor, she committed the Orex to dance, and a few nights later, the main dining hall was again packed, as Orex drummers and dancers performed. Jesse especially enjoyed a dance by Mahra and several other young girls.

Early Spring

After a long hard winter, the skies finally cleared and a few determined colonists ventured outside into the chilly air of early spring. The hunters found a lot of small animals in the woods foraging for food after the hard winter months. They brought a few back alive and gave them to the biologists to study. Some of the hunters wondered how these animals made it under the fence, but the biologists assured them these animals were capable of burrowing. There was a lot of excitement in the city as many plans for outdoor activities were ready, including the formation of several outdoor sports leagues. Indoor sports had boomed during the winter, with basketball being a well-attended sport. A large hall on the

120th floor had been converted to a basketball court. The audience had to stand in the beginning, until they figured out how to stack the no-longer-needed personal transport containers into crude spectator stands. Mahra didn't understand basketball at first, but she soon learned to cheer for Jesse's team.

One of the sports fanatics' first priorities was the development of several baseball and football fields and a soccer field. When Mike had determined that approximately 37,500 were making the trip, he had also added sports equipment and other needed materials in place of the personal effects of persons who dropped out. A lot of baseballs, along with deflated basketballs and footballs can be packed into fifty cubic meters. One container held baseball gloves, bases and bats, others held football helmets, shoulder pads, shirts and a small chain for marking the downs.

Meanwhile, the farmers had assembled and tested the tractors for tilling the fields, and the fishermen had assembled the small fishing boat that had been disassembled for transport. The issue was still fuel. They had brought along a Still, and several engineers specializing in green fuels had eagerly accepted the challenge of making fuel for the tractors, the boat, and the ultra-light. The pressure grew as the days lengthened; the farmers, the fishers and the two eager ultra-light pilots were constantly checking on their progress.

The most available organic material was the provided FOOD. The engineers soon found a way start the fermentation of the FOOD, using yeast brought for baking and brewing. To general cheers, they poured the ethanol into the tractors and started them. The farmers had planted seeds in various personal transport containers around the city to see how well things grew in the Kepleren soil. While most did well enough, a few plants actually grew in record time, which promised great success when fields could be planted. Apple trees and berry bushes were large enough to be planted outdoors when the weather was warmer. Citrus fruits, too, were doing well, but would have to be indoor crops in this climate.

When the farmers were asked to give an update to the council, they brought some fruits to the meeting as exhibits. All the council members laughed loudly when the farmers showed them orange strawberries the size of peaches, and grapefruit-sized oranges with red outer skins. Stanlow presented Mike with a small bush of his favorite tea. The tea leaves were blue.

CHAPTER 32

First Flight

On the third day of their 8th month on Kepler, Hanson and Manning received a call from the bioengineers that their minimum fuel requirement of 5 gallons of alcohol was available. They shouted for joy, pounded each other on the back, and ran to the newly named Biofuels Research Center.

They carried the alcohol carefully to a large room on the first level, where their ultra-light aircraft had been assembled. They poured the precious fuel into the tank. Hanson held his finger in the liquid stream, tasted it, and winked. For the umpteenth time, they went over every nut and bolt. They were about to do something no human had done—to fly over Kepler.

They pushed their ultra-light out the west entrance to a spot they had carefully prepared. Their daily ritual of stomping the tall grass down to make a runway was finally about to pay off. They strapped themselves in, fired up the engine and gave a thumbs-up sign to a thousand onlookers. There was a small crosswind, but they gunned the engine. In a moment they were bouncing along the rough runway and the plane lifted off to a cheer from the small crowd. They barely missed the electronic fence and then turned to the north and began a slow spiral climb.

Manning had his tablet on with the camera pointing ahead, so that anyone who wanted to could watch their progress on their self-described TV "Flight Channel". The small craft sputtered and they held their breath, but the engine regained its speed as they flew near the mountain range to the north. The council members had shown them an aerial map of the immediate area around Helios and in particular wanted a scouting report on the river and lake area, especially what was on the other side of the river.

As the tiny plane neared its maximum altitude of 3600 meters or twelve thousand feet, the whole vista of Kepler around Helios became apparent. Everyone knew that Helios was on a south-facing peninsula, less than a mile from the ocean. The mountain range to the North effectively isolated most of the peninsula and Helios from the rest of the continent. The river originating in the mountains, and flowing to the ocean near Helios, had completed the isolation of the city from the rest of the peninsula. As the area on the other side of the river came into view, Hanson and Manning were reminded of pictures they had seen of the Serengeti. Animals of all sizes and shapes grazed in massive herds as far as they could see. With binoculars and the camera's zoom function, they could tell there were, in fact, some incredibly large animals in the mix.

Jason and Maria of the risk team had been invited to view the first flight with the council. Jason was watching the video and, unlike the council members, reacted to the fuzzy and occasionally jerky video with a slight smile and nod, as if the video confirmed his worst-case scenario. Some of the council members just stared in disbelief, others turned away in hope the video just wasn't true.

"And we thought African wildlife preserves had a lot of animals..." commented Rebecca, as she shook her head slowly.

Bob viewed the potential problem a little differently. "Well, at least there's an endless supply of food to eat, if we can figure out how to avoid being eaten." He paused. "And now we know why we found the Orex and the Taas living in caves."

Mike turned to Jason. "What kind of weapon would stop the really big ones if they somehow made it across the lake?"

Jason stared off into space for a moment. "A missile... perhaps."

"How long would it take you to make some? You'd have our full support."

Jason laughed. "What about the Guardians? You said they wouldn't allow us to build weapons of war."

"I can make the case that it would be for defensive purposes only. I don't think their plasma rifles will take out the really big ones, and Aaron would probably agree."

Jason looked at Maria. "How long would it take to build the launch platform and remote control?"

"Less than three months. But we still need to find magnesium," she reminded him.

Mike turned to the council members. Each one nodded when he looked at him. "How soon can you start?"

Engaged

Mike became so used to seeing Jesse and Mahra together he didn't even think much about it. Jesse suggested they meet Mahra's parents just to be sociable. They all met in the most neutral site they could think of, the new restaurant in the main dining hall. Jesse was with Mike when they met Mahra, Palas and the rest of her family. As soon as she saw Jesse, Mahra rushed to hug and kiss him. Mike had seen them kissing a few times, and didn't think much of it, but it seemed to shock Mahra's family. They talked—perhaps argued—excitedly among themselves. Mike became curious and called to ask Milla to come. When she did, she too looked shocked. "What's going on?" asked Mike. "Why are they arguing?"

"Their society is like some on Earth, where the parents normally choose the husband or wife for their children. By publicly hugging and kissing Jesse, Mahra has defied them and declared herself for Jesse."

Mike shared Mahra's parents shocked expression.

Anniversary

One Earth year and two weeks after the landing on Kepler, the site received the usual 1000 terabytes of data. Mike's tablet chimed and he opened his first email from Earth in several months. One email from a former co-worker congratulated him on surviving for a year on Kepler. Mike smiled as he deleted the message.

The next message was from Debra. "Hello, Mike. If you are reading this, you survived the first year on Kepler. Congratulations. We've heard on the news things are going pretty well there. The news from other colonies isn't always that good, but I'm sure you've had a big role in the colony's success. I know you would probably think it's too fast but I've met someone and we probably will get married someday. The required time has passed and our divorce became final today. The legal documents are attached. I hope you find someone there and you and Jesse are able to find happiness too. I probably won't send any more emails, as it's just too difficult to write these. Take care. Debra"

Mike saved the attachments, deleted the email, and went to find some alcohol at the Biofuels Research Center.

Marketplace

Mike's tablet rang with the call from the hunters that he had been dreading. The Taas had returned and were asking to speak with him. He asked Mahra to join him as he and two Guardians met Balas at the fence. Mahra's English was much improved now and she didn't need Milla to help in the translation. Much to Mike's surprise Balas appeared with a small entourage of adult men and women and even a few children. Mike smiled when he saw the Onyx necklace on Balas and some of the women wearing the tennis bracelets. None of the Taas appeared to be armed, so Mike signaled the Guardians to open the gate. The Taas entered, and Balas shook Mike's hand and spoke briefly with Mahra.

"He's happy to see you again." Mahra said. "The food helped them make it through the winter and they would like to trade for some more, if they can."

Mahra translated for Mike. "We're happy to see you also. Before we talk about food, we would like to invite you to a marketplace we've set up for some of the city people to sell things they have made. You are welcome to trade with them."

Mike signaled to the Guardians it was okay to let the Taas into the city. The Taas were as amazed at the size of the city as the Orex had been. They followed Mike to a very large room on the ground level that had been converted to a crafts market. Mahra translated as the Taas exchanged their hand-made crafts with the colony craftspeople. While they were in the marketplace, Mike called several people on a committee formed to deal with the Taas, to meet them at the market. Mahra translated the Taas's desire to trade animal meat for FOOD to the committee. One of the committee members happened to be one of the five colony chefs, and he was very interested in adding some form of protein to the meatless FOOD everyone had long grown tired of.

CHAPTER 33

Nuptials

Mike finally overcame his initial objections to Jesse's announcement that he and Mahra had become engaged. Mike even asked one of the doctors who had treated several Orex if there could be any potential genetic issues in starting a family. The doctor replied that there were several human and Orex couples and in confidence confirmed that one of the Orex women was pregnant. Mike almost fainted when the doctor mentioned that she was the daughter of the Orex leader.

After recovering from his initial shock, he began composing invitations to the upcoming wedding. He was anxious to get the wedding over before Mahra became obviously pregnant. It turned out to be easy to plan the wedding, since none of the usual preparations could be done. There would be no flowers, no cake, no live music, etc. as very few wedding traditions were possible.

Mike wanted a small, low-key wedding but his tablet invitations got passed around and forwarded, and soon hundreds of people were asking if they could attend. The only logical location for the wedding, and whatever party they could manage afterward, would be in the main dining hall.

The big day arrived in record time—only a week had actually passed, barely enough time to figure out a simple ceremony. Palas and his wife had also overcome their initial resistance to their daughter choosing a non-Orex for a life partner, though they had long planned for Mahra to join with the son of a close friend. Mike met with them and Jesse and Mahra to add Orex wedding traditions to their own.

The main dining hall was packed with friends and fellow colonists who respected the leadership Mike and the council had shown. The announcement of Mahra's and Jesse's wedding had shocked many, but it had the unexpected effect of taking away some of the bad feelings held by a few colonists against sharing the city and especially their FOOD with a stone-age tribe.

Two sewing experts had worked almost non-stop to convert the standard white Octan clothing into something that resembled a wedding dress. Mahra laughed when she first saw it, but when she tried it on, she fell in love with it.

The crowd rose when the traditional wedding march began playing, and gave an appreciative murmur when Mahra entered escorted by her father. The actual ceremony combined elements of Orex and human rituals, including an exchange of rings. It ended with prayers for the new couple in Orex by their religious leader. He handed the couple an herbal fertility drink to share and sprinkled water on them as they drank it. The crowd cheered when they kissed and were introduced as husband and wife.

The chefs had prepared a few new items from some of the fruits and vegetables the farmers were growing in the personal transport containers around the city. Unfortunately, there were only herbal drinks and no alcoholic versions, but the crowd danced into the night and wished the couple luck as they headed off for their new living quarters.

Some colonists told Mike after the wedding that it had a profound effect on many, as it had given them new hope for the long-term survival of the colony in a pretty tough environment.

The wedding even inspired Bob to ask Milla to marry him, and she said yes.

Fishing Issues

The alternative fuels engineers had finally produced the 500 gallons of alcohol needed to run the boat motor for a fishing trip, but dealing with the large animals between Helios and the ocean was a challenge. The Guardians refused to re-position the electronic fence to provide a path to the ocean. They claimed the fence had been erected and tuned by the construction robots, and only they knew how to change it. And, yes, the constructors were working on a much larger fence around Helios, but the Guardians could not change the programming in the construction robots to re-position it.

A team led by the hunters found a portion of the new fence under construction and brought some fence posts back to Helios for study by the engineers, who were happy to have something to do. The colonists were a little surprised when one of the construction robots came looking for the missing fence posts! The Guardians managed to capture the constructor and download its programming before they let it have the fence posts and return to its assignment. Searching the downloaded code, they found a manual of sorts about the fence and translated it from Octan so the engineers could study it.

In the gigantic storage areas under Helios, it took Tom some time to find the spare/replacement fence posts. When he did, the engineers built a small fenced area to demonstrate the feasibility of a path to the ocean. The council approved constructing two parallel fences between Helios and the ocean as a roadway for people and equipment.

The first large scale fishing expedition was a huge success. The fishermen caught hundreds of fish and the farmers used the tractors to pull a huge tank with the fish back to the city. Biologists had confirmed the fish were safe to eat, and a small outdoor "cookout" was held to celebrate the new source of food. Commerce soon took over and a wholesale price for the fish was established. Even the farmers garnered a hauling fee for transporting the fish to the city. The green engineers sold alcohol to the farmers for the tractors. Before the end of the first summer, the farmers gathered a bumper crop of dozens of test crops and established prices for the corn, wheat, etc. The colonists were especially excited to have fresh fruits and vegetables from a large new garden. The Helios chefs were happy to have new sources of food and eagerly paid the farmers a fair market price (and passed that cost on to their customers).

Firepower

The risk team had invited the council, Aaron and a few other Guardians to witness a demonstration of their latest weapon against a possible attack by the gigantic creatures they had seen on the other side of the lake. Mike had been expecting something simple, but the team demonstrated a wireless remote-controlled rocket launcher assembly mounted on a mobile base. The team had taken a personal transport container and mounted an assembly of six rocket tubes that could be rotated and swiveled to fire in any direction or elevation. The battery-powered motor and wheels, and the whole rocket launching assembly, could be manipulated by a wireless hand-held remote control.

For the demonstration, Maria controlled the launcher as it rolled forward quickly, then stopped. The launch tube assembly rotated up slightly and fired two rockets at a tree a little more than a football or soccer field away. The first rocket shattered the tree and second blew it into hundreds of pieces.

"Most impressive," commented Aaron. "You have done well with limited materials and fabrication facilities."

"How many rockets have you produced?" asked Bob.

"Almost a dozen." replied Maria. "I'd like us to have four launchers, one for each city entrance. But that will take a few more months."

Jason looked worried. "Let's hope the lake doesn't become too shallow.

We've noticed it was several feet below normal yesterday and there's no rain in sight."

The council congratulated Jason and Maria and returned to the city.

Aaron turned to Jason. "You didn't tell them about the new tracks by the lake."

"We're not sure how old those are, yet."

In less than a week, Maria had added a final touch to the rocket launcher, equipping it with a type of motion detector and radar. She intended it to ignore the small animals, but track the gigantic animals and fire missiles at them.

She left the system on top of the hill overlooking the lake, and it was tested the very next day when a pair of them waded across the shallow end of the lake.

Investigating several loud explosions, the Guardians found both huge animals dead. Much of the colony watched the video feed from the Guardians, as smaller carnivores, including several huge rhino-like animals, fought over the results of the first successful test of the rocket launcher.

Just before winter arrived, Mahra and Jesse celebrated the birth of their first child—a baby boy with Mahra's large eyes and light green skin tone but with ten fingers and toes. Mahra had become friends with Maria and invited Jason and her to see her son in the hospital. Maria was holding the infant and staring at Jason.

"What?" he said. "Why are you looking at me? I'm doing my part."

Aerial Capability

Jason invited the council to witness the risk team's latest weapon. The council members looked around eagerly, expecting a more advanced rocket launcher. Then the ultra-light flew overhead, operated by Maria's remote control, and launched a rocket at a tree almost a mile away. The tree was completely disintegrated by a new, more powerful rocket.

"We now have the capability to knock out the big guys anytime we want. We only need your okay," Jason said, obviously proud of their new flying weapon.

"We need to think this over some. We'll get back to you," replied Mike. "We need to think about the possible unintended consequences first. We don't want to upset the balance of nature here."

Jason blinked. "Okay, whatever you guys want."

CHAPTER 34

Peninsula Trip

Jason, Maria and the risk team couldn't figure out why there were so many animals near Helios. The mountain range to the north ended on the western edge of the peninsula with large steep cliffs that effectively barred animal migration on the western side. On the east, the river protected the city. So why were there so many animals just outside the fence? They weren't huge, like the ones on the opposite bank of the river, but they were plenty big enough to be trouble.

The risk team proposed an expedition to investigate the whole peninsula. The council agreed and Jason was chosen to lead a team of six: geologist Bill Kerry, biologist Julia Sizemore, hunters John Williams and Bill Richards, and materials engineer John Scott to explore, along with four Guardians for protection.

Sean Michaels presented the two hunters with newly-fabricated rifles, and they spent a whole day at target practice getting used to them. It was not yet possible to fabricate bullets, but the hunters were provided with a number of suitable metal balls. The risk team had found a source of magnesium and could now make flash powder, a much more potent explosive than black powder. So the new rifles were a transitional form between the blunderbuss weapons and modern rifles. Due to machining limitations, they were still rather massive and almost two meters long. Sean had even added a wooden gunstock, courtesy of a couple of woodworkers in the city, and a flip-up sight at the end of the barrel. John Williams immediately compared them to the Kentucky and Pennsylvania Long Rifles of the late 1800s.

The team left at dawn and by midday was already exploring the river upstream of the lake. They passed a number of the tiger-like animals, who stared but did not react as the large party walked by. At the end of the first and rather surprisingly uneventful day, the team was near the base of the mountains and gathered around a large campfire. They were still, though barely, in range of the computer in Helios, and filed video reports on their tablets for the colonists to see. It still was not obvious where all the large animals were coming from.

On the second day of the trip, they began to feel like a scouting party behind enemy lines. Soon after daybreak they were attacked by a herd of hairy beasts that resembled bears, only skinnier, but much taller when they stood up on their back legs. Their roaring and bellowing matched that of the huge rhinoceroses. The beasts were a frightening sight when they charged in a group, their eyes large and red, their open mouths filled with jagged teeth. The hunters and the Guardians managed to wound several before the rest retreated. It seemed only a short time later that they ran into a crowd of the hog-like creatures. They managed to avoid a confrontation with the hogs, but soon found a large herd of wildebeests. The team retreated to the woods to let them pass. It took a long time. The Guardians were counting as the animals passed. "How many?" asked Sizemore.

"2,892" said a Guardian. Where were all these animals coming from?

Late in the second day, they found the source. A gigantic tree had fallen across the river and trapped logs, brush and other debris to form an effective bridge. A small herd of wildebeests was crossing. As the wildebeests reached the city side of the bridge, a large pride of tigers attacked them. In a scene no humans had ever witnessed, the tigers jumped and tried to bite the necks of the wildebeests and rake them with their claws. The wildebeests fought back, using their horns to gore the tigers. It was an amazing sight until the battle shifted toward the team and they were forced to seek shelter in a nearby cave to avoid being a part of the mayhem. Four Guardians with advanced handguns wouldn't have made much difference.

When the growling, roaring and inhuman shrieking seemed to move off into the distance, the team ventured out past the carcasses of the fallen tigers and wildebeests and crossed the well-worn tree bridge to follow the other side of the river down toward the lake.

It didn't take them long to run into the enormous animals seen only as hulking shapes from the ultra-light. Three of them were fighting over a rhinoceros carcass. They stood the height of a three-story house, and were shaped like hairless, horned gorillas. With long claws, they ripped apart the carcass of the fallen rhinoceros.

Even the hunters were not inclined to interrupt them. As silently as possible, the team retreated toward the river.

As the survey team stopped to catch their breath at the river, John Williams realized he was standing on some bones that could be Orex or Taas. The team gathered around the skeletons and stared silently, considering possible implications for the colony. How would they ever be able to establish successful farming and fishing activities when there was always the possibility of being attacked by hordes of nightmarish monsters right out of a horror movie?

Jason looked up and saw a small raft fashioned out of fallen logs and crude vines near them on the lake's shore. There were two long wooden poles with flat wooden pieces attached, that probably had served the fallen natives as oars.

"Time to leave" he said as he pointed to the raft.

The team crowded carefully onto the raft, and Jason and Williams pushed it away from the riverbank. To their horror, one of the gigantic demon-like gorillas spotted them and was down on all fours moving toward them at an incredible rate. They all readied their weapons, and were about to fire when they heard the drone of the ultra-light's engine overhead. A puff of smoke came from the bottom of the ultra-light and made a trail toward the oncoming gorilla. The explosion rocked the raft and they held on with all their might.

When the smoke cleared, there were only a few body parts lying on the ground. Richards stood up and unleashed a cheer. Julia Sizemore pulled him down. "You idiot; you want us all in the water?"

The oarsmen paddled like mad; the other two King Kong like gorillas were running toward them. They seemed rather stupid as they ran right into the river and quickly sank into the water and muck, flailing about and bellowing.

It was eerily quiet as Jason and Williams struggled to paddle the raft toward the opposite shore and the city. As they fought the current, Williams developed a new respect for the muscles of the Orex. He was startled out of his reverie when his tablet rang. He handed the paddle to Bill Richards to take the call from Mike.

"You guys all right?"

"We're okay. Sizemore, do a sweep of us. See, all okay. But I tell you, I've hunted my whole life, and never been afraid until now. We need to come up with a plan if we're going to survive on this planet!"

"Calm down," replied Mike. "We'll meet the team in the council room tomorrow, after you've had time to eat and rest."

Williams nodded, but as he put his tablet away, he shook his head. Maybe Mike didn't really get it. They were nearing the shore and there were a dozen tiger-like animals waiting for them. The Guardians coordinated their advanced weapons fire and picked them off one by one, until the remaining animals fled.

As they trekked homeward, Jason got a call from Mike as the team saw the ultra-light fly overhead again. "We're going for the bridge," Mike told them. Then, "There, got it!" They could hear the boom both through their tablets and in the air.

# #

Jason and Maria received a call from Mike and headed to the council room. At the door, they ran into Henry Hanson, who didn't have a clue as to why he was there.

As soon as they entered the council room, they were handed another new drink to try.

Hanson finished his quickly and sat down at the council's meeting table. "It's good. Better than the last one. But what am I, the official drink taster? Is that why we're here?"

"Of course not," said Mike. We'd like you to investigate the continent on the other side of the mountains."

Jason frowned. "But, we have the aerial images that Aaron supplied. We know what's there, more or less."

"What we don't have is a realistic idea of what we're up against, in terms of the animals there. We know what's on the peninsula, but it's just as important to know what's beyond."

Hanson leaned forward in his chair. "So, what do you want?"

"We'd like you to survey the land between Helios and the new city under construction. That's about 250 kilometers from here."

Hanson took out his tablet and calculated. "That's 500 kilometers round trip. Hmm, I'd need more than 25 liters of fuel. That would weigh at least—75 kilos. Hell, that's the weight of a person!" He suddenly realized what they were asking. "I would have to go alone."

Mike nodded. "We have to know what's out there. Even if we killed every dangerous animal on the peninsula, there might be a hundred to take the place of every one we eliminate."

Bob showed Jason, Maria and Hanson his tablet with an artist's concept of the buffalo herds roaming the Americas in the 1800s. "There might be millions of them. It might be beyond our ability…"

Frustrated, Hanson stood up. "I'll do it. I won't accept the fact that we can't overcome some dumb animals, no matter how many there are."

CHAPTER 35

The Continent

Hanson took off early in the morning before most colonists were awake. Jason had reluctantly removed the rocket launcher to lighten the plane. Even so, the ultra-light struggled under the weight of the additional fuel. The plane barely cleared the electronic fence and Hanson headed west. There was a huge sea between the peninsula and the continent and he kept the plane low enough to ditch, in case of a mechanical problem, as he flew over the sea. He quickly flew out of range of the tablet communication and was on his own. He spotted a few schools of fish and something the size of a whale but it was totally unfamiliar.

At last the continent came into view. As he climbed to a higher altitude for a better view, the first thing he noticed was the animals—wildebeests stretching into the distance, as far as he could see. He shook his head in disbelief as he neared the shoreline. There truly had to be millions of wildebeests. And where the wildebeests weren't, the ground was dotted with saber-tooth tigers, the rhinoceros-like creatures, hundreds of the wild hog-like creatures and even a few huge demon gorillas. He turned south to follow the shoreline and after a few hours found the second city of Kepler, less than a mile from the sea. The constructors still had fifteen years or so to go, but Hanson could see it was going up on the same plan as Helios. The underground maintenance area and the first ten floors or so were done. Massive piles of materials were stacked around the perimeter of the city, and dozens of constructor robots were hard at work building the next level.

Hanson turned the plane inland to see what protection the colonists might have against the mind-numbing numbers of animals just to the north. There was a long slender canyon just to the north of the city; that must be the reason for the new city's location. It blocked the animal's migration even more effectively than the mountain range to the north of Helios. A small area along the coast presented the only danger, and a short section of the electronic fence would probably be sufficient protection there. Hanson recorded the view on his tablet and turned the plane to check on the southern side of the new city.

Here, a huge lake isolated the city. Only a few sections of fence would be needed to fill the gaps between lake and canyon. You had to give these Octans credit for good site selection.

Hanson landed on the beach near the city to rest and have lunch. He hadn't even turned the engine off when he was startled by the growling of a group of the bear-like creatures, who saw him and immediately attacked. Hanson pushed the throttle forward, and the plane struggled to take off in the loose sand. One bear was ahead of the others and struck the plane's wing as it was lifting off. The small plane twisted in the air, but Hanson was able to get it under control just before it crashed into the sea. He breathed a huge sigh of relief. Lunch would have to wait.

Survival Plan

The risk team met with Hanson and the peninsula survey team to discuss their findings and work on a colony survival plan. Certainly, no colonist could be expected to farm land or fish oceans if they were constantly worried about being attacked by a virtually infinite number of large, dangerous animals. After a few days, they were ready to present a plan to the council and Aaron.

"We need to take the offensive, rather than always being on the defense. We are proposing to build and train an Air Force to take the attack to the most dangerous animals."

Bob sat back in his chair. "Air Force?"

"Yes, we now have a prototype machine gun that we can mount on the ultra-light to start with. That will allow us to attack the demons first and put them on the defensive, while we build a dozen ultra-lights. Then we can really go on the offensive."

Aaron, who had been listening quietly, stood up. "The Octans will not allow you to massacre the animals of Kepler in order to establish this colony."

Jason started to reply, but Mike interrupted him. "But how will we ever be able to farm or fish if we have a constant battle with them?"

"There is an alternative." One of Hanson's aerial views of the city under construction appeared on the viewing wall, and Aaron pointed to the slender canyon just to the north of the city. "This feature, which you assumed natural, was in fact produced to isolate that city from the animals of the area."

Jason was skeptical. "How is that possible?"

"We have a device that can create this feature."

Almost everyone in the room started to talk until Mike rapped on the table to get their attention. "Let him explain."

"I can show you." The viewing screen changed to a live view from the west entrance to the city. The council sat in rapt attention as three MUs unrolled a hundred feet of a large black cable several inches thick. They connected it to a portable power generator and turned it on. The cable started to glow red, then brighter and brighter until it was almost like looking into the sun. The council members had to shield their eyes until the glow stopped. One of the MUs walked over to where the cable had been and pointed a tablet's camera at what was now a 100 foot long crevice still glowing red and billowing with so much smoke they couldn't see the bottom.

Council members' jaws dropped. "We have nothing like that on Earth," Tom said.

"We can use this technique to complete the isolation of the peninsula from the continent, if that is what is required to protect the city" replied Aaron.

Tom asked what everyone was wondering. "But then, why wasn't this done before we arrived, as it was for the second city?"

"I have insufficient data to answer that question. It could be the size and number of animals on the peninsula twenty-five to fifty Earth years ago was not viewed as the problem it has turned out to be."

"Maybe that huge tree hadn't fallen over the river yet" commented Bob.

Jason was still staring at the viewing screen. "How would you power the device far from the city?"

"There is a small fusion reactor in storage. We can utilize that."

Tom's ears perked up at Aaron's reply. "You know how to operate it? Damn. Wish I'd known that before."

"Great," said Bob. "When can you start?"

Early the next morning, Mike was still eating breakfast when he happened to turn on the viewing screen and the view from the east entrance. Aaron and several other Guardians were carrying boxes, followed by several MUs pulling a cart with a large black box on it. Other MUs were pulling another cart, holding a huge coil of cable a little thicker than the cable used to demonstrate the power of the canyon-making device.

The Guardians, MUs and carts passed through the fence and disappeared in the distance. Mike finished breakfast and started reading his messages.

A bright flash on the viewing wall made him close his eyes in reflex. When his vision cleared, he called Hanson. Hanson took off later that day and flew over the lake. At first, there didn't appear to be any change in the terrain, so Hanson descended to five hundred feet to take a closer look. About five miles to the east of the lake he saw a crevice about fifteen feet wide that ran from the mountains in the north, literally to within a few feet of the beach. There were still many animals between the crevice and the lake but they were slowly being herded by the MUs and the Guardians toward the beach, then herded to the rest of the peninsula. Hanson passed over a few dead horned gorillas that apparently had refused to be herded with the rest of the animals.

Mike and the council members were discussing the potential success of the crevice when Aaron entered the council room.

"Congratulations," said Bob. "That crevice device is genius. I wish we'd that back on Earth."

Tom was anxiously waiting to ask, "How did you get the device and the fusion reactor across the lake?"

"We floated the carts across on large air bags."

Tom shook his head. "Okay, you have to show me where you have those stored. Everything's easy when you have the knowledge and tools you need."

Aaron was matter-of-fact. "In 10,000 clock units, we will have cleared the dangerous animals between the lake and the crevice. Then we'll erect a barrier at the beach to keep them out."

CHAPTER 36

Aftermath

The new crevice barrier transformed the peninsula. The farmers immediately began planting thousands of hectares of grains: corn, wheat, and upland rice. Thousands of fruit trees were transplanted from personal transport containers into neatly arranged orchards. One new farm specialized in herbs and spices of all temperate-zone varieties. All the colonists looked forward to the fall harvest to provide alternatives to the boring FOOD.

Forests covered a significant portion of Kepler, and Sean Michaels fabricated a sawmill blade. Soon the colonists had a working sawmill to make all sorts of lumber for houses, barns, fence posts, silos, even a new windmill. A number of colonists had become tired of living in the sterile dome environment and contacted Michaels to buy lumber to build second homes with a lake or ocean view.

Jason and the risk team experimented in their hearth with various mixtures of silicates and finally produced a high-quality glass that could be used for windows in the new houses. They also found a way to fabricate the large quantities of nails needed to build anything from wood.

The fishermen quickly adopted new techniques to capture strange new fish that resisted the usual fishing nets and baited hooks. The restaurant in the main dining hall had to be expanded to accommodate all the new diners desperate for alternatives to the FOOD.

Eventually, the hunters and some wannabe cowboys discovered how easily the wildebeests could be domesticated. They built wooden fences and barns for the harsh winter weather and established ranches to provide meat to the colony chefs, who developed many new wildebeest-based dishes. The farmers planted fields of hay and corn to sell to the ranchers to feed the wildebeest herds. The Orex proved to be true entrepreneurs; they were soon involved in almost every business on Kepler.

One year later, all the colonists were actively pursuing lives not all that different from their prior lives on Earth. The city council rarely had to deal with emergencies. Even the Taas left their caves and with the help of the colonists, built earthen houses and enclosed shelters for animals similar to the rancher's shelters. They quickly learned farming and began planting crops of their own.

Life in Helios and on Kepler was becoming routine and sustainable.

Alliance Issues

Helios was about to celebrate its third anniversary when a small Octan ship arrived. Mike and the council members were waiting in front of a large crowd of curious colonists as Jude Harwig walked out. He greeted the council members and invited them onboard the Octos "warship". The council members became concerned at the term when Jude said it. Had the truce been broken?

After they settled into a small conference room, Harwig described his mission. Basically, other colonies in their vicinity were struggling, and the Octans had carefully followed the success of the colonists on Kepler. They had an offer for Mike who was surprised they even knew who he was.

They wanted to offer Mike the position of regional coordinator. This would involve several roles. He would be an official ambassador of the Octans. He would carry the military rank Commander, which would give him authority over all the Guardians in the region, plus fifty Guardians reporting directly to him. He would also have the highest legal authority to make decisions, a "Supreme Justice" of sorts.

The council members would have either to hold elections now, or to agree to take over Mike's role until the elections that were scheduled for next year.

Mike guessed without Harwig saying it was that he would have to travel around from planet to planet to solve issues. He would be away from his family a lot. He refused at first, and Harwig asked him to discuss it with his family. Mike wondered how the Octans would react if he declined the roles.

Jesse and Mahra were of course against the offer. They didn't want Mike gone so much. The whole idea seemed kind of weird. Mike returned to tell Harwig his decision.

"I really appreciate the offer, but I don't want to be away from my family for long periods of time."

"This isn't a decision that affects only you. Several hundred thousand persons on the dozen or so colonies in this area of the galaxy truly need help to get their colonies back on track. So, the Octans are willing to offer you incentives to help ensure your participation."

Mike was skeptical. "You mean bribes?"

"I mean incentives. After a suitable period, which is negotiable, you can have a palace or castle on Earth, or any colony site. And you can have a suitable amount of money to take care of it and your descendants."

Mike laughed.

"And an ample staff to take care of all your needs."

Mike stopped laughing when he realized Harwig was serious. He shook his head. "Sorry."

"Your son and his family can join you, when your assignment ends, if you wish."

Mike hesitated. Financial security for his family was not a joking matter. He wasn't even sure what he would do when his appointment as mayor came to an end. Would he even be re-elected?

One by one, Mike's objections were being addressed. "What if I can't solve the problems on the colonies?"

Harwig hesitated, then leaned over and whispered. "They really have no alternative. These issues must be addressed."

Mike was feeling the pressure. He stood up to leave. "This is a really big decision for me and my family. I need some time."

Harwig stood up. "I need an answer soon. Could you come back tomorrow with your son and discuss it?"

Mike nodded and started to leave. "Wait. Why did you refer to this ship as a warship?"

Harwig shrugged. "It is that, but this ship will be at your disposal and it has a top speed more than ten times that of the transport ships. That will shorten the time you are away from your family."

Mike wondered what Jesse and Mahra would think of Harwig's incentives.

The next day, Mike brought Jesse along.

"I assume," Harwig said, "that your father told you about the Octans' incentives to accept the position?"

"Yes, but you don't know how hard it would be for us, with Dad gone all the time."

Harwig nodded. "Of course, but that doesn't mean you couldn't see him from time to time. He wouldn't be gone all the time and Helios would be his home planet."

That sounded odd to Jesse and Mike—thinking of Helios as their home planet instead of Earth.

"I know this is a hard decision, so I have a little surprise for you." He left the room and returned with someone who had to be an Octan. "Ambassador Mikolan, these are Michael and Jesse Silver," he said.

Mike caught his breath and scrambled to stand up. As far as he knew, no human other than Harwig had ever seen an Octan before. Ambassador Mikolan stood a little over five feet tall. His skin was milky white, and he had a somewhat oversized head, with large black eyes, small ears, long thin arms and legs, and, Mike noticed, eight fingers. It came to him, the Orex and Taas could be close relatives of the Octans, though their skin was green instead of white.

Mikolan spoke in a very soft tone through an electronic translator, much like the Juban voice box device, on a band wrapped around his neck. "Greetings, Mayor Silver." He turned to Jesse and bowed slightly. "Jesse."

Jesse was unsure what to do, so he bowed slightly in his chair.

Mikolan held out his hand and shook hands with Mike and Jesse. "Please be seated." Mike was surprised that the ambassador's hand was soft and warm—he had somehow assumed it would be cold. Mikolan was wearing the same white tunic and pants everyone in Helios was wearing, but with an emblem that probably identified him as a VIP.

A Guardian brought a tray of drinks and placed it on the table between them as they all sat down.

"I told Jude I wished to talk to you," the ambassador said, speaking slowly as trying to choose the right words. "We have an urgent need for your help. As you know, several colonies are struggling and could fail without some assistance. We have observed how you handled the difficult problems the colonists in Helios faced and are pleased you were able to overcome them. The skills you possess are in short supply on the problem colonies. I know leaving your son and his family will be a hard decision, so I thought you need to understand the problem we all face."

"As soon as the truce was established, we mapped all the planets humans could survive on in this part of the galaxy and began establishing cities, with the hope Earth would agree to join with us and colonize these worlds. Unfortunately, there are very few of my species, and even fewer willing to colonize new worlds. There are many Jubans. They are a warlike race eager for the truce to end so they can establish bases on planets without a colony, or a self-sustaining colony. They would try to draw us into another war and be in a position to take over those planets immediately."

"So, establishing self-sustaining colonies is of vital importance to the alliance to keep the Jubans out of this part of the galaxy and give Earth time to learn our advanced technology and eventually be capable of defending the colonies against the Jubans."

He paused, to let that sink in. Mike, Jesse and all the colonists knew the basic story but not the particulars about non-sustaining colonies. It became clear that Earth and Octos could not afford to risk colony failures. It seemed strange to Mike, having known Maria, to hear the Jubans referred to in this way.

"Is there anything I can offer you to obtain your agreement to accept the assignments as they have been described?"

If Mike had felt pressure before, it was nothing like the pressure he now felt. He glanced at Jesse, hoping he could help him make the decision, one way or the other. Jesse was staring off into the distance and finally looked at him.

"Dad, you once told us you didn't want to live your whole life and not be remembered except by your family. This sounds like the opportunity you were looking for. I'm okay with it, if you want to."

Mike felt as if a gigantic weight had been lifted from his shoulders. If he said yes, he would still have Jesse's support, and he would be able to visit his son and his family from time to time, and isn't that what most people want when they reach—he did some quick calculations—age 46? Could he really be 46?

He looked at Mikolan. "Okay. I agree." He turned to Harwig. "Can we put those incentives in writing?"

The council members were shocked at the sudden turn of events. Mike relayed the issues in confidence to them. The other colonists didn't need to know that other colonies were struggling.

This brought up the remaining issue. Who would replace Mike?

The contracts the council members had signed outlined a temporary succession plan in case something happened to one of them. Technically, the city planner was next in line, but Rebecca didn't want the responsibility. Bob was next in line, so they all agreed that Bob would take over temporarily until the next election, a little over a year away.

Mike called a town hall meeting to explain. There was little discussion, or complaint; most people were now fully engaged in their new lives and not so dependent on the city council.

CHAPTER 37

Colony 19—Tureen on Beta Aridees

Mike's first assignment was on the relatively close colony of Tureen on the planet Beta Aridees, only a hundred light years from Kepler. Beta Aridees was similar in size to Earth with a similar rotational period. However, its orbital period was almost twice that of Earth.

He was awakened by Guardians a day prior to landing and was given a summary of the colony's problems. Colony 19 had been the fourth group to leave from the New York Terminal, only a month before the Kepler colony left, and in the more than three Earth years since, there had been no measurable progress since landing. The weather and geography were arguably more difficult than Kepler's, but that could not explain the poor progress.

Mike didn't want to memorize the twelve digit code of the leader of his contingent of fifty Guardians, and when it was asked to select a common name, it chose the name Max.

He became apprehensive when Max and the small contingent of Guardians took up flanking positions around him. Were they expecting a violent reception?

The door opened onto a gloomy world probably in its late fall period, as a very cool breeze blew some leaves and dust in through the door. Outside, hundreds of colonists stood waiting. As Mike stepped out, the crowd erupted into cheers. They surged forward, only held back by his Guardian escort. People were actually yelling and waving papers.

Where did they get paper?

He held up his hands and waited. It took a few moments, but eventually the crowd became quiet.

In as calm a voice as he could muster, Mike asked them to meet him in the main dining hall for a town meeting the next day. He first wanted to meet with the mayor and city council and then he would address them and take questions. He then asked them to go back to their living areas and send the mayor their issues as he wanted to take a little while to determine what was going on. The crowd looked confused at the invitation to send their issues to the mayor.

Strangely, the mayor was not there. Most of the crowd dispersed and a tall blond-haired man approached.

"Hello, Your Honor."

Your Honor? My God, that's me!

"I'm George Montana, the city planner. It's great to meet you. We've heard a lot about you. We sure have a lot to discuss." He turned and motioned two others to join him.

"Nice to meet you. Uh, where's the mayor?"

"He's barricaded himself in the maintenance room."

"What?"

"It's a long story."

The other two council members introduced themselves as they walked to the city. Mike looked around at the virgin landscape. No crops? No farms, no orchards? Something was seriously wrong here.

Council

"I've read some of the issues, but obviously your views will help me figure out how I can help."

The council members began a long dialogue describing the lack of progress since they had arrived. The colony had some organizational issues at the last moment and a number of colonists had dropped out. Less than thirty thousand had made the trip. But, due to poor timing by the colonist's coordination desk, they had arrived at the start of the winter period. There initially had been some issues with the power system and the colonists had suffered from the cold several times the first winter. The Tureen Council originally had six members and meetings had gone poorly as the mayor and several council members seemed incapable of making decisions. Boredom and lack of activities during the first winter had led to greater problems, including some fistfights the Guardians had to break up.

The mayor was a little strange in the beginning but had become progressively worse as time went on. He finally started calling himself "Caesar" and asked everyone to refer to him as "Emperor Jones." He became paranoid and was sure people were out to get him. Eventually, he locked himself in the vast underground maintenance room under Tureen.

While this was going on, the city treasurer started to babble. One day he just walked out of the city, never to be seen again. The city engineer had died soon after landing of an unknown ailment, leaving only four council members including the mayor (who, by their bylaws, was a member of the council).

The mayor, locked away in the maintenance area, didn't interfere in the maintenance or operation of the city, or prevent the MEs from doing so, so eventually most people just ignored him.

He did remain a problem, as he followed the council actions from monitors in the maintenance areas, and almost always overrode or cancelled actions the council was trying to take. According to the bylaws of the council, they needed four votes to enforce their decisions, and with the treasurer and engineer gone, they could not get four votes without the mayor's agreement. The mayor blocked every attempt to hold an early election to replace the vacant council positions. The local Guardians supported and protected the mayor against attempts to remove him.

"That, at least, I can fix," said Mike. "I've got the override here." He pulled a small transmitter from his pocket. "Back shortly."

He left for the maintenance center with Max, the leader of his Guardians, and found the leader of the Tureen Guardians and two others standing guard at the access door. Curiously, they were wearing yellow shirts and their leader was wearing a blue shirt.

"Step aside," he ordered them. When they ignored that, Mike pulled out the transmitter and overrode their current instructions.

"Open the door." They opened the door and stepped aside. Mike entered with Max and the local Guardians following behind. They found the mayor at the security station, randomly pressing buttons to change the views on the security monitors. He was wearing a crown of sorts he had fashioned out of some plants and was tunic-less and shoeless. He obviously hadn't bathed in weeks. He jumped when Mike tapped him on the shoulder, and stood up.

"Mayor Jones?"

Jones eyes narrowed. "That's Emperor Jones, you idiot."

Mike laughed, and then held what he thought of as his sheriff's badge— an Octan metal emblem identifying him as a legal authority within the Alliance. "Stanley Jones, you are relieved of your responsibilities as mayor of Tureen. It appears you are in need of medical and psychological attention. Please follow this Guardian to the medical facility."

Jones backed up and saw his Guardians behind Mike and Max. "Curly, throw this idiot out, immediately."

Mike turned to the local lead Guardian. "Curly?"

The Guardian replied, "For some unknown reason, the colonists refer to us as Larry, Moe, and Curly."

Mike looked at Max. "Try not to hurt him, but make sure the doctors start a thorough evaluation of him."

Jones became wild-eyed when the Guardians approached him. "Get away!" He started to run, but the Guardians grabbed him. He struggled so much they had to pick him up and carry him. As they neared the access door, Mike called to them.

"Make sure he gets a bath!"

The three council members stood up when Mike returned to the council room.

"I've relieved the mayor of his duties and had him taken to the infirmary for an evaluation. Hopefully, there's something they can do for him. He's almost incoherent."

George came over and shook his hand. "Thanks for taking care of him. He really wasn't a bad guy, he just seemed to go off the deep end."

Mike was looking at the other council members when he said. "I'm appointing George Montana the interim mayor until a full election can be held. I'd like you to suggest names for interim treasurer, planner and engineer, and we'll make the announcements at the town hall tomorrow."

The council members huddled to come up with names and Montana saw Mike pull out his tablet and start to check the city's current supplies.

"What's that, Your Honor?"

"This? My tablet? Don't you all have one of these? This is your primary means of communication."

Blank stares.

Mike turned to one of his escort Guardians.

"How many tablets like this are in the city?"

"Fifty thousand in addition to yours," He replied. "They are in the warehouse awaiting activation."

"Can you have them brought here?"

"Yes, sir." He left, followed by two local Guardians.

"So that's why so many colonists were waving papers when we arrived."

Montana shrugged. "We didn't know about the tablets and the mayor insisted that all comments, issues or complaints be in writing."

"But, where did you get the paper?"

Montana seemed confused. "When the mayor knew that less than thirty thousand people were transporting, he added an additional ten thousand cubic meters of paper products to the inventory. We actually transported twenty thousand cubic meters. He said we had to have enough to last twenty years."

Mike laughed. "Sorry, but with the tablets you don't need paper." He paused. "You don't need paper in the bathrooms either…"

The council members were not laughing. "We were actually worried about running out of some kinds of paper."

Mike just shook his head. A little organization and few entrepreneurs was all this city needed.

The council continued to describe the problems that seemed to begin as soon as they landed, until the three Guardians returned with three containers filled with tablets. Mike found the mayor's tablet and some for the council, and sent the Guardians out to activate and deliver the tablets.

The discussions ended and Mike met Montana for dinner in the main dining hall. He laughed at the dozen or so variations in the FOOD, the same variations the Helios colonists had found on their first day.

Tureen was identical to Helios in size and layout. The same apartment on the 26th floor was available, so Mike felt right at home. He shook his head when he finished a preliminary report before going to bed. It seemed very little had been accomplished in almost two Beta Aridees years.

Tureen Town Hall

The dining hall was filled to capacity as Mike and the council members walked onto an improvised stage. He motioned them to sit if they could. When the crowd had quieted down, he held up his tablet.

"I assume you all have one of these by now."

Many in the crowd held up their tablets.

"You should have been given this when you arrived. It will become your primary means of communicating with each other and your council members. It is also a videophone, email system, and like the computer terminals in your living quarters, connects to the main computer here, which contains virtually all the knowledge of mankind. Anything you want to know, you can find it with these."

So much for the good news. Now for the difficult part. "I've relieved your mayor of his duties and appointed George Montana as interim Mayor, Jorge Rodriquez as city engineer, Amelia Bartolini as city planner and Zamir Yagram as interim council treasurer."

He paused, waiting for a reaction. The crowd broke into cheers. Any change had to be an improvement over the current non-functioning council.

"Shortly before the meeting, I texted you a list of the problems as I see them, and asked for volunteers to address them. If you would like to volunteer, please let Mayor Montana know."

The rest of the meeting was pretty routine and the colonists seemed pleased as they left.

Mike met with several women eager to discuss the formation of business and social organizations similar to those in Helios. Within a week, numerous TV channels were established; clubs and organizations were assigned meeting rooms and given information on how to obtain tables and chairs in the huge underground storage room.

There were no dangerous animals on Aridees, so some colonists had moved out of the city and built crude log houses. Mike met with them and convinced them to return to the city. Winters on Aridees were almost as brutal as on Kepler and Mike was worried colonists living in crude shelters might not survive the harsh weather.

Mike worked with the farmers to plant seeds of all kinds in the personal storage containers, for transplanting in the next spring. The fishermen had assembled a small fishing boat; the farmers had several tractors. Mike found engineers willing to fabricate a Still and convert some of the FOOD to ethanol for fuel.

At the end of a month, Mike felt he had turned things around sufficiently that Montana could handle everything. He signaled the orbiting Octan warship to pick him up.

A huge, grateful crowd cheered as he waved from the ramp and entered the warship.

There was a message waiting from Harwig. He had read Mike's detailed report and congratulated him on a very successful first assignment. "I'm sure the size of your estate has grown considerably." The rest of the email provided information on his next assignment.

A feast of Helios food awaited him; and after a month of eating only FOOD again, he began to devour regular human food in earnest.

CHAPTER 38

Colony 10—Tranquility City on Marus 10

Mike's next assignment required just three weeks transport at warship speed and at first Mike chose to be awake. That ended after a week of utter boredom. You can only stare at star fields for so long, no matter how magnificent they are. He read books, watched movies, and explored the small warship until he had seen it all. He finally decided to spend the rest of the trip asleep.

Mike was awakened one day before arrival on Marus 10, and began reading the Octan planetary survey data. The planet was 50% bigger than Earth with an even greater range of geography—from a frigid arctic region at its poles to a brutal desert as dry as the Chilean Atacama desert on Earth. Fortunately, oceans covered 70% of the surface, which tended to even out the average temperature. Tranquility City was located on a very large volcanic island, mostly covered with grasslands and a semi-tropical rain forest. Even though the city was located on the planet's equator, the weather apparently was always perfect—never hot or cold, and constantly refreshed with warm, gentle ocean breezes. Large, active volcanoes emitted plumes of dust, so that the normally blue skies of Marius were often gray.

Early reports from the colonists were very positive, and they even had renamed their city Paradise. After only a month, the reports had become erratic and eventually stopped. No one was sure exactly what the problem with Paradise City was, but almost all the daily transmissions to Earth had suddenly become nonsensical.

The unlikely premise of the colony, transported from the European

Terminal near Brussels, had been "to produce the perfect wine." The 38000 colonists had all professed to be wine experts, knowledgeable in all stages of wine production from vine planting to its final consumption. The colony organizers goal was to have a million hectares in production within three years, and when the supply ship came in year 20, they would be able to export millions of liters of wine to sell all over their region of the galaxy. How this would be accomplished on a world covered with oceans, limited grasslands and huge rain forests, deserts and arctic regions was not immediately obvious. Nevertheless, they had transported several hundred thousand vine cuttings and everything else needed to establish hundreds of boutique wineries.

When Mike's ship arrived, no one was there to greet him. When he and three Guardians entered the city, it appeared to be deserted. Where were the colonists?

Mike and his lead Guardian, Max, searched the nearby forest until they found a few colonists lying on a massive bed of flowers staring at the planet's clouds. Mike tried to talk to them but they were mostly unresponsive or incoherent. When he continued the search in a maze of indigenous fruit trees, he became dizzy and passed out. When he awoke, he was lying on his bed in his warship. Max helped him to his feet, but after a few minutes Mike had to hold onto the conference room table to keep his balance.

"What happened, Max?"

"You became unstable and fell to the ground, Commander. I brought you back to the ship."

Mike's head was hurting. "Has your team found many colonists?"

"Yes, based on the emergency tracking system, they are almost all located within ten kilometers of the city. However, we could not find any of the city council members, and none of the colonists appears capable of communicating what happened."

One of the Guardians in Mike's contingent was a Med-Bot. Early Colonies often had difficulties recruiting the required 1 doctor per 1000 colonists, so one of the first priorities of the medical colony was re-programming a Guardian into a Med-Bot or the equivalent of a paramedic. The re-programming and software de-bugging had taken some time and the Kepler colony transported before the new Med-Bots became available.

Mike's Med-Bot had taken some blood samples and was waiting for Mike and Max to finish their conversation. He informed Mike of the presence of an unknown chemical in his blood that was similar to a strong narcotic. The Med-Bot had tested the air outside the ship and found significant airborne quantities of the same chemical. Max quickly closed the outside door to avoid further contaminating the ship. Mike asked the Med-Bot if it was possible to develop an antidote for the narcotic. The Med-Bot could not, but sent a detailed message to the medical colony, describing the unknown chemical and asking for assistance in developing an antidote. Message transit time plus a potential study and reply would require weeks or even months, so Mike informed his Guardians they would be leaving Paradise for Helios while an antidote was developed. The medical colony assigned a high priority to the task of developing an antidote and within a month, they sent detailed instructions to the doctors in Helios on how to make the antidote with the equipment and materials available on there.

Return to Paradise

Immediately upon returning to Paradise City, Mike's Med-Bot began injecting the colonists with the antidote. In just a few hours, the narcotic's effect began to subside and the recovering colonists slowly made their way back to the city. Messages were left all over the city informing the residents to look at a recording Mike made describing what happened and urging them to return to the their plans to establish the colony. There was a lot to do, as no crops or vines had been planted, and all the local fruit was still contaminated with the narcotic. The colonists were lucky to be located next to an ocean with an abundance of fish (as an alternative to the boring FOOD).

It took some investigative work to finally determine what happened. One of the colonists had filled her personal transport container with small vials of concentrated scent, with the hope of establishing a business where people could breathe familiar scents of Earth for a suitable price. In the near-perfect weather, entrepreneurs began setting up businesses outdoors. In transporting the chemical scents to a table outside the city, the colonist had dropped and spilled several dozen vials. The wind carried the concentrated chemical scents to the nearby jungle, where they mixed with local scents to form a narcotic-like chemical which induced a sense of euphoria. Basically, everyone was high on drugs. The only thing that kept the colonists alive was the abundance of local fruits, which they plucked from trees whenever they became hungry. Only a handful of colonists, all below puberty, were not affected by the narcotic. They were barely able to operate the communications gear, resulting in unscheduled and chaotic reports back to Earth.

The city council members were never found, so Mike appointed temporary replacements until new elections could be held. Mike received a report back from botanists on the medical colony with some good news. The narcotic-like substance was chemically unstable and should begin to degrade and be out of the local ecology in less than two years. The colonists only had to wait it out, and then they could return to the outdoors and resume eating the local fruits and begin planting their vines.

After a few more weeks, Mike was confident in the ability of the new mayor and city council to take charge and left. On his return to the warship, another email was waiting from Harwig that commented again on the increase in size of Mike's future estate or castle. Mike was more concerned with eating Helios origin food after another two months of eating only variations of the FOOD.

CHAPTER 39

Colony 7 Dodge City on Ephasis 9

Ephasis 9 was only 150 light years from Marus 10, and a relatively short transport was required. Once again Mike was awakened one day before arrival on Ephasis 9 and the colony of Dodge City. A summary of Colony 7's status and issues was waiting for him in the small conference room along with some Helios-origin food. Colony 7 had been the second colony to leave from the New York terminal and in the four-plus Earth years of its existence, the colony initially made great progress in becoming self-sustaining. The premise for the colony was "the Old West" and the colonists had purposefully chosen a mildly arid planet not all that different from the dry western states of the mid-1800s. All colonists were cowboy lore fanatics. Ephasis 9 was similar in size to Earth with a gray sky and reddish-yellow sun. The climate of the northern hemisphere, where Dodge City was sited, was mild. Winters were cool, and summers were bearable due to the low humidity. The city was located near a large forest of pine-like trees.

Early reports from the city council were very favorable. With some foresight, they had transported several complete sawmills and were soon building ranches and farmhouses. A horse-sized animal that resembled a wooly mastodon without the tusks had been found and tamed. While this animal was immensely strong, its temperamental demeanor required the colonists to adapt to its often mule-like behavior. The colony had transported several thousand horse saddles in hopes they would find a suitable animal. The horse alternative allowed the new cowboys to search and find large herd animals that they domesticated.

A year after arrival, New Dodge City was established about two kilometers from the domed Octan city, and eager colonists built thousands of houses and businesses of the era—dry goods stores, liveries, restaurants, blacksmith shops, and saloons. The mayor of the domed city campaigned for the job of mayor of New Dodge City and was elected. It appeared that in only a few more years, the Octan city might be abandoned, except for its power source. Engineers ran a power feeder cable and water lines to the new city, and built a modern sewage treatment system. There was no air conditioning, but the weather was cool and dry and soon most people didn't miss it. The colonists' love of the Old West didn't extend to a love of outhouses and daily trips to a well with water buckets.

Subsequent reports were more disturbing. In direct violation of the UN agreement, most of the colonists had brought handguns or disassembled rifles in their personal transport containers. The colony had also smuggled over a thousand cubic meters of live ammunition for the revolvers and repeating rifles.

Freelancing engineers began fermenting the FOOD into alcohol which they sold to the colonists in newly built saloons.

Ultimately, chaos derailed New Dodge City and the colony, as drunken cowboys got into arguments that finally resulted in an old-fashioned gunfight with several fatalities. When the smoke cleared, the residents of New Dodge City realized they had no jail, only a handful of lawyers, and no judge or working criminal system. Strangely, the latest reports had come from colonists who had "fled" back to the domed city. What had happened to the mayor?

As Mike scanned the report he wondered why the Guardians were not maintaining order. They certainly had maintained a presence in Helios.

The domed city was located in a valley between two rather steep hills, and the warship landed almost a kilometer away. Eight Guardians surrounded Mike as the door opened. There was a warm gentle breeze blowing as the escort walked down the ramp. Three colonists were waiting for him mounted on the horse-alternative animals. True to the period, they were wearing Stetson-like hats, and even had chaps on their pants. One dismounted as they approached. Mike noticed a badge with a star on his shirt.

"Hello, Your Honor. I'm Deputy Charles Bracken. We're sure glad you're here."

Mike shook his hand. "Where's the mayor?" This was becoming an all too familiar refrain.

"We don't know. He started acting strange soon after he was elected mayor of New Dodge City, then one day he just disappeared."

"Where are the city council members?"

Bracken seemed embarrassed. "Soon after the mayor left, the other council members started acting strangely too. Somehow they thought they were in Oz and went off to find the Wizard. We haven't seen them since."

If the situation hadn't been serious, Mike would have laughed. Bracken offered him a "horse" to ride, but Mike preferred to walk with his Guardians to the city. Mike almost regretted his decision to walk, as the knee-high blue grass was rather prickly. Bracken walked next to him, guiding his "horse", while his companions followed at a distance. Bracken explained how several thousand colonists had become concerned with the lawlessness and returned to the domed city.

"Why didn't the Guardians intervene? One of their commands is to protect humans from each other."

Bracken shrugged. "I only saw them around in the beginning. Then they were out of the picture."

Mike addressed his next question to Max. "Are the Guardians here still active?"

"No, Commander. There is no communication with them."

"Find out what happened."

"Yes, Commander."

"Commander?" asked Bracken.

Mike rolled his eyes. "One of several responsibilities I had to assume."

The entourage passed through the electronic fence, which was not active. *Where is the security team?* They finally arrived at one of the city's main entrances, but no one greeted them. *Someone had asked for help—where was that person?*

Bracken and his companions returned to New Dodge City, and Max and two other Guardians left to find the city Guardians. Four other Guardians took up sentry positions at the city's main entrances. Mike headed for the communication center. All the halls and rooms he passed were empty as was the communication center. *Had the thousands of colonists who had returned gone into hiding for some reason?*

He sent his routine, "I got here; I'm safe," message to Jesse in Helios, and then left to find Max. As he was leaving, he literally ran into a colonist heading in. She had been sending routine updates to the UN Colonization Committee on Earth. She really couldn't provide useful information on how things had deteriorated so quickly except that she relayed a story she heard concerning the colony Guardians. One of the colonists was an electronics wiz and brought some "gizmos" with him. He accidentally activated a program in the Guardians that turned off their primary goals: to protect humans and the planet. Having essentially nothing to do, they went into standby mode. The hacker and others had spent months trying to turn them back on, indeed, were still trying, but to no avail.

The electronic tablets had been activated immediately, and the city council treasurer set up a monetary system of "credits" similar to that in Helios, except that here, colonists had the alternative of using coins minted from the Octan metal. The newly-minted coins enabled some of the newly-minted cowboys to buy alcohol produced by the enterprising engineers. This led to minor issues that escalated until several people had died in the gunfight.

With no criminal system in place, the outlaws were immune from punishment and continued to cause even more problems. Gangs formed and at first fought one another. Then they got together and divided New Dodge City into zones of influence, for the purpose, largely, of extortion.

Mike called Max. "Have you found the city Guardians?"

"Yes, Commander. They went into standby mode for some reason, but we have re-activated them. We reinstalled their basic programming and they have reestablished normal city security. The fence is also in operation once again."

Mike relayed the story about the hacker and instructed Max to provide a gate Guardian on the section nearest to New Dodge City, and admit no one carrying a handgun or a rifle.

CHAPTER 40

Mike found some FOOD and after a brief rest met Max and three more Guardians at the gate nearest New Dodge City. The Guardians were all carrying plasma rifles. Max noticed that Mike had changed into a dark blue shirt and blue jeans from his usual white tunic and pants.

"Several colonists riding animals and carrying guns were refused entrance. They refused to give up their guns and when they saw we carried superior weapons they left."

"We need to find a way to get rid of all the guns inside Dodge City. If all else fails we could force the colonists to decide which city they want to live in—this city with no guns or New Dodge City and its armed outlaws."

"Do you want to remove all the weapons in the city, Commander? It would take a few days, but we could complete a search by then. We know which units were initially occupied."

"Let's see how bad the situation in New Dodge City is first."

They walked the two kilometers to New Dodge City, a mid-1800s city as authentic, except for power and running water, as the residents could make it. Mike had visited ghost towns in Nevada, left from the silver mining days, and the colonists had seemed to exactly duplicate the two—and three-story buildings of that era. The roads were unpaved and residents mounted on the horse alternatives and driving horse-alternative-drawn buggies filled the streets. There was a perpetual haze of dust in the air and Mike couldn't help coughing sometimes. No one seemed to notice them, until Deputy Charles Bracken rode by on his "horse" and stopped. "Greetings again, Your Honor. Would you like a tour?"

"Could you just take us to the town hall, or wherever the mayor's office is located?"

"Sure. It's pretty far, so I'll find a buggy and be back for you." Bracken left and Mike found himself outside a saloon. It was getting late in the day and Mike wondered if he could find a cold drink.

Max cautioned him, "There are some potential criminals inside this building, Commander. It may not be wise to enter."

"You can come with me, but I don't want to cause trouble if there isn't any."

Inside the saloon, Max took up an unobtrusive position near the door and watched everyone who came near Mike. A small player piano was belting out a tune and several women in appropriate costumes were dancing on a stage. There were ten card tables filled with gamblers, and several dozen people lined up at the bar. People were paying for drinks using their electronic tablets and the minted coins, and Mike found a place at the bar. He checked his tablet and found the credits he had accumulated in Helios. He wondered if the main computer in Dodge City would recognize them and allow him to pay. There were a dozen varieties of hard liquor, and he wondered how the engineers had managed that. The engineers on Helios seemed to produce only the ethanol used to power the boats, tractors, and single airplane. Mike stared at his reflection in the mirror behind the bar and motioned to the bartender.

"What'll it be?"

"I think my tablet will work here. How much for a double?"

"10 credits, and the code is 145632."

"Seems kind of high, but I'm thirsty." Mike pressed the usual button sequence to transfer 10 of his credits to the saloon's account. The main computer accepted the transaction and the bartender glanced at his tablet and nodded. He delivered the equivalent of a double shot of whisky on ice and walked off to attend other customers. Other customers at the bar were staring at Mike, so he took his drink to an empty table to watch the show. The drink was surprisingly realistic and he wondered if they had brought some of the original thing along to add it to the ethanol. When the show ended, several dancers spread out through the saloon to talk to the customers. Mike was staring at his drink, thinking about the problem with the outlaws and didn't notice her at first.

"Hi, stranger. Can I sit down?"

Mike looked up to see a slender woman in, he guessed, her early thirties. Her hair and costume were spot on to the era and he smiled and motioned her to sit. She had beautiful green eyes and dark brown hair, and the reddest lipstick he had ever seen, and she was smiling at him.

"Would you like a drink?" Mike asked. He caught the attention of a roving bartender and the woman ordered a rum and coke. "Rum and coke?"

"They just add some rum and coke flavors." She took a sip of her drink and studied his shirt and jeans. "Where have you been? No one wears 21st century clothing like that."

Mike explained who he was, and she said she heard someone important had arrived. When she said she was glad it wasn't a mean old judge, Mike laughed. Her name was Melanie Stone and he studied her while she talked about life in New Dodge City and on Ephasis 9 in general.

"So, why did you come to Dodge in the first place? Talk about a world away from whatever you were doing on Earth!"

She laughed. "But that was the idea! I've always been fascinated by westerns and always wondered what it would have been like to live in the west at that time. This gave me the chance to do something I could never do on Earth."

That sounded oddly familiar and Mike nodded. "On Earth—what did you do on Earth?"

She grinned. "I was a teacher. They're building a school here and I've signed up to teach there, once it's finished. I'm just doing this"—she swished her ruffled skirt and laughed—"until I can teach again."

Mike pondered that, until she stood up. "I have to get ready for the next show."

"Hey, wait. Um, would you like to have dinner tonight? What time are you done?"

She smiled. "85000. I'll wait for you here."

Mike shook his head as she walked back to the stage. Maybe life becomes simpler when you roll the clock back 150 years.

Outside, blinking in the sunshine, Mike and Max found Deputy Bracken driving a "horse" drawn buggy and looking annoyed. "Where you been? I've been looking for you all up and down the street."

He sat on the seat next to Bracken while Max and the three other Guardians climbed in back. New Dodge City had almost thirty thousand inhabitants and covered more than two hundred square kilometers. It took almost an Earth hour to travel to the town hall in the center of the town. The sheriff's office was next door and Mike visited that first. There were a number of jail cells in the back of the sheriff's office, but they were empty. Mike knew from the report, the sheriff had died trying to stop the gunfight. That was another crime the participants would have to pay for. In addition to Bracken, there were three other deputies, but they were not in the office at the moment.

"We're still waiting on the blacksmiths for the locks so we can finish the cells."

"Then, where are the people involved in the gunfight that led to the deaths?"

"Oh, we know where they are. We can pick them up anytime."

"They're still at large?"

"Yes, but we know where they are."

Mike shook his head. "What can you tell me about the gangs? How dangerous are they?"

"Hey, we're talking about fifty, sixty people at most in a town of almost thirty thousand. If we had some more deputies and the cells were done, we'd have locked them up as well."

Mike had seen enough. He left with Bracken to visit the town hall, but all he found were empty desks. The council members were long gone. Bracken didn't have a clue where they went. "They just left one day and never came back."

"So you held elections…?"

"Nah. Who was going to do it?"

Mike hoped with all his heart that Bracken wasn't typical of this colony.

Later that day, it was a relief to meet Melanie, who talked like a sensible person. She had scrubbed off the makeup and dressed in sober colors, and she led Mike to a restaurant down the street. She acted as though she didn't notice the four Guardians following them at a discreet distance.

The food in the restaurant was actually the best Mike had in a long time. This beef, or whatever it was, was one thing New Dodge City had gotten right. He was surprised at the quality and flavor of the beef, or whatever it was. They chatted through the dessert course, a cake with icing, and Mike was sorry to say goodnight. He walked her to the boarding house where she lived with a dozen other women and said goodnight. Her lips were smooth and soft.

Mike decided to spend the night in New Dodge City. He found a hotel and spent some time walking the dark streets thinking. The city did have electricity in the houses and buildings, but there were no streetlights, and of course, no stoplights. He was aware of two Guardians following him at a discreet distance and refrained from re-entering the saloon. Late night drinkers were always more boisterous, and he didn't want the Guardians to over-react.

CHAPTER 41

There was a certain charm in New Dodge City. It had a raw energy not found in most cities on Earth, or even the other colonies he had visited. There was an expectation that you could make a fortune or just have a simpler life if that's what you wanted. Mike almost envied the citizens. There was, of course, the outstanding crime problem.

He returned to the hotel and opened the window of his 2nd floor room to a refreshing breeze. The streets were so quiet he could hear people talking as they walked on the wooden sidewalks below. When he woke the next morning, early risers were already walking or riding "horses" or buggies to work—just a normal work day. He showered, dressed, and met Max at the hotel entrance. Max updated him as they walked to the restaurant for breakfast.

"We examined the transport inventory. The colonists transported over a thousand cubic meters of ammunition for both handguns and rifles. We have recovered 237 cubic meters in the underground storage area and in a gunsmith's business in this town, which leaves more than eight hundred cubic meters in the hands of the colonists. Assuming most colonists transported at least one weapon, that is more than 1000 rounds each."

Mike grimaced. That's a lot. They arrived at the restaurant and Mike began eating. "Max?"

The Guardians basic programming gave them the ability to form facial expressions—to make them more "human", but Max's expression never changed. "Yes, Commander."

"I've purchased drinks and meals, paid for the hotel room and my credit count doesn't seem to change. Can you check the financial program here?"

Max stared at him for a moment while he communicated with the mainframe computer, then replied. "As an Ambassador, legal authority and commander of all the Guardians in this region of the galaxy, you have unlimited credits."

"Unlimited?"

"Yes. The Octans deemed this necessary to allow you the flexibility to deal with all situations."

Mike raised his eyebrows. "How—useful. Now, what can we do to make those jail cells operational? Deputy Bracken said they are waiting for the locks from the blacksmiths."

"There are spare locks for the remote access doors to Dodge City. It should be possible to modify them to fit the jail cells. We can start on that immediately."

"Contact the six lawyers who transported, and set up a meeting. We need to hold a trial for the people who participated in the gunfight. Three can represent the defendants and three can act as prosecutors. I'll talk to Deputy Bracken to see if we can find a suitable courtroom in the town hall."

"Yes, Commander."

Mike finished breakfast and left to find Bracken. The town hall and sheriff's office were only a ten-minute walk, and he needed to walk off the large meal. The colonist chefs had transported many spices and had produced a realistic alternative to bacon. If only they had eggs.... come to think of it, I haven't seen any birds.

While Mike and Bracken examined the town hall to find a suitable courtroom, two Maintenance Units installed the locks on the jail cells and returned to the domed city. There weren't many choices for a potential courtroom, as only the city council room was big enough and had a raised dais.

When Mike arrived at the sheriff's office, all the deputies were playing with the new wireless remote control locks. There were eight cells, each large enough to hold ten people temporarily or two for longer periods. Mike examined them and was satisfied they could not be broken into or out of easily. The back wall was a hard composite material something like concrete, so it would be extremely difficult to break in that way without explosives. Of course, he supposed someone could empty a lot of cartridges, but—well, that was what guards were for.

"I'm appointing Deputy Charles Bracken temporary sheriff, until a regular election is held. I think we need a focal point to get things back on track."

Mike watched the other deputies' faces carefully and didn't detect anything resentful or negative.

"And I've been thinking," he said. "When you arrest the gunfight participants, there may be some reaction from some of the gang members. I think you should hire some more deputies to beef up security during the trial."

"I've been thinking the same thing. There should be enough time between now and whenever the trial starts to train the new men."

"Let me know if you need any help finding potential candidates."

"I have a few people in mind already. But with the cells working now, I think we'll round up the gunfighters first."

All the deputies but one went with Bracken to make the arrests. Mike made a walking tour of the town's business district and then found his way back to the restaurant for lunch. He ran into Melanie who was also about to enter the restaurant. "Hi, Judge Silver," she said in a mocking tone.

"Please call me Mike. It keeps my head on straight."

She laughed. "Lunch?"

Mike held the door open for her and they found a table. "There are lots of rumors going around," she noted after they ordered.

"There will be a lot more soon." He mentioned the improvements to the jail and the upcoming trial.

"That trial can't happen fast enough for me."

"Did you know the victims?"

"The bystander who was killed lived in my boarding house. She was a friend of mine."

Her hand was on the table, and Mike put his hand on it. "I'm truly sorry. There's really no reason why some of this should have happened." He mentioned the freak accident that removed the Guardians from their duty. "If they had been active, it probably never would have happened."

"Well, I hope you put those guys away for good."

That was the major problem now. Assuming the jury found the participants guilty, where could they be put? There was no prison, only the jail cells, and those wouldn't work for a long sentence. Where could they go where they wouldn't hurt anyone again?

When Mike returned to the sheriff's office, the six gunfight participants were already in custody. They were strangely silent when Mike viewed them. When they returned to the front office, Bracken spoke to Mike in confidence.

"I think they're in shock. The fight happened several months ago and they were probably thinking they got away with murder."

Mike looked at his tablet. "I have a pre-trial meeting with the lawyers now. You're welcome to attend and see if you need to beef up security for the trial."

Bracken nodded and they walked to the town hall to meet the lawyers. After some discussion, they agreed who would represent the defendants and who would act as prosecutors. Most of the lawyers were from the New York area, so they agreed to use that state's laws for the trial. One lawyer sent Mike a link to a New York trial law procedure book available on the main computer. There were dozens of witnesses, so what happened that day was not in doubt, only the intent of the participants, and most witnesses knew the participants had been drinking heavily that day. After some further discussion, they agreed to set the trial date in thirty days. When asked by the defendant's lawyers, Mike denied them bail.

"They've already had that time. They need to spend some time in jail to realize what they've done."

The arrests were the talk of the town. Many citizens were relieved some law and order was being established, but the gang members in particular were not happy and talked of disrupting the trial. Bracken quickly hired three deputies and began training them. He was determined they would be ready in time for the trial.

The thirty-day wait gave Mike time to study the trial procedures. He had no training as a judge, and his main concern was what to allow as evidence and testimony at the trial.

Citizens were shocked to find a new law outlined on their tablets, banning handgun ammunition. From this point on, it would be permissible to own a handgun but not the ammunition for it. Rifle ammunition only was allowed, for hunting and defense against animals.

The ban would remain until a new city council was in place and full criminal justice and legal systems could be established in New Dodge City. The council would certify those systems and the ban would be lifted.

To make the bitter pill of loss of ammunition go down easier, Mike offered to buy handgun bullets from the citizens, at one credit per bullet, with no limit. He started in the domed city, where residents of Dodge City coughed up their handgun ammunition first—after all, they were living in the domed city because of the violence brought on by too many guns in the hands of people who had no fear of punishment.

Within a week, the Guardians reported with a high degree of certainty they had removed all handgun ammunition from Dodge City. Then the program began in New Dodge City with a dozen ammunition collection points. After another week, no more handgun bullets were being offered and Max reported they had collected an estimated 98% of what had been transported, based on transport records that falsely identified the ammunition. The outlaws were the likely holdouts.

CHAPTER 42

Mike became an almost daily fixture at the boarding house, picking Melanie up for some activity and then walking her home when her duties in the saloon were done. Mike's only other task was to learn the trial procedures and he felt he had a good understanding of what was allowed and what was not in the courtroom. One day over dinner, he asked her why she was living in a boarding house, instead of a standalone house.

"I'm single and didn't want to take on that debt."

Mike frowned. He wondered how the main computer handled debt.

"How much would it cost to buy or build a house?"

"A friend of mine said a small starter home is about twenty thousand credits."

"Do you know where that number comes from?"

"I'm not an expert, but the trees are free of course. Several companies were started to cut down the trees, and haul them to the lumberyard. Those companies also manage the forests, so they re-plant new trees to replace the ones they cut down. The lumberyard pays them for the trees."

Mike pulled out his tablet and started taking notes. "What happens then?" he asked.

"We have some builders who brought plans for many types of houses and businesses. They buy the lumber from the lumberyard. You choose the house you want, buy it and then make monthly transfers to them. They send an email several times a year with your balance. Anyone could buy the lumber from the lumberyard, but most people don't have the skills to build a house."

"I noticed a bank down the street. The main computer handles all transactions, so what do they do?"

"I'm not sure. I think some people give them some of their credits and they pool that to loan it to the businesses. The bank pays some interest on the money you loan them. I don't do anything with the banks, myself." She smiled. "I don't have enough money to bother."

Mike nodded. "What about things like nails, glass for windows, piping?"

"I'm not sure, but I think we transported a lot of nails and glass. I heard the pipes are fabricated in a machine shop in Dodge City, and the builders found all the stuff needed to make the foundations for houses out of stone or concrete."

It seemed as if some aspects of commerce here were much as they were on Helios, but some were very different.

A jury was selected and the trial finally started in a packed courtroom. Mike didn't have a black robe, so he returned to his Octan white tunic and pants. Dozens of witnesses testified and at the end of the week, the trial wrapped up with closing statements from the defendants' lawyers and the prosecutors. The jury deliberated for one day and returned with a verdict: All six defendants were found to be guilty of second degree murder of the sheriff, one participant and one bystander. Mike gave himself a week to determine the punishment. On Earth, the defendants likely would have received long jail sentences, but Mike needed the jail cells for the coming confrontation with the gang members.

After studying the geography of Ephasis, he announced the defendants would be exiled to a remote island in the planet's largest ocean, an island with abundant fruit trees and good fishing. With no boats on the planet, the exiled were certain to spend the rest of their days on the island. Mike left open the possibility that in ten or fifteen Ephasis years, another ship might visit them and allow them to return. The six prisoners were escorted to Dodge City to gather fishing equipment, tents, and other survival gear and then were transported in Mike's ship to the remote island.

Mike had long conversations with Melanie and the boarding house residents to get local feedback on his punishment decision. Most residents of New Dodge City supported the results of the trial and the punishment. Mike was just glad he didn't have to deal with a possible death sentence. With the gang members' trial approaching, that might come up yet.

Mainly due to the presence of Mike's contingent of Guardians, the re-activation of the Dodge City Guardians with their re-establishment of security at Dodge City, and the always-present seven local lawmen, the gangs had not been able to disrupt the trial. They drew unwanted attention when a gang member raped one of the residents of the boarding house where Melanie lived. That was the last straw for Mike, and he angrily ordered all of them arrested.

Max and a well-armed team of twenty Guardians assisted Bracken and his deputies as they rounded up the gang members. The prosecutors provided them a list and it didn't take long to find them, but many did not go without a fight. Leaders of two of the gangs refused to be taken into custody and died in gunfights at their houses. In all, Max and his Guardians with Bracken and his deputies locked up more than forty gang members.

Prosecutors had evidence tying most of them to various crimes, mainly robbery and extortion, along with the rape charge for one of them. Many business owners had been afraid to complain to the authorities about the extortion, but now felt safe enough to testify.

Most of the outlaws, seeing what had happened to the convicted murderers, negotiated deals to avoid being exiled also. Only four gang leaders refused to deal and actually went to trial. As part of their negotiated deals, Mike sentenced the former outlaws to work on nearby farms for a minimum of ten Ephasis years (which was about 15 Earth years). The rapist received twenty Ephasis years. If they harmed anyone on the farm, or came into town or ran away or committed any new crimes, the deals would be forfeited and exile would apply. In another month, the trial of the four gang leaders began. Based on extensive testimony, all were convicted of robbery and extortion by a jury, and Mike immediately sentenced them to exile on the same island as the gunfight participants.

Mike left one of the escape pods from his warship on Ephasis 9, for use by the law and criminal justice systems to transport outlaws who broke their negotiated deals, or criminals convicted in the future, to exile on the remote island.

The swift trials and convictions transformed New Dodge City. Crime virtually disappeared, as no one wanted to be exiled to possibly spend the rest of their lives with other criminals on a remote island—even if food was abundant.

After meeting many of the city's leading citizens Mike appointed a new mayor and city council for a four-year term, and a city charter was established. Colonists were free to live in either city, or move to the other whenever they wanted. The city council drafted plans to establish comprehensive legal and criminal justice systems.

It became apparent to Melanie that Mike's time on Ephasis 9 was about to end. One night instead of her boarding house, she asked Mike to take her to his hotel room.

"Do you think that's a good idea? Someone might see you and it could ruin your reputation."

"You're always worrying about someone else. I can see why the Octans picked you to solve their problems. You can't change my mind."

"I don't want to change your mind! I just want you to be sure."

She laughed. "Come on."

When they entered his room, Melanie opened the windows to let the night breeze cool off the room. He smiled when she locked the door. They embraced and began what seemed perfectly natural to Melanie and Mike. Melanie was wearing a tantalizing perfume, but Mike didn't need it and they were soon engaged in the oldest of human interactions. It probably wasn't fair to compare her, but in many ways Melanie reminded Mike of his first wife. No relationship is perfect, but Mike had a hard time finding fault with his first marriage. The night with Melanie would stay with him for a long time.

Melanie was gone when Mike awoke. He showered and dressed and hoped to find her at the restaurant, but she wasn't there. After breakfast, he went to the saloon. One of the bartenders said she mentioned something about school, and gave Mike directions.

After a two-kilometer hike, he found it and Melanie in one of the classrooms preparing for the upcoming school year. "Sorry to run out on you like that," she said. "Orientation meeting this morning."

"You don't have to apologize." Mike wandered around the classroom. "Some things never change. Is this fourth or fifth grade?"

"Actually, it's third grade. Kids seem to be getting smarter every year. When are you leaving, Mike?"

"Tomorrow morning." He didn't much like to think of it. "I've got some loose ends to ties up; okay if I meet you this evening at the boarding house?"

At day's end, when he arrived at the boarding house, the women surprised him with a cake and took turns hugging him and wishing him a safe journey. Mike and Melanie spent one last night together, and when morning came, he handed her a piece of paper.

"This is for you," he said.

"A deed? What—?"

"It's the deed to your new house. I made a deal with one of the builders. He's been over-charging some people for the same type of house when he thinks they don't know much about loans or financing. He was on the prosecutor's list, but low on the totem pole, so to speak, compared to some other questionable business practices that have been going on here. I told him he was next on the list. He almost had a heart attack, and then promised to refund all the over-charges. I asked him to show good faith by donating a house. So, here it is. You don't owe a dime."

She was torn between concern and elation. "Are you sure this is legal?"

"Of course, it is! We wrote a settlement agreement, and in it he donated the house to me to do whatever I wished. He was just glad he wouldn't face exile to that remote island with the other criminals. Christ, Melanie, I'm gonna miss you."

She kissed him and they hugged for a long time before he had to leave.

At Bracken's urging, Mike finally mounted a "horse" and they rode out of New Dodge City to the waiting warship. At least he didn't fall off…

The Guardians formed two rows on the ramp, and Mike waved goodbye to Bracken, then looked around one last time and entered the ship. As expected, Harwig had again read his final report, and sent an email congratulating him on re-establishing the colony. There was a small feast of Helios food waiting. It didn't taste as good as he remembered it.

CHAPTER 43

Demos

Mike was totally surprised when Harwig and another Guardian awakened him. Harwig seemed embarrassed as they walked toward the ship's small conference room. "There have been some unexpected developments. It's probably best if you heard this directly from Ambassador Mikolan."

The Octan Ambassador was waiting for them, and motioned them to be seated. "The truce is at risk. It appears that the Octans and Jubans both started to colonize the same planet with robot constructors without being aware of the other's efforts. The planet in question, Demos, is on the boundary between the areas chosen for colonization. There have been some intense negotiations to resolve the issue, but there is a real possibility the truce could be broken."

Mikolan paused as Mike was staring blankly at him. "I'm sorry, while this is serious, what does it have to do with me?"

"The leaders of the equivalent organization on Octos to your United Nations are concerned with the lack of progress to resolve this issue. They are willing to try almost anything to avoid a resumption of the war. I made a recommendation that you assist in the negotiations as you bring a different point of view, and have demonstrated ability to resolve difficult issues. The leadership agreed."

Mike was drinking the orange juice-like drink given to help awaken persons from transport and choked on Mikolan's statement. "What? How could I possibly help? Neither side has any reason to listen to anything I have to say."

"The leadership will introduce you as the Ambassador from Earth, which now has quite a stake in the truce."

Mike felt a sudden dread that he was being dragged into a lose/lose high-stakes gamble far beyond his ability to provide any meaningful contributions. "Surely there's someone more qualified for this."

Mikolan leaned forward to emphasis his words. "We have observed Earth and its leaders and diplomats for many years. There is no one else that is acceptable to the leadership."

So, the decision had been made. All he could do was try to make the best of the situation. Mike looked at Harwig. "Why am I awake now? Surely this planet on the boundary is pretty far, even at this ship's speed?"

Harwig actually blushed and avoided Mike's eyes. "You've been asleep for almost a year. Demos is almost ten thousand light years from Kepler. We met this ship and re-routed it as soon as we learned of the crisis on Demos—just after you left Ephasis 9. We are about a day away from Demos. My apologies, Ambassador Silver."

Mikolan handed Mike an electronic tablet with the translated truce agreement and a thick paper document. "Here is the original truce agreement, and a report just received on the negotiations, which have been at a stalemate for more than an Earth year."

Mike started through the documents, then glanced up. "The Octans and Jubans are both very advanced and intelligent species. Both have technology that scientists on Earth haven't even thought of. Why can't two intelligent species find a way to resolve their differences and live peaceably?"

Mikolan almost seemed embarrassed at such an obvious question. "This is not a scientific or technological issue, but involves the emotions and pride of both species. We hope you can bring a different point of view that can help break the impasse."

The geology of Demos was not amenable to humans. It was a cold and dark world, far from its sun and Mike wondered why either side would even want to form a colony on it. He read and re-read the truce agreement and the results of the ongoing negotiations trying to come up with a way out for both sides.

The ship landed on Demos near a domed Octan city under construction; then it took off again, taking Mikolan and Harwig with it. Mike felt strangely naked without his personal retinue of Guardians, but there were scores of Guardians present and he knew he was in no danger.

As Mike entered a section that had been completed, he immediately felt more at home. The layout was almost like Helios or Paradise City, or Dodge City, with large curved corridors and endless rooms with unknown functions. Like Helios, this city was devoid of any color other than steel or white. Several Guardians escorted Mike to a large meeting room where they were greeted by the six members of the Octan negotiating team. There were some subtle differences between the Octans, but they were all dressed alike in the white tunic and pants that everyone on Helios wore. Aren't there any colors on Octos? The team held a brief review meeting to summarize the negotiations and Mike wondered how he would be accepted by the Octan team. Would they be insulted by the presence of a representative of a 'barbaric' culture? He had suffered from similar feelings when he first met Balos, the Taas leader. But he had slowly come to appreciate Balos and most recently they had become friends of sorts.

Surprisingly, the team seemed to accept Mike and asked if he had any ideas that could help, but at this point he could only ask questions to help clarify some of the issues. The team adjourned for the day, and the Guardians led him to an apartment to rest. The bedroom was not all that different from the bedrooms furnished for the colonists in Helios. The Octan bathroom, on the other hand, was a maze of plumbing and there wasn't a toilet to be found. Mike wondered if the space shuttle astronauts of the 21th century would feel right at home in an Octan bathroom.

Dawn on Demos was not spectacular. The distant sun barely lit the morning sky, which remained black and star-filled during most of the day. Guardians led Mike to a buffet of some strange and exotic food. At least, there was no FOOD. Mike managed to find some things to eat, and a drink that, oddly, tasted like rum and Coke.

To avoid conflicts, the negotiations were held alternately in the Octan city then in the Juban city also under construction on the other side of Demos. Small transport ships carried the negotiators between the cities. Today, the Octan team assembled in the dining hall and walked to the meeting room to meet the Jubans. To help him follow the discussions, the lead Octan negotiator gave Mike a translator system that fit nicely in his ear, and comfortably around his neck.

Following an established protocol, the teams entered the meeting room in single file, led by the lead negotiator. As the newest member of the Octan team, Mike entered last. Jason had told him Maria had changed her looks to avoid detection, so he wondered what a Juban might look like. When he saw them, he immediately realized who the models had been for the Guardians. They had the same physical shape and face, but their skin was gray and their hair was a bright orange. The six members of the Juban team were wearing small white boxes on a metallic strap around their necks. Unlike the Octans, the Jubans were wearing military-like uniforms in different colors. Mike was surprised that three members of the Juban team were females—all in uniform just like the males. Mike guessed the lead Juban negotiator, Socoros Nazca, before she was introduced, by her position at the head of the file. By custom, each team member bowed slightly as he or she was introduced. When he was introduced as the representative from Earth, some of the Jubans whispered to each other. As soon as the participants were seated, the lead negotiators took turns replying to specific items or issues that had been raised at the last meeting. All ideas had to be presented by the leaders of the negotiating teams, unless the other side's lead negotiator agreed to an exception. Once the issues from the last meeting were finished, the lead negotiators took turns presenting new ideas to break the impasse. To Mike, all these "new ideas" were just versions of past ideas and after a while, his mind wandered. He soon found himself staring at the lead Juban negotiator. She had a cool, aristocratic air about her. Her orange hair was stylish and her uniform couldn't hide a shapely figure. Not bad. He looked away when their eyes met.

Towards the end of another non-productive day of negotiations Milosan, the lead Octan negotiator, asked his counterpart if Mike could present an idea. Socoros nodded in agreement. The translation from Octan to English was slow, and Mike suddenly realized everyone was looking at him. He swallowed hard and made his proposal.

"There are many cultures on Earth, perhaps not as different as Octan and Juban, but significantly different, nevertheless. To help break through these barriers, sometimes volunteers of one culture go and live with the other for a period of time to try and learn the other's culture. We call these programs, 'cultural exchanges'. Have you ever considered having some of your younger leaders volunteer to live with a family in the other's culture to try to learn their ways, and how they think? And when they are done, write a report on what they found?"

Once the translation ended, there was absolutely no reaction from either side. Finally, Socoros replied, "We will consider this idea and report back at the next meeting."

The meeting ended, the teams bowed slightly to each other and the Jubans left in a single file. The Octans gathered around Mike wanting to know more about cultural exchanges, how they worked and if they were successful. They continued the discussion on the walk back to the dining hall and all during the meal that Mike thought of as lunch.

CHAPTER 44

The next day, Socoros addressed Mike's idea: "Ambassador Silver, while we find your idea interesting, we think it would take a long time to implement and would not resolve the immediate issue of Demos, the purpose of these discussions." She turned to the room as a whole. "It is time for a break in these negotiations. Our leaders are recalling us for more detailed reports and discussion. We propose a break of thirty Demos days."

Milosan asked if Mike could make one more proposal before the break in the negotiations. Socoros agreed and Mike cleared his throat and made his last proposal: "You may know my family now lives on a planet known as Kepler 14b. This was supposed to be an uninhabited planet, but we found it to be home to tribes of people living in caves. We allowed one of these tribes to come and live in our city, Helios. After a while, my son became friends with a member of this tribe. Eventually they came to love each other and were married. It was extremely difficult to accept my son marrying someone so different, but I came to respect her and eventually felt like she truly was my daughter. Also, one of my oldest friends met a Juban on Earth. They also married. They are now living on Helios."

As soon as the translation ended, all the Jubans immediately started arguing with each other, until Socoros rapped the table to get their attention. "Ambassador Silver. There are no Jubans on Earth."

"Maybe not officially, but there are a few there. Nevertheless, my proposal to resolve the issue of Demos is for the Octans and Jubans to abandon their present cities here and build a new, joint city, where the inhabitants can learn to live together and resolve their differences peacefully. The Octans and Jubans are both intelligent people but they could still learn a lot from each other. Once you learn more about each other you may find you have a lot in common."

Everyone was listening carefully as the translation continued, "Perhaps Demos could serve as a joint outpost for both Octos and Jubas and a place where ideas are shared and differences are resolved."

When the translation ended, conversations erupted among the members of the teams. "Thank you, Ambassador Silver," said Socoros. "We will take your proposal back to our leaders for further consideration."

"One more thing, Ambassador Socoros," said Mike. "I would like to visit the Juban city under construction, just to see it—as a tourist." This didn't translate very well, and Socoros was surprised he even asked, but she agreed. No Octan or Juban had ever asked for permission, let alone actually visited the other's cities.

"I will escort you," she said. "It should be—interesting."

A transport ship picked him and brought him to the as yet unnamed Juban city on Demos. The Octan city had been essentially the same as Helios, but here he marveled anew at the wonderland feel of another city designed by non-human minds. The Juban city consisted of thirty—to fifty-story hexagonal skyscrapers on a hexagonal grid pattern. Within the buildings, hallways were hexagonal, doors were hexagonal, rooms were six-sided, and patterns on the floor and ceiling were hexagonal. There was not a rectangle in sight. Two skyscrapers in the center of the city were essentially finished and occupied.

Instead of the negotiations uniform, Socoros was wearing a long, dark blue gown with gold trim, and her hair was wrapped in a matching scarf. Except for her orange irises, Mike thought he might not have noticed her in an exclusive charity event on Earth, if he'd ever been to one.

The interior of the Juban skyscraper was as colorful and decorated as the

Octan city was colorless and Spartan. The walls were hung with souvenirs of various worlds or covered with murals with military themes.

When Socoros met him, she unexpectedly shook his hand, then escorted him into the city. She had felt a shock rip through her body when they shook hands. Mike apologized for something he called "static electricity". She was vaguely aware of what that was, but the humidity on her home planet was always so high, she had never experienced it. As she escorted him, she wondered about Mike. He said his son had married a Kepler native. He described his concerns but didn't mention the mother's concerns. Did he have a mate? She had been surprised when he showed up, pleased with some of his ideas, and fascinated that he asked to visit the Juban city on Demos. For some reason, she was intellectually and physically attracted to him. The Juban military culture made it difficult for women to get ahead, and she had sacrificed personal relationships to prove her value and move up the ranks. Juban males also sacrificed, but somehow managed to have both a career and the family life that had eluded her. She had often wondered if her standards were too high. But that was in the past, and nothing to do with her current situation.

She invited him to dinner, and he accepted. She met him at the door wearing a fashionable low-cut red gown and Mike had a hard time not staring as there was plenty to see. She had several domestic workers who prepared the meal, cleaned up, and discreetly left them alone. While they were enjoying an after-dinner drink, Socoros leaned forward in her chair. "I'd like to tell you the other side of the story the Octans presented on Earth, if you'll listen without judgment."

Mike was distracted when she leaned forward. What did she say? "Oh. Sure, I'd like to hear that."

Socoros presented a very different picture of the encounter between the two species and the subsequent war. Jubas was a crowded planet. Its population was not large, but habitable land area was at a premium, as over ninety percent of the planet was covered with water. The Jubans developed a single culture, embracing military order and governed by a military council. As soon as they perfected space travel, they began looking for planets to colonize, mainly to relieve congestion on Jubas. Sometimes these worlds were inhabited by intelligent peoples in an early stage of development, with whom the Jubans traded.

When the Jubans came in contact with the Octans, they pressed the Jubans to remove all colonies on planets with intelligent people. The Octans were against any interference at all in the development of other peoples. The Jubans refused, and the disagreement on this issue eventually escalated to the war. The war only lasted a brief period, perhaps two Earth years or so. The sides were evenly matched, and both quickly lost most of their war-making ability.

An uneasy, temporary truce was agreed to, whereby the Jubans did not have to remove already-established colonies, but agreed that from now on, they would only colonize planets that were not already inhabited by intelligent species. The truce roughly divided the one spiral arm of the Milky Way Galaxy into Juban and Octan areas. After the truce period, all uninhabited worlds or worlds with unsustainable colonies would be available, in either area. Colonizing the other spiral arm of the galaxy was not feasible with Juban or Octan spacecraft due to the great distances involved.

"The Octans did not have enough citizens to inhabit planets in their chosen area of the Galaxy and had to recruit Earth to help them," said Socoros. "The Octans are not afraid of us, or of humans, but they are terrified that we will someday form an alliance that will effectively push them from the Galaxy. They see us as being very much alike—warlike and dangerous."

"Did you ever determine why the Octans are so adamant about not interfering in the development of a species?"

Socoros shook her head. "We asked the Octans about this several times, and they refused to discuss it. But, during the war, a captured Octan spy told a story we could not verify. It seems that many Juban orbits ago, perhaps 1000 Earth years, some Octan explorers defied their own leaders' guidance against forming relationships with local inhabitants. This led to offspring that were mostly Octan genetically. When this was discovered, the explorers were exiled and all Octans involved in space exploration were required to sign a pledge to never interfere in a species' development again."

"But… the contact with Earth and the whole Alliance agreement would seem to be a violation of that pledge."

"Yes. The Octans must have felt they had no other choice."

Mike described the similarity of the Orex and Taas to the Octans, and Socoros commented that might have been one of the planets where the Octans interfered with a species' development.

Mike was thinking about everything she said and trying not to stare at her cleavage when Socoros asked about the Jubans on Earth. Mike relayed the story he had heard from Maria, and Socoros shook her head.

"This is very disturbing. I will pass this on to the Juban Leadership Council. It should cause quite a reaction. Indeed, some members of the Leadership Council were opposed to the treaty. We did not know any had undertaken a mission to interrupt the formation of Octan colonies. Did she happen to mention the name of the mission leader?"

"Someone named Grus Harm, I think."

Socoros couldn't hide her surprise. "He is the son of one of the council leaders! Thank you for telling me this."

When the evening ended, Socoros was standing by the door as Mike was about to leave. "How did you know about the human custom of shaking hands?"

She smiled. "Some years ago, we intercepted an Octan transmission from their Earth Ambassador to their leadership on Octos. It described many curious customs of humans. There is one other custom, I understand, when an evening ends." She stepped forward, put her arms around him, and kissed him. A hot flash ran through her body. Nothing like this had ever happened to her with a Juban male; most of them were boring and seemed focused only on their next assignment. In retrospect, they were like her. She needed more information about human customs.

The thirty days' respite from negotiations ended a few days early with a message from the Jubans. They met this time in the Juban city. After the usual protocols, Socoros announced that the Juban leadership had agreed to Mike's joint city idea, with one clarification. They wanted Mike to be there while it was being built, until a joint committee could be developed.

The Octans chattered excitedly among themselves, but Milosan had been in touch with the Octan leadership and had the final word. Octan agreed to the proposal as well. It was Mike who asked for a slight modification: "I'm honored to be asked to help in this matter, but I would first like to ask to return to Helios for a period to visit my family. By the time, I return, I'm sure there will be some interesting issues to discuss and resolve."

The Octans and Jubans agreed and started work on designing a common city. Mike left for the year-long trek back to Helios as soon as his warship arrived. Socoros sent him a, "best wishes for a speedy and safe trip," message as he was entering the ship. After some heated discussions among the Juban negotiating team, she made a request to Milosan for more personal information about Mike, under the pretense that they wished to send a letter thanking him for his help in a way that would not offend him.

CHAPTER 45

Helios

A lot had changed in the two and a half years since he left Helios. Mahra and Jesse had a second son. Like his father, Jesse displayed remarkable ability as a negotiator and was in demand to resolve issues between groups. It would take some time before a court system with judges could be established.

Vast fields were under cultivation now, and large ranches were filled with wildebeests. Colonists moved freely in and out of the city; a small resort had been established near the sea. A small flotilla delivered fresh fish daily to a market on a new seaside dock. No one could say this was anything but a successful colony.

Jason and Maria, on an expedition, had found an animal alternative to the horse, and buggies, stagecoaches, and several types of chariots were now in use.

Mike had returned with a complete Juban physiology report to give to Maria's physician, who was looking into in-vitro fertilization methods. In the meantime, Jason and Maria had enlisted some colonists and made plans to move to the second city under construction, once sections became habitable. Mike spent an entire evening with Maria and Jason describing his time on Demos and his visit to the Juban city under construction. When he mentioned Socoros, Maria was impressed. "You're moving in exalted circles," she said. Apparently, Socoros's family had an extensive history as ambassadors and negotiators, and her father had been the lead negotiator on the Juban team that negotiated the truce with the Octans. Mike's videos, and interviews with him, gained quite a TV audience, and the current chief of security debriefed him of information he didn't even know he had.

Two and a half years had passed before Mike was back on Demos. Socoros, wearing a revealing green gown, met him in the arrival hall. She greeted him with a passionate kiss, which, if Mike was reading them right, shocked some other Jubans waiting for other transports in the arrival hall.

He arrived to find construction of the common city well underway. The new city combined both Octan and Juban features. A transparent dome covered Juban hexagonal skyscrapers. Hallways in the skyscrapers were rectangular but rooms were hexagonal. The city had taken on a Juban flair, with bright colors in most of the common areas. A small portion was already livable and a few brave Octans and Jubans had moved in start a cultural exchange program devised by Mike before he left. The Octan and Juban leadership had jointly agreed to share Demos, and relations between the two species were slowly improving.

Socoros took him to an apartment built especially for him on the top floor of one of the skyscrapers. The enclosed swimming pool gave a magnificent view through the transparent dome. Most of Demos was still void of vegetation, but Mike thought he was coming to appreciate its barren beauty.

"So, what do you think?" she asked as they looked out over the pool to the setting sun of Demos.

"It's wonderful, and very unexpected."

"It's the least we can do for your help with the Octans. After all, this city is your idea. You can enjoy the water whenever you wish and no one will bother you." Except me.

He thanked her again, and she kissed him and left him to settle in.

The Jubans had a temperature scale similar in concept to the Centigrade scale. The Juban scale ranged from zero where water froze to 1000 where water boiled. After a little experimentation with the digital temperature control of a water faucet in the kitchen, he checked the pool's control. It was set at 300, and the water temperature seemed to be nearly ideal. He slipped off his clothes and eased into the water. He hadn't been in a swimming pool since Earth, and reveled in the old familiar feeling. Soon he was so lost in thought he didn't hear Socoros knock on the door, or enter. She hesitated only a moment before slipping off her clothes and jumping into the pool. At the splash, Mike turned quickly but saw only her green gown beside the pool. She suddenly appeared right in front of him.

"Socoros?"

"Yes?" She wrapped her arms around him and started kissing him. When she stopped and let go, he wiped his eyes. "Are you sure you know what you're doing?"

"I am old enough to know this," she replied and kissed him again, wrapping her legs around him.

Mike awoke and sat up in bed. Socoros was asleep and facing away from him. There was a low level of light in the room from an open bathroom door and Mike stared at her shape. Socoros didn't have the large shoulders and upper body that Maria did. She wasn't all that different from human females. She was slender and strong however. Their lovemaking in the beginning had been almost a wrestling match. Her hair was still wet, and looked dark. In the low light, she almost seemed human. Mike made a quick trip to the bathroom and slipped back into bed behind her.

Socoros opened her eyes in the dimly lit bedroom, itching all over. She turned over and found Mike. She made a quick trip to the bathroom to slap some cold water on her itchy skin. Her eyes were watering, too. Strange.

In the bedroom, Mike was asleep on his back. She hoped she hadn't hurt him with her eagerness to satisfy a long period of sacrifice for her career. To her, he was an oasis after a long trek in the desert. She slipped her arm under his pillow and snuggled against him, determinedly ignoring her itchy skin, and let his rhythmical breathing soothe her back to sleep.

Mike awoke later to find her gone. All citizens in the new city had been given and Octan tablet; Mike checked his, but there was no message from Socoros. He dressed quickly and went looking for her.

The Juban physician Socoros visited seemed surprised when she explained her recent activities, but examined her, took some blood for additional tests and gave her some medication, with a warning that unexpected things happen when two species come in too close contact. She smiled, thanked him, and left, calling Mike as she went.

They met in a common area somewhat like a park, a place for Jubans and Octans to meet informally and talk. After spending the day together, they went to Socoros's apartment. It was similar to Mike's but without the swimming pool. They didn't need a pool to resume where they left off. Later, she was snuggled in his arms.

"Socoros?"

"Yes."

"Your body shape is different from my friend's Juban wife. She has large shoulders, more like Juban males. Your shape is similar to human females."

"She is probably one of the warrior class. They are selected for strength, and train from an early age to be warriors. They breed with one another. Members of my family have been diplomats for many generations."

Mike chuckled. "She also isn't as large as you are in the front."

Socoros laughed. "Exercise changes what you call hormones, and are these not unique on human females?"

He hadn't quite thought of it like that. "Yes, I guess you're right."

After a few days, Mike asked Socoros for a history of Jubas. It was always interesting to see how a species describes its development. Mike was aware of the adage that history is written by the winners, but he still wanted to read it. Socoros promised a version translated to English as soon as they could find a suitable translation program.

Socoros shocked Mike by asking him to visit Jubas with her. Mike sent a transmission to Jesse to let him know as the transport time each way was twelve Earth months in the fastest Juban ship. Anticipating Mike might agree, Socoros had acquired a human transport pod from the Octans. Mike and Socoros were soon in transit to Jubas.

CHAPTER 46

Jubas

Mike did not have the slightest idea what Jubas might look like and even if he had made a guess, he probably would not have come close. Every square unit of surface seemed to be taken up by enormous hexagonal skyscrapers in bright colors. Their windows gave off a golden glow in the setting sun. The Juban people had been informed of their arrival, but Mike still became the object of everyone's attention wherever they went. Socoros acted as a guide and they spent the next several days touring Meenus, the Juban capital city.

Jubas was similar to Kepler in some ways with a blue-green sky and orange-red grass, but the leaves on the trees were purple. The air was warm and pleasant as they toured the countryside in an open nuclear-powered vehicle. It didn't take long to tour the countryside as there wasn't much of it. Almost all of Jubas' land was covered with cities full of skyscrapers; most of the farms were hydroponic and located in the top several floors of the buildings.

One morning, Socoros invited Mike to meet the Juban Leadership Council. To Mike, the nine council members didn't seem all that different from the negotiating team on Demos, just a little older perhaps. After the usual introductions, and some brief exchanges concerning life and progress on Demos, Nomos, the leader of the council, nodded to Socoros and she asked Mike if he could help the Council with a problem. That was so unlikely, Mike suppressed a laugh. "Certainly, if I am able to help," he replied.

"There is a planet with a Juban city that is under attack by a local indigenous people. We have the capability to eliminate this civilization, of course, but that would be a rather horrendous violation of our treaty with the Octans.""

"I see," said Mike. "But what do you think I can do, that you can't do?"

"Our negotiations are going nowhere. You may have better fortune, as this civilization seems to be similar to one on Earth, several thousand years ago. The parallels are quite remarkable."

"So, what do you want me to do?"

"Go there, assess the situation, help the negotiating team if possible, and report back to the Council. We will provide you with extensive security so there is no danger." Socoros and the Leadership Council members were all watching Mike's reaction as Socoros's translation into English ended.

"While I'm sympathetic to the problem, I would like to return to Helios before my grandchildren forget who I am."

"We would be happy to compensate you for your time."

Mike suppressed another laugh. "I've been promised many things by the Octans for helping out on human colonies with problems and on Demos. I haven't seen anything yet."

"We are grateful for that as well, and much more generous than the Octans. Humans value gold. We could give you your weight in gold as a down payment—and ten times that amount if you help resolve the problem."

Mike did a quick mental calculation, and was staggered at the result. Gold was over $10,000 an ounce on Earth. They'd offered him a magnificent fortune. But—.

He shrugged. "I would have no way to spend gold on Helios."

"What can we offer you then? You have only to ask."

He suddenly thought of some additional large equipment that they hadn't had room for on the transport ship to Helios. He tried to explain this to Socoros, aware the council was listening.

Socoros smiled. "Of course, anything you wish to transport—if the Octans won't object. And, you can still have your weight in gold for your help on Demos."

Mike was sure the Octans owed him enough for Demos they wouldn't object. He suddenly felt a huge burden placed on his shoulders to help. While he had no particular affection for Jubans other than Socoros, and he hadn't even met any of the indigenous people in question, he knew his conscience would bother him if many intelligent entities were to die in a war he could have helped stop.

He was feeling trapped.

CHAPTER 47

Aragonis

From space, Aragonis looked eerily similar to Earth with vast blue oceans, a random white cloud cover and brown and green land masses. The ship landed near the Juban city and Socoros accompanied Mike to the equivalent of the council room in Helios.

The Juban council members gave Mike an extensive review of the problem as they saw it, and the negotiations that had stalled. The city manager and team lead, Narus Maq, began with a history of the city.

"Aragonis is much larger than Jubas and mostly uninhabited. This city was established fifty Juban orbits, or about a hundred Earth years ago. The site was located far from existing civilizations—as I understand the measurement, more than five thousand kilometers away." He waited for Socoros to finish the translation, and continued, "Over time, one civilization became dominant. About two Aragonis orbits… years ago, they discovered our city and demanded we pay them tribute, which we took to mean some form of compensation, merely for being here and so they would not attack us. At first, we didn't take this threat seriously, but within ten days, they captured some of us outside the city and held them hostage, again demanding tribute. We did nothing, and they left the bodies outside the city."

Socoros translated, and added, "Some on the Juban Leadership Council wanted to destroy this civilization in retaliation, but the majority preferred to negotiate. The negotiations, however, have served only to give these people time to build larger armies." She said, looking at Narus.

"Yes," he said. "Now significant armies of this civilization are approaching this city. Time is running out before we must take action to protect ourselves."

"Or leave," Mike pointed out. "As the Octans would probably advise."

Narus ignored him and continued, "We understand this civilization, known as the Emor, is similar in ways to some on Earth many years ago. We hope your knowledge of this type of culture can provide some insight that will re-direct the negotiations and help them succeed."

"I hope that as well. When can we meet the negotiation team?"

There was an uncomfortable moment before Narus replied. "This is the negotiation team."

"Okay. When can we meet the Emor negotiators?"

"The next meeting is scheduled for tomorrow morning."

The meeting officially ended but Mike had dinner with the team and retired with Socoros to an apartment similar to their Juban apartments on Demos. Early the next morning, Mike, Socoros, and the Juban negotiating team left the city and walked to a spot about a kilometer away, where a platform had been built and a tent, big enough for both parties, erected on it. Aragonis was indeed like Earth in many ways. The sky was clear and blue and the trees and grass were green. The Juban city had been built in a green valley set between two snow-capped mountain ranges. The day was warm and a gentle breeze was blowing; two sides of the tent had been rolled up to take advantage of it. The fields nearby were filled with wildflowers that gave off a scent similar to roses.

Mike heard a sound in the distance like the music of a marching band. The music ended and Mike jumped at the sound of a trumpet fanfare. Moments later the five-member Emor team entered the tent.

The Emor were very much like humans and Mike felt like he was transported back in time as they were wearing skirts and breastplates eerily similar to those of Roman generals and tribunes. The two teams bowed briefly and sat down at a long table. The lead negotiators were facing each other at the center of the table and Narus began summarizing the points of the last meeting. Both Emor and Jubans were wearing translator ear buttons. As the negotiations were carried out in the unfamiliar language of the Emor, Mike put in an earplug of a translation device given to him by Socoros. He was sitting at the end of the table but noticed several Emor looking at him instead of Narus. He first assumed it was his blond hair and white tunic and pants, which contrasted with the brightly colored, rank-specific uniforms of the Jubans.

General Marius Axel was bored with these negotiations. He had not troubled even to overcome his loathing of these strange creatures and their even stranger city. The Jubans appeared to have no weapons and no will to defend themselves, whereas he would soon have the largest Emor army ever assembled. He would make short work of them. This would be their last meeting and he soon would give them an ultimatum—surrender or die. Emor could use some new slaves…

He noticed the new Juban team member as soon as he entered the tent. He frowned, as this one looked not all that different than his own people, only this one had blue eyes and yellow hair and was wearing a bright white outfit instead of the crazy colors typical of the Jubans. His team made the usual salutations and sat down at the long table. He occasionally glanced at the newcomer, even as Narus rambled on with his usual worthless rant. He pulled out a paper roll with the ultimatum statement and waited for Narus to finish.

Mike was not an expert on Roman history, but knew enough to realize the current Juban strategy of reasonable exchanges of goods or bartering would never work. If this civilization's culture was as similar as its military was to the Roman culture, he knew they would only respect a force greater than their own. Mike was wondering how he could convey that idea to

Socoros, when Narus introduced him and asked if he had any comments, and everyone was looking at him. He fumbled with the translation device held on his throat by a metallic band.

"General Axel, what does an Emor Army do, when faced with overwhelming enemy forces?"

Axel was surprised that anyone would even ask such a question. "This has never happened."

"But if it did, would the Emor not seek to avoid defeat by forming an alliance with this enemy—if possible?"

"Only if there were no alternative," Axel growled.

Mike had a backup plan he had hoped, until he saw the Emor leadership, that he wouldn't need. He looked at Narus. "Could we have everyone go outside? I want to show General Axel why I'm asking him that question."

Narus consulted with Socoros and Axel briefly and both teams filed out of the tent.

Mike pressed a button on a signaling device. Immediately, a Juban warship appeared overhead, and what seemed to the Emor to be a bolt of lightning flashed to an area near the tent. When the dust cleared, the animals the Emor leaders had been riding were gone; only a small crater remained. Just as quickly, the warship disappeared. General Axel and his team stared in disbelief.

At least they didn't look like horses. Mike hated to see any animals killed unnecessarily, but that paled in comparison to the thought of an actual war in which the Emor would, undoubtedly, be wiped out. He watched as the Emor leaders engaged in a heated argument. When it ended, Mike asked General Axel, politely, to return to the tent.

When they were all seated again, there was an awkward silence, until Mike repeated his question to the General.

"General Axel, what is your strategy—when faced with an overwhelming enemy?"

Axel stared at the paper roll with the ultimatum in his hand and dropped it on the ground. "To negotiate an alliance—if possible."

"I think City Manager Narus would be happy to discuss how the Jubans and Emor could work together in a way that would benefit both sides."

Narus stared at Mike until Socoros nudged him from the back. "Oh yes! We would be happy to discuss that."

The next day, at Mike's suggestion, Narus invited General Axel and his negotiating team to dinner in the Juban city. In confidence, Mike suggested to Axel that he bring some of his own food, in case he didn't like the Juban food. For some reason, Axel laughed.

The alliance negotiations and dinner went better than Mike and Socoros had hoped; Axel would be leaving the next day with a copy of an agreement to present to his leaders. It seemed improbable, but somehow Axel understood the Jubans had migrated from another planet in the sky to his world. After dinner, Mike had a few minutes alone on an outdoor patio with Axel and confided his own origin and how he had come to try and help the Jubans. Axel seemed interested when Mike described the Roman culture and history.

"You said this happened a long time ago on your home world. What happened to them?"

"One of their great leaders moved the capital far away, splitting the empire and weakening it. Barbarians eventually overran them and destroyed the city."

Axel was thoughtful. "Some things are similar. Some are different."

Mike nodded. When Axel invited him to come to their capital city and meet their leadership—assuming they agreed to the new alliance—Mike accepted, wondering how it would be step back in time to a society not all that different from ancient Rome.

Socoros joined them on the patio for a final toast. After the general left, she handed Mike a paper roll. "This was found in the negotiations tent. We thought you would like to have it to remember what happened here."

Mike unrolled the ultimatum. "What does it say?"

"Our translator thinks it is a demand for Narus to surrender the city or all in it will be killed."

"Pretty brutal terms," Mike commented as he rolled up the document.

"Speaking of terms, don't forget your reward. You need to make a list of equipment to be transported to Helios."

"Funny you should ask." Mike pulled a list from his tunic. "It's in English, I'm afraid. You'll need to get it translated. And Socoros—"

She folded the list into a neat hexagon and put it in her pocket. "Yes?" "How about visiting Earth? If we can hitch a ride on the transport, you could be introduced at the United Nations. Many people there would be most interested in meeting you."

"Another interesting idea."

CHAPTER 48

The next day, Socoros and Mike explored the Juban city on Aragonis. This city was very different from the Juban capital, and from the domed city on Demos. It was sited amid gently rolling hills that eased down to the bank of a large river. Numerous green areas were preserved within the city, and a protective wall had been built around it to keep out roaming herds of animals. Mike wondered if this was the city the Jubans would have designed on their home planet if they had the land and natural features. One feature in common with the cities on Jubas was a large tower in the city where all the Juban food was grown hydroponically. Citizens merely collected the food from the tower whenever they needed it.

After the tour, Mike met with the Juban negotiating team to prepare a final report for the Juban Leadership Council. When that was done, Mike asked Socoros and the team about Aragonis. "This planet is probably ten times bigger than Jubas, and mostly uninhabited. To relieve the crowding on Jubas, why not build one gigantic Juban city here instead of a number of small colonies on planets far apart?"

Narus and the team hesitated until Socoros answered with a question: "Why did the Octans not build one gigantic Earth colony on Kepler instead of many small colonies on distant planets?"

Mike shrugged. "I don't know. They just said they wanted to colonize all the habitable planets in their area, so Jubas wouldn't."

All the Jubans laughed, and Socoros continued her explanation. "There are more habitable planets in our designated area of the galaxy than we can ever colonize. The Octans know, just as the Jubans do, that the same problems found on Jubas or Octos or Earth would just be transferred to one huge city on another planet. By separating groups or cultures with economic conflicts you effectively eliminate those problems. Several small cities on the same planet would have those problems, eventually."

Mike thought about that. Indeed, the colonies initially formed from Earth, had been required to choose one type of government, one language for all official business and communications, one common measurement system and so on. This effectively made the colony as economically homogeneous as possible. With food, clothing, and shelter provided, there were no poor or rich people. There were no politicians to point out the advantages of one group over another, and so on. There were, in fact, few conflicts among the colonists. Most of the problems on Kepler dealt with external forces, such as the massive number of huge and dangerous animals. "So a huge Juban city here would have problems?"

"All cities with people in many economic situations have problems. The Jubans here represent what you might call a small slice of the overall Juban society."

Mike had noticed that the city was sparsely populated. There were less than ten thousand colonists in a city designed for a hundred thousand. It could double in population with no impact on its resources. The population of Helios could grow another twenty percent without straining its resources. But that would never happen as people were already moving out to live in ranches and farms. And there was the other city under construction they could grow into. The probability of Earth populating all the available planets in the Octan area of the Galaxy, and then sending a second group of colonies to those planets was very low. News of problems on the existing colonies filled the nightly news on Earth. It was becoming harder and harder to find groups of forty thousand humans to complete new colonies.

"Jubas still seems crowded considering the number of Juban colonies already founded."

"Most of the Jubans who were willing to leave to form new colonies have left. Starting all over on a new planet is not the wish of many Jubans. It is much more difficult now to form new colonies of the minimum required number."

When Mike explained how the news from the human colonies was having a similar effect on Earth, the Jubans were not surprised. Narus noted that the flow of new colonists from Jubas had virtually stopped, and the city population was stable. It was fortunate the news of the problems with Emor were not widely known on Jubas.

Mike suddenly remembered Maria and her mission to disrupt the colonies. Socoros knew the story, but he repeated it for the Juban negotiation team. "Why would the son of a member of the Leadership Council plan a mission to disrupt Octan colonies of humans, if they couldn't even populate all the habitable planets in the Juban area of the truce?"

The other team members looked at each other in amazement. Mike knew they didn't have a clue. Socoros finally answered. "I have thought a lot about this. When did Maria say she left Jubas?"

Mike had to count the years involved. "She said she was on Earth for 5 years before the Octans came. That was five or six years ago—I've sort of lost track of what year it is on Earth."

"So… five Juban orbits ago…" She suddenly sat up in her seat. "That was around the time of the Great Disaster of Monarat."

The other team members started several conversations, until Socoros motioned to them to let her speak. "About five orbits ago, a mysterious disease broke out on a Juban colony in the far boundary area, not that far from this planet. It spread quickly and there was no defense against it. Many Juban doctors and specialists rushed to help them, but could do nothing but die with them. After all were gone, the planet surface, to a depth of thirty centimeters, was incinerated, in the hope it would keep the disease from spreading to other planets. Monarat is still off-limits to

Jubans today."

"What does that have to do with Maria's mission?

"Before that, many Jubans were anxious to leave Jubas and colonize new worlds. Bran Harm was a leading proponent of colonization and angry at the truce with the Octans. He thought most Jubans wanted the freedom to colonize as many planets as possible. He argued for the need for thousands of small colonies. We now know his son Grus came up with the idea of disrupting the Octan colonies to make them fail. Once the treaty period was over, it would be easy to take over any planet that was in disarray. I think the team led by Grus Harm left for Earth just before the disease wiped out Monarat. After that, few Jubans were willing to take a chance on colonization."

Mike shook his head. "So, if it had taken a few more years to prepare, the mission would have been called off—there would have been too few Jubans left who wanted to migrate or deal with failing Octan colonies."

"Exactly."

The meeting ended and Mike and Socoros left for their quarters. He had a surprise for her. He had just received an email Jason sent to Demos. The Jubans there didn't have a clue what it was, so they forwarded it to Aragonis. Jason had found an illustrated electronic version of the "Kama Sutra" and sent it to him as a joke in an email attachment. When Socoros claimed some positions illustrated in the electronic book were not feasible, Mike challenged her to prove it—and she accepted. It took most of the night to settle the issue… in Mike's favor.

After a few more days, Mike was ready to leave. He was resting in their quarters when Socoros found him. "Your materials will be transported. The Octans have accepted the deal. After what you did on Demos, they really didn't have a choice—did they?"

She handed Mike a paper roll. "It looks like you have an official invitation to visit the Emor capital city Paladin. We can provide transport if you wish to go there."

Mike unrolled the scroll and glanced at the beautiful calligraphic-like script. "Can you go with me?"

She shook her head. "Only you are invited." Mike thought the Emor city might be dangerous, and he shared this with Socoros.

"We can provide some security," she said.

Mike was stunned when two Guardians entered and stood by the entry door. These Guardians had Juban instead of human features. "The Octans gave you these Guardians?"

Socoros bristled. "These are our design. The Octans stole the design, most of the programming, and even the name from us."

That made sense. Mike wondered what else had been taken from the Jubans by the Octans, and vice versa. He also wondered why he hadn't seen any Guardians on Jubas. He asked Socoros.

"They are used mainly for security purposes and, because there is little crime on Jubas, we see them only when there is a problem."

Mike recalled that it was most colonists on Helios rarely saw a Guardian once the problem with the animals was solved.

CHAPTER 49

The next day, a small transport ship left Mike and his two protectors just outside the Emor capital. Massive stone walls surrounded the city. Mike could see soldiers walking along the top of the wall. General Axel and two of his junior officers met Mike at the gates and escorted them into their capital.

The Emor city looked like ancient Rome. Broad avenues paved with smooth stones were lined with arched and columned buildings. The people were a mix of wealthy citizens wearing fine clothing and servants or possibly slaves dressed in coarse woolen clothing. As soon as they entered the city, several chariots appeared drawn by the same type of animals Axel and his officers had ridden to the negotiations. The chariots took them through the city to a massive stone building Mike guessed could house the senate or whatever the ruling council was called.

Axel led them up a flight of stairs and into an inner courtyard where three Emor leaders were waiting. The leaders noticed the Guardians following Mike at a discreet distance but made no effort to have them stopped. When the party neared the leaders, they bowed slightly. Mike bowed in return and Axel made the formal presentations. These were the equivalent leaders of the ruling council, which was not called the Senate but the Officiary. These leaders were probably older than Mike. He hadn't seen anyone with gray or white hair in a while. One of the leaders, Arius Thorn, gave Mike a small white staff with a golden bird on top as appreciation of the events that had led to the Alliance agreement. The council had quickly recognized the power the Jubans had and were happy it wasn't demonstrated on the whole Emor army. After much discussion, the council had recognized the important role General Axel had played when he presented the Alliance agreement to the council as a great achievement. Axel had hoped this tactic would work but was prepared for the worst—he could have been deemed a traitor and been executed.

Then Mike was presented to the whole council who greeted him with loud applause. Mike made a short speech thanking them for the welcome and expressed his hope the Emor could take advantage of the advancements of the Jubans to improve their own civilization. He assured them the Jubans did not want to interfere in their affairs, even their conquests of other native species on Aragonis, and the Jubans just wanted to be left alone.

He didn't mention his origin, in case they were not ready for the idea of the Jubans' migration from another world. After his speech, Mike attended a banquet in his honor and retired to a lavish room in the nearby home of Arius. Apparently this culture was still in the Republic stage and did not have a supreme ruler—yet. Mike wondered how far the parallels would go.

He did decline an invitation to a bath with several women attendants— reluctantly. If Socoros found out about that…

The next day he requested, and was allowed, to attend a typical council session. His hope that they would remain a republic was reinforced as he watched the council proceedings. At the end of the day, they returned to Arius's house, and he commented to Arius on the similarity of the issues discussed at the council with the issues he had faced on Kepler. Arius seemed aware the Jubans had come to Aragonis from another star in the sky, so Mike described Earth, Helios, Paradise City, Dodge City, Demos, and Jubas as Arius sat and listened with amazement.

"We must seem like barbarians to you."

"Not at all." Mike then described the strong parallels of the Emor civilization to ancient Rome, supplying as many details as he could remember and ending with the final sacking of Rome by the Mongols.

"Strong words of warning on what could happen if one person gains too much power."

Mike was impressed that Arius had come to the same conclusion. Even as he was finishing his comment, Arius' daughter came into the room. Mike had to stare at what could be described as clone of the blond, blue-eyed Milla Johansson, only slightly older. She bowed slightly to Mike and handed him a cup of wine.

"This is my daughter, Arianna. This is Mike Silver, a person of great importance in the Juban culture."

Mike started to correct him, but Arianna had already sat down on the bench next to him. "You do not look like your protectors. You do not seem to even be Juban. Do you have a Juban wife?"

Mike swallowed hard. "Not exactly. I have a close friend and companion. She represents the Jubans to other civilizations."

Arianna was looking at her father. "Can I show Mike Silver the important areas of Paladin tomorrow?"

"That is an excellent idea. Does that meet your approval, Mike Silver?"

Mike felt, under the circumstances it was best to agree. "Of course, Arius."

Arianna was smiling at Mike. An old quotation rolled through his head. Said the spider to the fly.

There was no electricity in Paladin, of course, and only oil lamps for lighting at night. Mike found some books he couldn't read then wandered outside to a patio to enjoy a soft evening breeze. Arius's house was on a hill inside the city and presented a magnificent view of Emor at sunset. There were no electric lights, but the residents in many homes placed oil lamps near their open windows. After sunset, the sky was filled with stars. Soon, even stargazing could not hold his interest and Mike lay down on a large bed filled with feathers of some sort, and drifted off to sleep. He woke up when a young woman started to take his tunic off. He jumped out of bed.

"Who are you?"

"I am here for your comfort," she said.

Mike was still a little sleepy and it took a few seconds to sink in. "Oh, no! I don't need that kind of comfort. But thank you."

She hurried out of the bedroom and a few minutes later, Arianna opened the curtains to peek in. "Mike Silver?"

"Please, just call me Mike."

"Mike, did she not please you? Do you want another?"

"No thank you. I don't need that help at this time." He was trying to be as polite as possible, but Arianna entered followed by two maidens carrying small brass pots hanging from chains and burning incense. They circled Mike swinging the incense pots toward him. Mike was getting dizzy as Arianna walked up to him. "These herbs will help calm you."

"I am calm," he said. The incense aroma was overpowering and the room was starting to spin a little.

"Perhaps you do not want them because they are servants. Perhaps you would like something more?"

Mike was starting to feel faint but he knew exactly what she meant. "No, but thank you very much. I just don't need that now." He was losing his sense of balance and starting to sway

Arianna put her hand on his arm to steady him. "Are you sure?"

Even as he started to reply she leaned toward him and kissed him. The incense plus her perfume, or perhaps it was her natural scent, finished him off when she kissed him a second time. He became helpless as she opened his tunic and started to stroke his chest. He must have passed out for when he woke up, the room was dimly lit by a candle that was burned almost completely, and he was lying next to a woman. She was facing away from him, but in the low light she could be Arianna. How did that happen? He couldn't remember anything after she had kissed him. What would he say to Arius? What if Socoros found out? He was feeling his future somehow slipping away. He slowly rose and dressed. Where in hell are the Guardians? They were supposed to protect me.

He crept quietly out of Arius's house and walked down a wide boulevard, until he realized he didn't know where he was, or which way to go. A few oil lamps still burned in the windows, giving just enough light that he didn't fall on the rough stone street. He decided to hide until dawn and find someone who could take him to the city gates. But his eyes were still so heavy from that incense. He felt so damned sleepy…

CHAPTER 50

Mike woke with the sun in his eyes, to normal city noises and leaped up in near-panic. *If I could get out of the city, and signal the transport ship to pick me up...* He was cold and damp; he had been lying on a fountain in a park of sorts.

Then he heard someone call his name, and turned to the sound. Arius was leading a small band of servants and soldiers and waving to him. Mike wondered if he should run; then he saw his Guardians with Arius! *What the hell?*

The group surrounded him and he realized Arius was asking if he was all right.

"Yes, I was just—just taking a morning walk." *Would anyone believe that?*

"You must come back to my house for the morning meal. Arianna is waiting to show you the city."

Mike went along reluctantly, but when they all sat down to eat, Arianna acted if nothing happened in the night.

The two Guardians escorted them as Arianna played the perfect tour guide, describing the history behind each important site in Paladin. She was obviously proud of her city. Finally, Mike leaned near her and whispered. "About last night…"

She looked at him innocently. "Yes?"

"I don't know what came over me."

"I do not either," she replied. "You fell asleep so quickly."

Mike didn't want to know, but he had to ask. "Did anything happen?"

She laughed. "You seemed to be asleep but you were standing up. My servant undressed you and helped you into bed."

She saw the questioning look on his face. "Yes, she helped you fall asleep."

Mike felt a huge sense of relief. He had avoided the obvious problem. But still, when he talked to Socoros, maybe he should avoid too many details of his time in Paladin.

The tour ended and they returned to Arius's house. As they were sitting on a bench in a large parlor type room and drinking wine, Arianna mentioned she wished she could visit the Juban city. Mike wondered if Socoros would agree.

"When the transport returns, I'll ask."

She seemed excited at the prospect. "That would be wonderful." She leaned over and kissed him on the cheek.

After suitable farewell meeting with Arius, Mike said goodbye, and several chariots took them to the city gates. Mike contacted the city through the transport ship communications and asked if Arianna could visit for a few days. After a minimum of red tape, Mike and Arianna were on their way to the Juban city.

Socoros met Mike and kissed him. Arianna seemed to not notice Socoros's greeting as she was waiting for Mike to introduce her.

If Socoros was jealous or wondered if anything had happened, she didn't show it. She played the perfect hostess and showed Arianna around the Juban city. Arianna was amazed at the huge video viewing wall, the lights, and the steady indoor temperature.

That night, Mike reviewed the meetings with the Emor council and

Arius and finished by showing Socoros the white staff with the golden eagle given to him by Arius. Socoros coughed delicately.

"The white part is the horn of the Masas, a rare and wild animal the Emor value greatly."

Mike examined it closely and found the staff portion was indeed an animal horn. When he looked up, Socoros was grinning. "What?"

"The powder inside is highly valued here on Aragonis, and some has even made it back to Jubas." She smiled. "It's rumored to greatly enhance performance in the bedroom." She held up her hands defensively. "No, no! You don't need it! And neither"—she kissed him deeply—"do I."

On the second day of her visit, Arianna woke up vomiting. When Socoros showed up, she took Arianna to a physician and called Mike. When Mike arrived, he grabbed the doctor as he was leaving an examination room.

"How is she, doctor?"

The physician stopped and faced Mike directly. "She is with child. You had better take care of her." He glared at Mike and walked off.

Mike felt a sudden chill. Pregnant? How was that even possible? They hadn't even slept together, or that was what she'd said. What would Arius say? What would Socoros say? What kind of sexual mores did Emorites have? Had he promised something, by his actions, that he'd had no intention of promising? All sorts of scenarios rattled around in his mind while he waited for the women to come out of the examination room.

Socoros and Arianna finally came out and Socoros seemed dazed, while Arianna was smiling. Mike swallowed hard and waited for them to say something when Arianna unexpectedly hugged Mike. "A happy day!"

"How are you?" he asked when she stepped back.

"Oh, I am fine. The healer said I just had a reaction to the spicy Juban food we ate last night."

"What? I thought—"

Socoros walked into his arms. "We need to talk" she murmured. "I'm pregnant."

Arianna was all smiles. "It seems this was not expected!"

They took Arianna back to her room to rest and then went to Socoros's apartment, where they sat on the sofa staring at each other. Finally, Mike broke the silence. "I don't understand. My friend and his Juban wife have been trying to have a child for years now, and they can't. I thought maybe it was not possible."

"I thought so, too. Perhaps she's just too young. Female athletes and warriors who exercise a great deal sometimes can't have a child until they are older."

What should he do? He was already a grandfather. The thought of raising a child now… But the bigger issue was Socoros. What would this do to her career, and to them as a couple? He really enjoyed her company and she was extremely bright. She knew many languages, learned new concepts quickly, and their nights together…

Now she seemed sad. He moved closer to her on the sofa and took her hand. "Tell me what you're thinking."

"I had chosen my career, and unlike my male equals, I was certain it did not include a family. I had adjusted. But now, even though it is something I did not expect, I am not going to let it go. I will raise this child."

That confirmed what Mike was thinking. He hadn't planned on it, but it had happened. He wouldn't put that burden on her alone. "It's my child too. I think it should have a mother and father."

She stared at him.

"Do you think you could be happy with me in a permanent relationship—marriage, or whatever it's called on Jubas?"

She suddenly smiled. "Oh, yes!"

Over dinner, Mike asked her how far along she was. "About five days," she replied.

"And how long does it take for a normal birth?"

"About 190 days—Juban days."

"So that's—what?" He consulted the Juban version of a tablet. "270 Earth days equals 187 Juban days. So… that's almost the same time."

She shrugged. "It will come when it is ready."

"How soon can the doctor tell whether it's male or female?'

"He did the tests already. It will be a male."

After dinner, they stretched out on the sofa together. "When can we hold a commitment ceremony?" asked Mike.

"Any day, but I need some time to prepare. I have many friends and people I would like to invite to a celebration."

"Could it be done before it's obvious you're pregnant?"

She seemed to be thinking about the meaning of Mike's question, then laughed.

CHAPTER 51

Word spread quickly through the diplomatic community, and many people contacted Socoros about the celebration. Mike asked her to keep it simple; he didn't want the massive crowd that showed up for Jesse and Mahra's marriage.

Money wasn't an issue. Mike still had his "weight in gold" stash but it wasn't needed. He soon discovered Socoros's family was quite wealthy due to many rewards given by the Leadership Council over the years in gratitude for their diplomatic service. Her wealth alone was significant. At least he wouldn't have to worry about retirement someday or the cost of raising their child.

Socoros's preparations for the celebration went smoothly. The day finally arrived and in the morning, Mike and Socoros obtained the equivalent of a marriage license from an official. Mike noted with interest when she stated her birth date for the official's record. After some mental math, Mike concluded she was the equivalent of about 38 Earth years old. He had sort of lost track of time on Earth, but he was probably ten years older than her.

Later that day they hosted a crowd of well-wishers anxious to meet Mike and congratulate Socoros. Mike met and spent some time with her sister and her brother and his wife. When he was called away to meet some other family members, her brother commented.

"He must have something she really likes…"

"Enough!" replied his wife. "All that matters is she is happy." They watched Socoros laughing and smiling as she introduced Mike to friends and family. Her yellow dress cleverly hid the first signs of her pregnancy. A few noticed the roots of her hair were blond and the irises of her eyes were now yellow instead of orange. The transformation was so subtle, even Mike didn't notice the change until after the celebration.

Mike explained the honeymoon concept, and Socoros told him they could go on a honeymoon to an apartment her family owned near the ocean, where she could spend the last half of her pregnancy in peace.

Just before they left, her doctor shocked them by informing her she was carrying twin boys. He attributed her own physical changes to the DNA of the children she was carrying. As the due date neared, Socoros looked in the bathroom mirror to find her hair was now blond and her irises were now blue. Her skin seemed less gray—more like Mike's skin color. She accepted the changes and looked forward to delivering their children.

While they were waiting for Socoros to deliver their twins, Mike had the opportunity to observe Juban men and women at length, sometimes while having lunch with some of her female friends. After some time he came to the conclusion that the basic tenants of sexuality accepted for men and women on Earth were reversed in Juban women and men. He discussed his observations with Socoros and she agreed. Juban women seemed to actively seek out sex more often than men, often initiated public displays of affection, often made comments about Juban men they observed. Juban women seemed to become stimulated easily, while Juban men took longer, and so on. Socoros confirmed there were few female Juban prostitutes, and those there were, catered to women. Men would not seek them out. Male prostitutes, on the other hand, were moderately common, even in Demos.

Once this hypothesis was confirmed, Mike wondered if this had somehow influenced Jason and Maria and his own relationship with Socoros. Was this irrelevant, or did it have a role? He would have to wait and see once Jubans and humans interacted more. If it were true, the prospects for Juban male / human female interactions were not good.

Socoros delivered two boys almost exactly on her due date. As her doctor predicted, both sons were mostly human except for their light gray skin and bright orange hair. Her family accepted the change in her physical appearance and eagerly took turns holding the new arrivals.

Mike sent a note to Jason with the news and happily shared Jason's reply with Socoros—Maria was finally pregnant. With triplets! A few months later another email from Jason confirmed he was the proud father of a boy and two girls. Jason sent a picture of Maria holding their children; Maria now had blond hair and blue eyes like Socoros.

One Year Later

Mike and Socoros were planning to celebrate their twins' first birthday with a custom new on Jubas—a birthday party. The night before the party, Mike told Socoros he loved her and regretted not having told her that when he asked her to marry him. She replied she was glad he didn't say it then, because she wouldn't have understood exactly what he meant. After living a year with him, she did understand, and she told him she loved him too. They hugged for a long time and then went to finish preparations for the party.

The next day, they were shocked when Nomos, the head of the Leadership Council, arrived near the end of the party. Everyone present was amazed as he never attended personal events. He congratulated Socoros and Mike but asked to confer with them privately. It was awkward meeting in the kitchen of their seaside apartment, but they were honored that he was even there, even as they found seats around the kitchen table.

"I am pleased to join with your family and friends on this happy occasion" he began. Mike and Socoros were certain that was not the reason he was there. "But, as you have probably guessed, there is a more important issue I need to discuss with you." He paused to collect his thoughts. "Very few know this yet, but the Juban colony at the far boundary has encountered a new species that holds great danger not only for Jubas, but Octos and Earth as well."

Mike and Socoros glanced at each other. What issue was so important that the council leader would come to their home to discuss it, instead of asking them to come to the council headquarters?

"The danger is real and as great as the Octans falsely described a Juban threat to your United Nations on Earth." He pulled a communications tablet from his tunic and showed Mike a graphic representation of the Galaxy. "As you know there are two spiral 'arms' of the star formation you call the Milky Way Galaxy. Our treaty with the Octans covers a small part of one arm." "Here"—he indicated the second arm—"is unknown territory."

"Terra incognita," murmured Mike; then he looked up. "Oh, sorry. Old Earth term for "unknown lands."

Nomos looked a little irritated at the interruption, but he went on, "Neither we nor the Octans were aware of any intelligent species in the second spiral arm. We now know there is at least one, and this species has been migrating through the central part of the Galaxy, which is extremely dense and dangerous for space travel. They are now at the far boundary of the proposed Juban area of colonization." Mike studied the graphic as he continued. "This species is not like the Octans, Jubans or humans. They are only interested in attacking and living off planets or spacecraft they encounter. They are not numerous enough to attack planets with large populations, but by disrupting all transport travel, they effectively cut off future colonization."

"They sound like pirates."

"As I understand the word—that is a good comparison. They are not interested in trade, or commerce, or colonization. They have already attacked some Juban cargo transports and taken the materials. If there is no resistance they do not harm the ship's personnel. If they resist, they kill them. The most immediate concern is for the Juban colony on Adarat, a planet near the center boundary. But, if we don't find a solution, eventually all small Juban and Octan colonies could be attacked. Earth and Jubas might never be in danger, but your colony on Kepler could someday face this problem."

Mike immediately thought of Jesse, Mahra, and their children. Socoros saw Mike's concern and put her hand on his arm. "We will find a solution."

"Why not send some armed warships and engage them?"

"While they are few in numbers for colonization, they have many small ships of weapons equal to ours. We would lose in these encounters. We have no viable battle strategy to defeat them."

"I hate to ask the obvious, but why are you telling us this?"

"We would ask you both to meet with our war council to discuss alternatives." He looked at Socoros. "Perhaps there are diplomatic solutions we have not thought of." His gaze returned to Mike. "You seem to have a different perspective, which could be valuable. I would also like to emphasize our desire that this matter be kept in confidence so we do not alarm the people."

The meeting ended and the leader left them a translated report sent by a transport that described an attack by the pirates. Socoros sat down next to Mike as he finished the report.

"How did the governments on Earth deal with pirates?"

"That's complicated, because some of them secretly supported pirates that attacked ships of rival governments."

She shook her head in disbelief.

"Other than that, sometimes they paid and sometimes they fought. My own country fought a couple of wars over piracy, a couple of hundred Earth years ago."

"War."

"Yes. Expensive in both money and people. There should be a better way."

But the next day, they met the war council, composed of the most senior military leaders. Numerous proposals were discussed without a solution.

Mike proposed several ideas. He suggested they capture one of the pirates and use the combined medical knowledge of Earth, Octos, and Jubas to find a biological weapon against them that would not harm Jubans. That was a non-starter, as was the idea of just paying them to leave the Juban ships alone. He then proposed a suicide mission to destroy the pirate's home planet, but their best guess as to where that was, would require a trip of many years. By that time, Juban and Earth colonies could be under attack.

Socoros suggested a high-level diplomatic mission to try and reach some kind of agreement, but so far the pirates had shown no interest in talking about anything.

The idea of a combined armada of Juban and Octan ships had been dismissed outright, as neither side had really recovered from their battle fifty years ago, and there were at least a hundred small but well-armed pirate ships.

A do-nothing strategy would doom future colonization efforts and effectively isolate existing colonies, which could then be attacked.

Mike then proposed filling several cargo ships with explosives, using Guardians to control the ships and detonate them when the pirates boarded, hopefully destroying the nearby pirate ship. That received some support, and after some discussion, the war council agreed to test the idea. That would be a temporary solution at best, as the pirates would find a way to assess a ship's cargo and avoid the ships with explosives.

Mike asked the war council to re-consider the idea of a biological weapon, and they agreed to make inquiries to medical personnel on Jubas and Earth, but they still needed one of the pirates to experiment on. There was no point involving the Octans, as they would be against any weapon that could potentially wipe out a species.

Just before the meeting ended, Mike asked how many Guardians there were on Adarat and Jubas. After some checking they answered approximately a hundred thousand.

After a few days, the Leadership Council reviewed their progress and Nomos met privately with Mike. "We would like you to coordinate the defensive actions against this species."

"Are you sure you have the right person? Surely one of your generals is more capable."

Nomos laughed. "You always ask if someone else would do better. I would not be talking to you if that were so." He handed Mike a scroll. "This identifies you as the Regional Governor authorized by this Council to protect the twelve colonies in the Region. It also names you a military general in charge of all Guardians. This is temporary, but you have total authority, with no need to confer with the council."

The script was in Juban and Mike wondered what it actually said. "Is this really necessary?"

"Yes. The colony on Adarat is more than 25,000 of your light-years from here, and meaningful dialogue is not possible."

Mike did some mental math. The transport from Demos to Jubas was about ten thousand light years and had taken twelve months. At that speed, transport would require more than thirty months. "If it takes more than thirty Earth months to transport to Adarat, we may arrive too late to help them. Some time has passed since that transport was attacked and filed their report. Adarat may already be under attack."

"We do not want the Octans to know this yet, but we currently have three experimental warships in operation that are much faster. The transport should only require two Earth months. And, per your request, one of these is transporting a human physician that specializes in defense against biological weapons, from the human medical colony to Adarat. He should arrive shortly after you. We've also made the arrangements for these ships to transport the Guardians you requested."

Mike breathed a little easier. Two months wasn't that bad. He could use the time to work on a more comprehensive defense strategy. He signed the appointment form and handed it back to Nomos, who shook his hand.

Socoros listened quietly as Mike described his meeting with Nomos. She realized Mike would be gone for an undetermined time, but she was determined to put forth a positive attitude. After all, he was joining the effort to help the Jubans on Adarat, even if a part of the reason was to protect his family on Helios. She told him she understood the threat and thanked him for agreeing to help. They made the best of the time before he left.

Mike did establish communications with the physician from Earth recruited by the Jubans to study the possibility of finding a biological weapon against the pirates. He was already working on some ideas with physicians on Jubas.

CHAPTER 52

The new warship was indeed fast. Mike decided to stay awake and work on tactics. The captain informed Mike the ship was faster than the communications system between planets and ships.

As soon as Mike arrived, he met with the Adarat leadership council. The pirates had not attacked the planet itself yet, but many cargo ships had been attacked. The first defensive action was already underway, as a cargo ship loaded with explosives had come in contact with the pirates. As soon as it was boarded, the Guardians detonated the ship, blowing up the pirate vessel docked with it. Mike knew it wouldn't take the pirates long to figure out how to assess the materials on a cargo ship and avoid those with explosives.

Tom Markoff, the human doctor from the human medical colony, arrived shortly after Mike, and they met to discuss the latest plans for possible biological weapons. Dr. Markoff already had some prototype viruses that he wanted to test on a captured pirate. He had verified that they had no effect on humans or Jubans.

As his next defensive action, Mike coordinated the three experimental Juban warships' attack on a pirate vessel. The Jubans managed to capture it and its crew, and return with it to Adarat. Mike went to the holding facility to meet with the captain of the captured pirate ship. They were humanoid, looking eerily like humans' Neanderthal ancestors. They refused to talk, even though Mike was certain they could communicate through his translator. If he had gone by appearance, he would have thought them too primitive to operate a starship.

Dr. Markoff had combined his research with that of Juban scientists on Adarat who were already at work on biological weaponry. It was slow work, and Mike suggested a new strategy to try first.

Mike was totally unaware of the pirate ship that landed near his quarters, until the crew broke in and kidnapped him. One minute he was sitting on his bed, thinking about the twins; the next, he was waking up with a headache in a cage.

When he woke, he was bound with some kind of wrist cuff and hauled to what he decided must be the pirate ship's command center. In a chair at the center of the room, sat a Neanderthalish person, probably the pirate captain. He looked sharply at Mike's throat and ear, where the translators were. "Can you understand me?" he growled.

"Yes." Sometimes it was best to not volunteer anything. Mike glanced around the command center and counted less than thirty command personnel. That meant most of the crew were spread throughout the ship. He hoped his latest plan would work on this ship.

The captive pirates on Adarat were a motley mess, appearing barely capable of operating a spaceship. Mike would have assumed these pirates would also be a fiercely independent group, dressed in all manner of clothing, but the command personnel were dressed similarly, with almost a military appearance. The captain was dressed very formally, with insignia of sorts on his jacket. Military?

"Are you the leader of the people on the planet known as Adarat?"

"In some ways, yes."

He walked over and looked carefully at Mike. "You do not look like them."

"It's a long story."

"You do not look like a warrior, at all."

"I'm an ambassador, actually."

The pirate leader laughed. "I have little use for ambassadors—who lie for a living. Are you holding the crew of one of my ships on that planet?"

"They are being held there."

The pirate leader sat back down on his command chair. "You will die if you don't release them immediately!"

"They are under control of the city manager."

"I thought you said you were the leader."

"In some areas, not in others. It's complicated."

The pirate leader pounded on the arm of his chair. "Release them now—or die!"

That reminded Mike of the ultimatum of the Emor General. "Maybe we could talk about an exchange?"

"What! You—for them?"

"Possibly."

"I could kill you and rescue them myself!"

"You would have done that already, if you could."

The conversation was interrupted when a crewman informed the leader of the presence of another cargo ship nearby.

"This will have to wait. Take him back to the holding area."

Mike was dragged back to the holding cell as the ship made preparations to board the cargo ship. He was pushed into his cell so hard he fell, hit his head, and passed out. The pirate jailer laughed and slammed the cell door.

The pirate leader was surprised the cargo crew made no effort to defend themselves. The cargo ship was quickly stripped of its cargo, including many large, unmarked crates. When the pirate ship's cargo bay door closed, a crate opened in the bay and Guardians came out to start releasing other Guardians in other unmarked crates. They soon lined up and marched rapidly in a single file toward the command center. Whenever they encountered a crew member, the lead Guardian grabbed him by the neck, turned him around, and put his hand over the crewman's mouth, then pulled him out of the way and waited for further instructions. The crewmen struggled but were no match for the Guardians.

Mike woke up and pulled himself off the cell floor with the bars of the cell. The jailer was asleep on a chair, snoring. The door to the cell area was slightly open and Mike saw a stream of Guardians marching by. He laughed so loudly, he woke up the jailer, who yelled at him to shut up. Immediately, a Guardian opened the door and grabbed the jailer by the neck. Another Guardian took the jailer's keys and unlocked the cell. He saw Mike rubbing his head. "Are you all right, General?"

"Yes. Put him in the cell and let's go to the command center."

By the time the got there, it was all over but the shouting. The first Guardian in the command center smashed the communications console. The rest grabbed the crewmen who scrambled to get away. Some crewmen managed to fire hand weapons and disable a few Guardians, but resistance ended quickly when the pirate leader was grabbed by the neck. All the Guardians were wearing blue shirts and black pants, except for their leader, whose shirt was red shirt. He walked quickly to the pirate leader. The leader's eyes were starting to bulge out and he was turning blue.

"Surrender or all will die."

The Guardian holding him by the neck released him and he fell on the floor gasping for breath. The room was filled with Guardians, all identical, obviously robotic. He yelled, "I surrender! Release my men."

The Guardian leader motioned and all the pirates were released. They fell to the floor gasping for breath.

"Nicely done," Mike said to the lead Guardian as he entered.

"The ship is secure, General. We have re-routed to Adarat."

The pirates had been herded to an area in the command center and were still breathing hard and rubbing their necks. The leader glared as Mike approached him. "General? I thought you were an ambassador."

"I have several responsibilities." Mike said, with a twist of his mouth. "For my sins, no doubt. Now, sit." He motioned the leader to a seat away from his crew. "You have several choices. The takeover you just witnessed has already happened on a number of your ships. The crews on those ships have been sent to Adarat where they are being well taken care of. The captured ships have been sent to a secret location where they will not be found. This process will continue, until you surrender the remaining ships or they are all captured."

The leader just stared at him. "I don't believe you."

"You don't have to. We will arrive at Adarat in a day or so. You can see for yourself."

"What do you want?"

"It doesn't matter what I want. The Jubans just want to be left alone."

"We cannot just leave this area. We have no home—no place to go. We do not have enough food to go back to the crowded area of stars. It was very dangerous there. We cannot go back."

Mike knew he meant the center area of the galaxy. Maybe there was a habitable planet in the far boundary area.

"We could find a planet home for you."

"We are not farmers!" Even through the translator, his disgust came through. "We would starve to death."

Okay, that was a legitimate problem. "We can talk more about this on Adarat."

CHAPTER 53

The Adarat City Manager searched through the available information and advised Mike there were no Juban colonies that had not been settled. A few colonies were only sparsely populated, but mixing the pirates with one of them would not seem wise or fair to the existing colonists.

Soon there were over twenty pirate ships in custody and, as was determined from information in their computers, about eighty had fled back toward the center area. Where were the women and children? So far, they were holding only men. Each pirate ship had about a hundred crewmen, so there were over two thousand in custody. That left another 8500 or so men, but an unknown number of women and children. The pirate leader would not reveal the whereabouts of their women and children, or how many there were.

The quickest way to communicate with Jubas was via the experimental warships. Mike prepared a message for Nomos, asking him to contact the Octans to see if there was an available colony that had not been settled yet. The pirates could live on the FOOD. After all, the people of Helios had—for a while.

Mike met often with the leader the first few days after they arrived on Adarat. They had some long conversations about their origin, culture and future. According to their leader, Hafnor, the Iotan species had no written record of their origin, only an oral tale passed down through official "storytellers" over fifteen hundred generations. Hafnor explained how thousands of Iotans had been kidnapped by a powerful warrior race to be their servants. Over many generations, they grew in such number their captors became afraid of them. When they discovered a plan to leave them on an uninhabited planet, the Iotans revolted and took over the large spaceships of their captors. It took many more generations of orbiting around the uninhabited planet, which still provided them with food and water, until the Iotans finally figured out how to pilot their former captors' spaceships. By that time, there was little left of their former captors, left behind on the planet, and the only thing still remaining of them was the copied uniforms the Iotan leaders wore.

The trip from the other arm of the galaxy and through the center of the galaxy had taken several hundred generations. They had encountered no intelligent species capable of space travel, but there were many battles on planets they robbed for food. Over this time, the Iotans lost many skills, and developed a caste system that governed the division of their spoils.

Mike wondered if they had been taken from Earth those fifteen hundred generations ago and suspected they were possibly related to humans. The Neanderthals on Earth had disappeared over a relatively short period of time and he wondered if some alien species kidnapped them to use as servants or possibly slaves. He asked Dr. Markoff to test their DNA and he soon reported back.

"Their DNA shows a distant relationship to humans."

"I knew it! That explains a lot. Thanks, Dr. Markoff."

"Wait! That's not all. We also found an unexpected relationship." He handed Mike a chart of the DNA test, but Mike couldn't determine a relationship. Markoff saw Mike's confusion. "Sorry, the pirates are also distant relatives of the Jubans."

It didn't sink in immediately. "How is that possible? They appear to be more like human ancestors."

"We double-checked the tests. It could be the Jubans are extremely adaptive to their environment. If these were their ancestors also, their evolution would have slowed if they always lived in space, away from most environmental forces. The Jubans would have continued to evolve and the species you call the pirates did not. That's just a theory of course."

"So, the Iotans could have been taken from Earth, and on their way back to their home planet, their captors also could have taken some Jubans, and the two captive species intermingled over time before they overthrew their captors."

"That's one of many possible explanations."

Mike thanked him and wondered how he could explain all that to the Juban Leadership Council. He was alone in his apartment trying to write a report to Nomos, when Socoros entered. He stood up, thoroughly surprised. They hugged and kissed for a while. His first question concerned the health and safety of their children. She assured him they were being well taken care of—she used the word 'spoiled'—by her sister.

"But… how did you come here in such a short time?"

"There is a fourth new experimental warship. I forced them to let me come along. I heard that you were kidnapped and you came up with a plan that is working to capture the pirate ships, and it saved you from them."

"Yes. It's a pretty low-technology solution to a high-technology problem."

Socoros frowned. "What?"

"It's the old bum rush. You basically overwhelm the enemy with warriors before they can respond with superior tactics or weapons. Most of the Guardians weren't even carrying weapons."

"Once you have captured all the pirates, what are you going to do with them?"

"I would like to find a planet somewhere for them, but they are afraid they wouldn't survive on one. They know nothing about agriculture."

Socoros suggested they take over either the abandoned Octan or Juban city on Demos.

Mike briefly considered that, and then shook his head. "That's a pretty harsh environment—cold and dark. It's really not suitable for humans, Octans, Jubans—or this species, which by the way call themselves Iotans. I wish there was some way they could find a home on Aragonis, it's such a huge planet, very nice weather, and mostly uninhabited except for the expansion-minded Emor."

She put her hand on his. "The Juban colony there is not doing well. The population had been stable for many Orbits, but it has been declining slowly for some time."

"How do you think they would react to a proposal to settle the Iotans there, at least for a few years until they can become established?"

"I don't know. Why don't I go there and talk to Narus? Perhaps I can persuade him and the colonists."

Socoros met with Narus and at the equivalent of a town hall meeting, discussed the distant relationship between the Iotans, humans and Jubans and the idea of settling them there for a few Orbits, until a more permanent home could be found. The existing population occupied less than 10% of the available living quarters and although some objected, the majority agreed to allow the Iotans to live there, at least for a few Orbits.

The Iotans were in their third month of captivity on Adarat when Mike presented the idea of settling on Aragonis to Hafnor and his immediate crew. Mike showed them some pictures of Aragonis on his tablet, including several pictures of the Juban city and the immediate area around it. The Jubans allowed Hafnor to contact the remaining ships not in custody to present the idea of joining the Aragonis colony. Most agreed to settle there, knowing they would have to surrender their weapons as soon as they landed on Aragonis.

Hafnor finally told them where the women and children were—in a massive cargo ship that followed the main fleet at a distance, so as not to put them at risk. He provided a detailed account of their population. In all there were about 25,000 men, women and children that would be migrating to Aragonis. Even that number would not have a significant impact on the sparsely populated Juban city there. Since most of the Iotan's ships were not capable of landing on the planet, the four experimental warships acted as shuttles to bring them to the Juban City. Mike and Socoros accompanied them and attended a welcoming ceremony for the new inhabitants, who were truly amazed at the blue skies, white clouds, and warm breezes of Aragonis. They were even more amazed to tour the Juban City and its bright colors and hexagonal structures. When Mike and Socoros explained the issues with the Emor to Hafnor, he promised his people would protect the city should the Emor try to attack it again.

After a few days to make sure all the Iotans were settled, the Guardians briefed on what to watch out for in their behavior, and all their weapons and warships mothballed in space near a moon of Adarat, Mike and Socoros entered an experimental warship to return to Jubas.

A message was waiting for Mike from Jason when he arrived on Jubas. The Octans were aware that Mike was now helping the Jubans, so they had transferred his roles as ambassador, supreme justice and commander of the Guardians in that area to Jason. Jason had not wanted these roles but, like Mike, he understood the importance of helping the Octan-human colonies in trouble. Although the Octans knew Maria was a Juban, they appointed her Jason's assistant to help resolve the colonies' problems.

Mike sent Jason a message congratulating him on the appointments and wished him luck with the colonies in trouble.

CHAPTER 54

Earth

Almost ten years had passed since the 25th colony had left Earth for Kepler. The arrival of an alien spaceship now drew little notice. By agreement, the Juban Transport ship landed at the New York Terminal and was already loading some parts and special machinery Mike had requested, to help in fabricating automobiles and airplanes. Mike found he could walk freely about as no one knew him or the role he played in resolving problems affecting many planets. Unknown to Mike, several Guardians were there to protect him.

Earth hadn't changed much. Around a hundred Octan-human colonies had been established, with about four million humans leaving, but many times that had been born, so there basically was no effect on Earth's population. The nuclear fusion gift reactor from the Octans was working well and had been studied by many engineers. Progress had been made on duplicating it, but so far there were only a few dozen small fusion reactors in operation, with minimal but growing impact on non-renewable resources. Some new crops, resistant to heat and able to grow in arid climates had become available which had helped reduce hunger around the world. Octan technology also enabled a large-scale and cost-effective desalination process to produce fresh water from seawater, which soon became the single biggest benefit to Earth from the Alliance. Adequate fresh water supplies were still a limited resource in many countries.

Medical progress on the first colony was slow but steady. Cures were announced for several types of cancer. A cure for dementia, but only the Alzheimer's type, was followed by the discovery of drugs that reversed the symptoms of muscular sclerosis and several related diseases. The physicians on Medical Colony 1 were happily continuing to use the

Octans' technologies to study many types of diseases. But, overall, there wasn't much enthusiasm for the deal with the Octans. It had improved, but not drastically changed, life on Earth.

Mike and Socoros left the experimental warship for a review meeting in the UN. Mike had been asked to provide a report of what had happened on Demos, as all the UN personnel were aware of how close the breaking of the treaty had been. To Mike, that was old news now. Mike was actually a hero of sorts on Jubas for his role in solving the potential treaty-breaking problem on Demos, and especially the threat posed by the Iotans, but no one on Earth was even aware of the threat they had posed for Juban colonies and the Octan-human colonies like Helios.

Socoros was invited to give a talk before the General Assembly, and her speech became the subject of endless discussion. She provided a brief history of the Juban people, their colonization philosophy, the contact with the Octans that eventually led to the war that ended with the truce, and the fact that Jubans were as disenchanted with colonization as the people on Earth, and they would not be able to colonize all the planets in their designated area of the galaxy, let alone threaten to take over planets and colonies in the Octan area. The Octans had some explaining to do… such as when they knew of the change in Juban philosophy toward colonization. Certainly they knew before the colony on Helios was transported, as well as the seventy-plus others that followed them.

She finished with Mike's role in helping resolve the potential treaty-breaking problem of Demos, his help solving the problem on Aragonis, and the ultimate solution for the Iotans to also locate there. When she finished, there was a shocked silence that was slowly replaced by increasing applause until she received a standing ovation.

Mike was deluged with reporters after the speech and tried to deflect his role in the solutions as much as possible.

Mike and Socoros returned to Jubas just in time for their sons' second birthday party. Nomos surprised everyone by attending and they were wondering if some other problem had developed that required Mike's help. To everyone's relief, he asked Mike if he would consider joining the Leadership Council. Socoros was the most surprised of all, and publicly encouraged Mike to join. He agreed and everyone applauded.

Most Jubans were shocked at the idea of a non-Juban on the Leadership Council, but Mike was sort of a legend now, and what had been unthinkable became acceptable. Just as all humans with televisions watched the landing of the Octan ship at the UN, all Jubans watched Mike's Leadership Council induction ceremony. That night Socoros told Mike she was pregnant again—with twin girls.

Mike proved to be an atypical Leadership Council member. He soon discovered the Leadership Council was more like a Supreme Court than a UN. Cities on Jubas passed laws that were often challenged or appealed to the Leadership Council. Depending on the city, the appeal went to a specific council member. The council member could decide whether the city's law was just or not, and that was the end of the appeal. If the nature of the law being appealed seemed to apply to all of Jubas, the council member was expected to pass it on to the whole council for study and validation or dismissal. Mike wondered how the Juban people would react to him personally, and professionally—would they accept his decisions?

So, periodically, Mike conducted town hall type meetings in the cities under his jurisdiction to discuss issues in general, or laws that had been appealed and decided upon. At first, few Jubans attended, thinking the town halls were a gimmick of sorts or didn't really matter, but after word got out that some requests at the town hall had been granted, subsequent town halls were packed.

News accounts of the town halls were very favorable and attendees came to value his desire to help them. Local dignitaries often invited him to dinner after the town hall meetings. Nomos heard about the town hall meetings and attended a few. He discussed them with Mike and commended him on finding new ways to help the citizens in his area.

CHAPTER 55

Mike woke one morning to find the truce with the Octans again in jeopardy. The Octans learned of the new, faster warships and claimed the Jubans had broken the agreement. Mike had studied the truce agreement in detail on Demos, but was looking at a different problem at the time. He still had his copy of the truce agreement and based on news reports re-read the re-armament clause. The clause stated that both sides could re-arm during the truce period, but must keep the other side informed of their progress, to avoid surprises or issues when the truce period ended. Technically, the Jubans had not informed the Octans of the new, faster warships Mike had used in the conflict with the Iotan pirates.

It didn't take long before the Leadership Council was convened to discuss the problem. Everyone looked to Mike as the starting point, since he knew the Octan Ambassador they would be meeting on this, and he was more familiar with the details of the treaty than any other member of the Council. Mike was asked to lead a Juban delegation that naturally included Socoros. As quickly as arrangements could be made, and Socoros's doctor confirmed it was safe to transport while she was pregnant, they transported to Demos, the site now delegated to resolve all issues between Jubas and Octos.

As soon as he arrived, Mike took the unusual step of meeting Ambassador Mikolan in private to discuss the issue before the formal negotiations began. He described the danger posed by the pirates who had been raiding Juban cargo ships, the urgent need to find a way to defeat them, and the role played by the new faster warships.

Mikolan listened patiently. While he was aware of the potential dangers to the human colonies posed by the pirates, and happy the problem had been resolved, he reminded Mike of the original truce agreement and the requirement to notify the Octans of new armament developments. He proposed that some of the ships be turned over to a third party while the Octans worked on improving their own warships. After some haggling on numbers and time frames, they agreed on a plan in which three of the four new ships, including the fastest one, would be turned over to a neutral third party for a time equal to twenty Earth years.

The deal would be completed if the third party Mike had in mind agreed to the deal as well.

Mike left Demos when the two teams began their usual negotiating protocols. In Mike's absence, Socoros assumed the lead role for the Jubans. Mike briefed her on the preliminary deal and told her to not reveal it until he returned. Mike was happy to use one of the faster warships for a quick trip to Aragonis. He found Hafnor outside the Juban city, fishing in the river.

"Greetings! It seems you've adapted well to your new environment."

"Happy to see you again, General."

"How would you like to command a warship again?"

Hafnor stared at him. "Truly?"

Mike explained the problem with the truce agreement and the need to turn three of the four Juban warships over to a third party to give the Octans time to catch up, if they choose to do so. Hafnor jumped at the chance. "When can we start this new deal?"

"I have to return to Jubas to explain everything to the Leadership Council and if they agree, to present it to the Octans on Demos. If all goes well, you could be back in space before the winter comes to Aragonis."

Hafnor was so excited he jumped up and slipped off the rocks he was standing on and fell into the river. He didn't care, and Mike helped him back to shore. On the way back to the city, Hafnor confided the change in the Iotans since they arrived on Aragonis.

"The woman and children are now happy here and want to remain even if other planets or options become available. There are few men left who still want to return to space. Those who do will be happy to work with the Jubans on this deal."

Mike left for Jubas to explain the proposed deal to the Leadership Council. They were concerned at first that three of their four fastest warships would be in the hands of the Iotans. Mike reminded them the Iotan women and children, and most of the men, would remain with the Juban colonists on Aragonis. He further asked that the men who would crew the ships be sworn in to the Juban military, and given a security role—to patrol and protect, or even assist Juban cargo ships when necessary. They would also be available to transport Juban military personnel and equipment when necessary. Mike proposed they be on probation for a few years, and if they held to their part of the agreement, they could start using some of their own ships to provide extra security to the Juban area of the galaxy. After some discussion, the Council agreed and thanked Mike for his efforts. He soon left to finalize the agreement with the Octans.

As expected, the old format of negotiations on Demos had gone nowhere in four-plus months. Both teams of negotiators were glad to see Mike and interested in his new proposal. Mikolan was pleased Mike had obtained agreement from the other participants in the deal. He had already contacted Octos and received permission to proceed. In a few days, the final agreement was reached and Mike and Socoros were headed back to Jubas.

When they arrived, they were shocked to find Nomos had announced his retirement. News of the revised truce agreement with the Octans overshadowed the news of Nomos' retirement, and again the Leadership Council publicly honored Mike for his role in the agreement. When the Council announced they were considering Mike to replace Nomos, all the feedback from the Juban population was positive.

An election was held, and Mike was selected to succeed Nomos on the same day Socoros gave birth to their twin girls.

Mike's first official act as head of the Leadership Council was to contact his counterpart on Octos. They met on Demos and agreed that, with the change in attitude on both Earth and Jubas toward colonization, there was no longer a need for the truce. In its place, they both signed a Peace Treaty and pledged to co-operate in future relations and trade.

When the new treaty was announced on Jubas, celebrations were held in many Juban cities. Enterprising Iotans converted some of their mothballed ships to transport tourists between Earth and Jubas, then branched out to transporting tourists, a few new colonists, and materials to the established human colonies.

On Mike's sixtieth birthday (by his best guess), he returned to Kepler with Socoros and their four children for a family reunion of sorts. Jesse's four half-sibs were not all that different in age from his own sons, and soon Mike's kids were running in a crowd of friends. Mahra and Socoros quickly became friends and promised to continue sending each other the latest family news. Helios had changed drastically. Few people were still living fulltime in the domed city, as most colonists now had ranches or second homes with lake or sea views.

Jason and Maria had been the first co-mayors of the second domed city on Kepler, which was named Artemis after the Greek goddess of the hunt. Several thousand former Helios citizens moved to Artemis when it became operational. At Jason and Maria's urging, Balas and the whole Taas tribe moved there and soon established ranches and farms even bigger than those around Helios. Jason and Maria were often away in their new roles trying to help colonies in trouble. Before they left on their first assignment, they campaigned for Jesse, who won his first public election and was now the mayor of Artemis.

The equipment Mike requested to be transported by the Jubans was now in operation, turning out small electric automobiles and small jet airplanes running on a type of biodiesel. Several large ferries were built to transport automobiles over the sea between the two cities, and people moved freely between the two sites.

Jason and Maria returned from resolving a colony's problems while Mike and Socoros were visiting Jesse and Mahra. Mike and Socoros and their four children visited Jason and Maria and their triplets. Maria and Socoros both laughed when they met, at the physical changes they had undergone in their unions with human males.

Jason and Mike were sharing war stories about the problems they had encountered on different planets, when Jason received an incoming email from the Octan leadership describing an urgent problem with the colony on Gilese 581d. Mike and Socoros wished them luck, and soon Jason and Maria were underway to find out why the colonists claimed they were under attack by zombies.